A Sam & Friend's Mystery

Book Three

Mummy Mayhem

MARY LABATT • JO RIOUX

KIDS CAN PRESS

Kids Can Press acknowledges the financial support of the Government of Ontario, through the Ontario Media Development Corporation's Ontario Book Initiative; the Ontario Arts Council; the Canada Council for the Arts; and the Government of Canada, through the BPIDP, for our publishing activity.

Published in Canada by
Kids Can Press Ltd.
29 Birch Avenue
Toronto, ON M4V 1E2

Published in the U.S. by
Kids Can Press Ltd.
2250 Military Road
Tonawanda, NY 14150

www.kidscanpress.com

Based on the book *The Mummy Lives!* by Mary Labatt.

Edited by Karen Li
Designed by Kathleen Gray

Manufactured in Buji, Shenzhen, China, in 3/2010 by WKT Company

CM 10 0 9 8 7 6 5 4 3 2 1
CM PA 10 0 9 8 7 6 5 4 3 2 1

Library and Archives Canada Cataloguing in Publication

Labatt, Mary, 1944–
Mummy mayhem / Mary Labatt ; illustrated by Jo Rioux.

(A Sam & friends mystery bk. 3)
ISBN 978-1-55453-470-8 (bound). ISBN 978-1-55453-471-5 (pbk.)

I. Rioux, Jo-Anne II. Title. III. Series.

PS8573.A135M86 2010   jC813'.54   C2010-900107-9

Kids Can Press is a *Corus*™ Entertainment company

To my family — M.L.

To Keith — J.R.

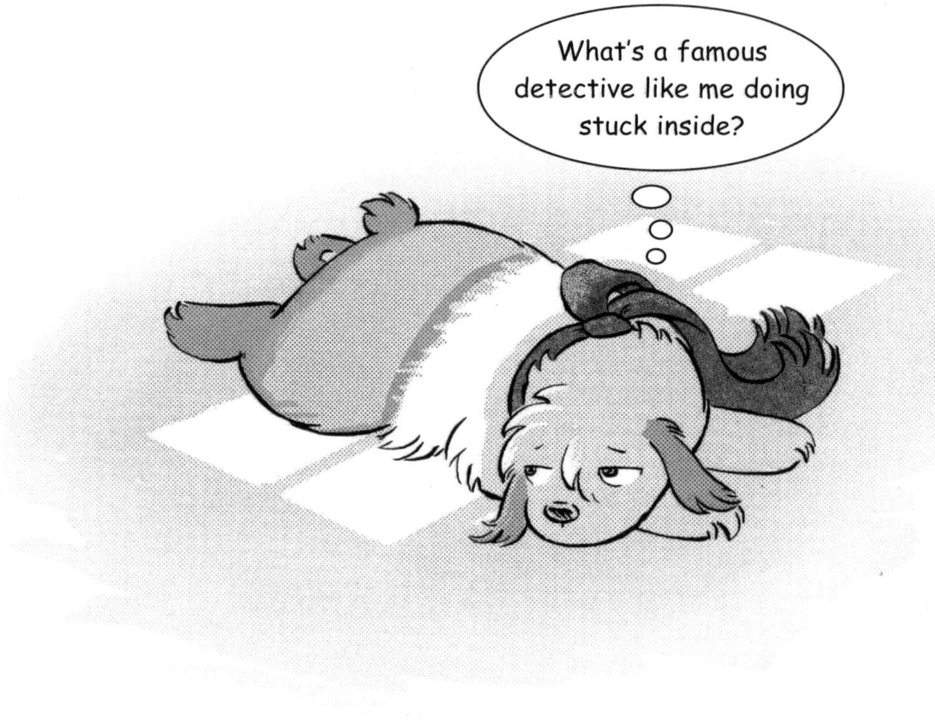
What's a famous detective like me doing stuck inside?

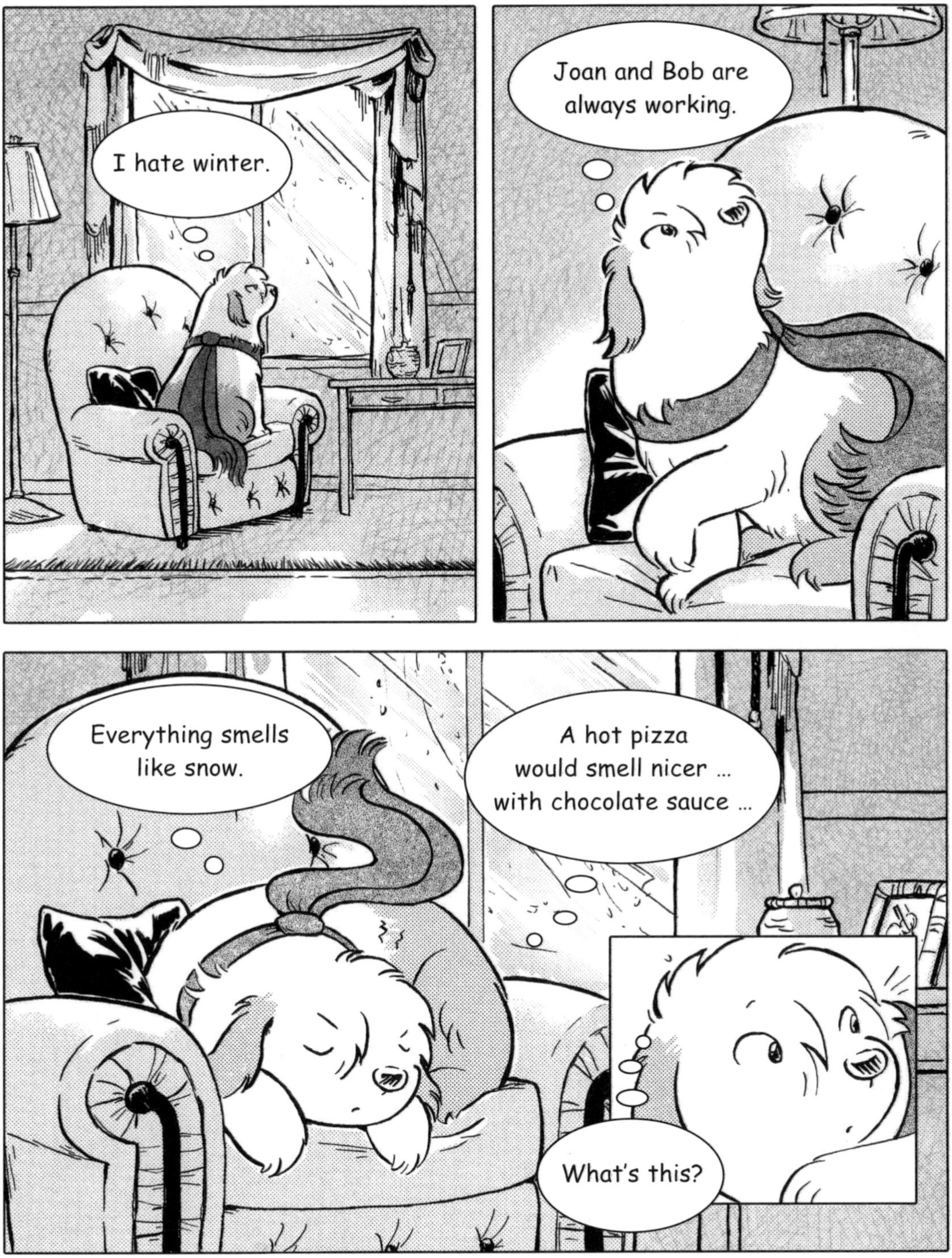
I hate winter.
Joan and Bob are always working.
Everything smells like snow.
A hot pizza would smell nicer ... with chocolate sauce ...
What's this?

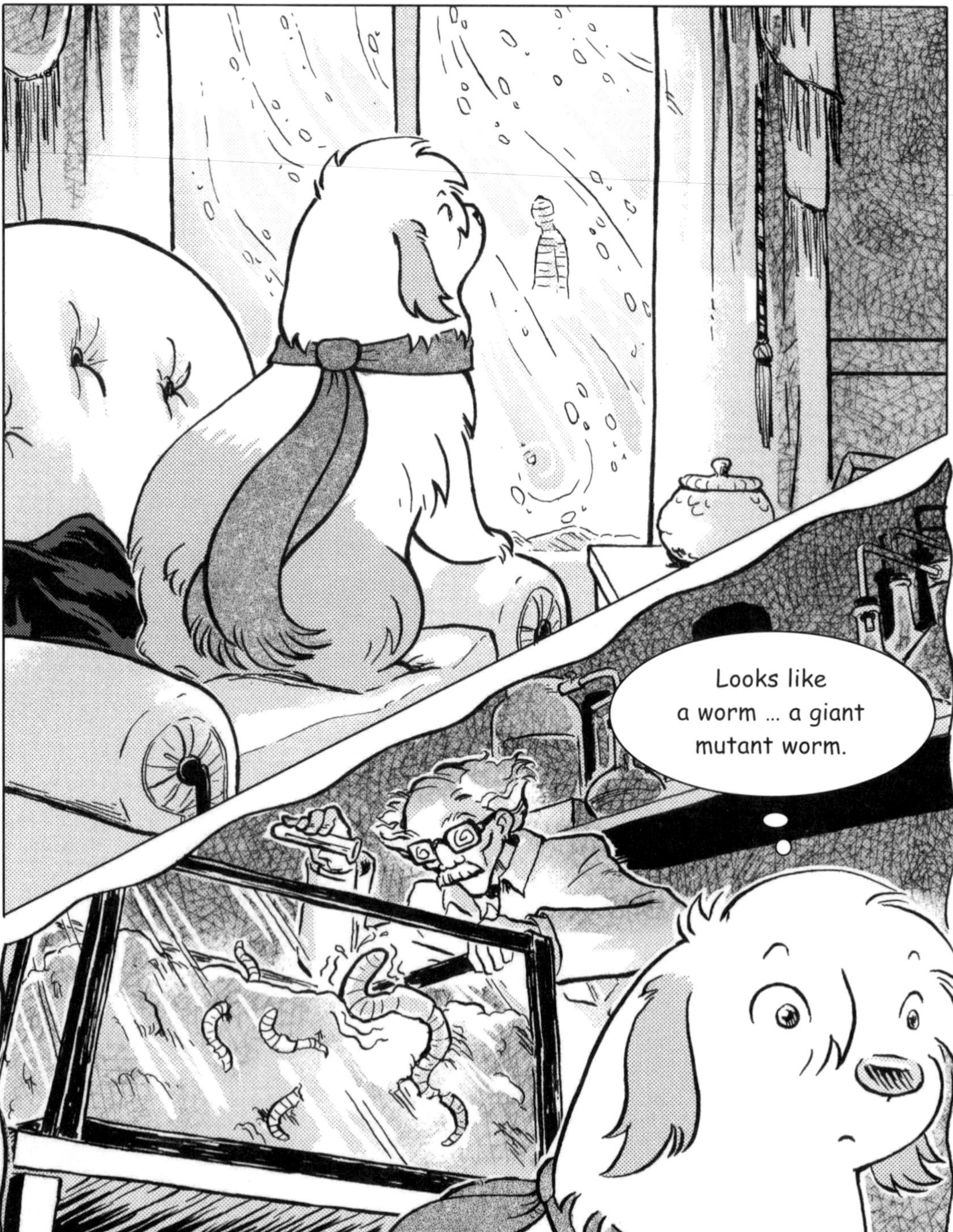
Looks like
a worm ... a giant
mutant worm.

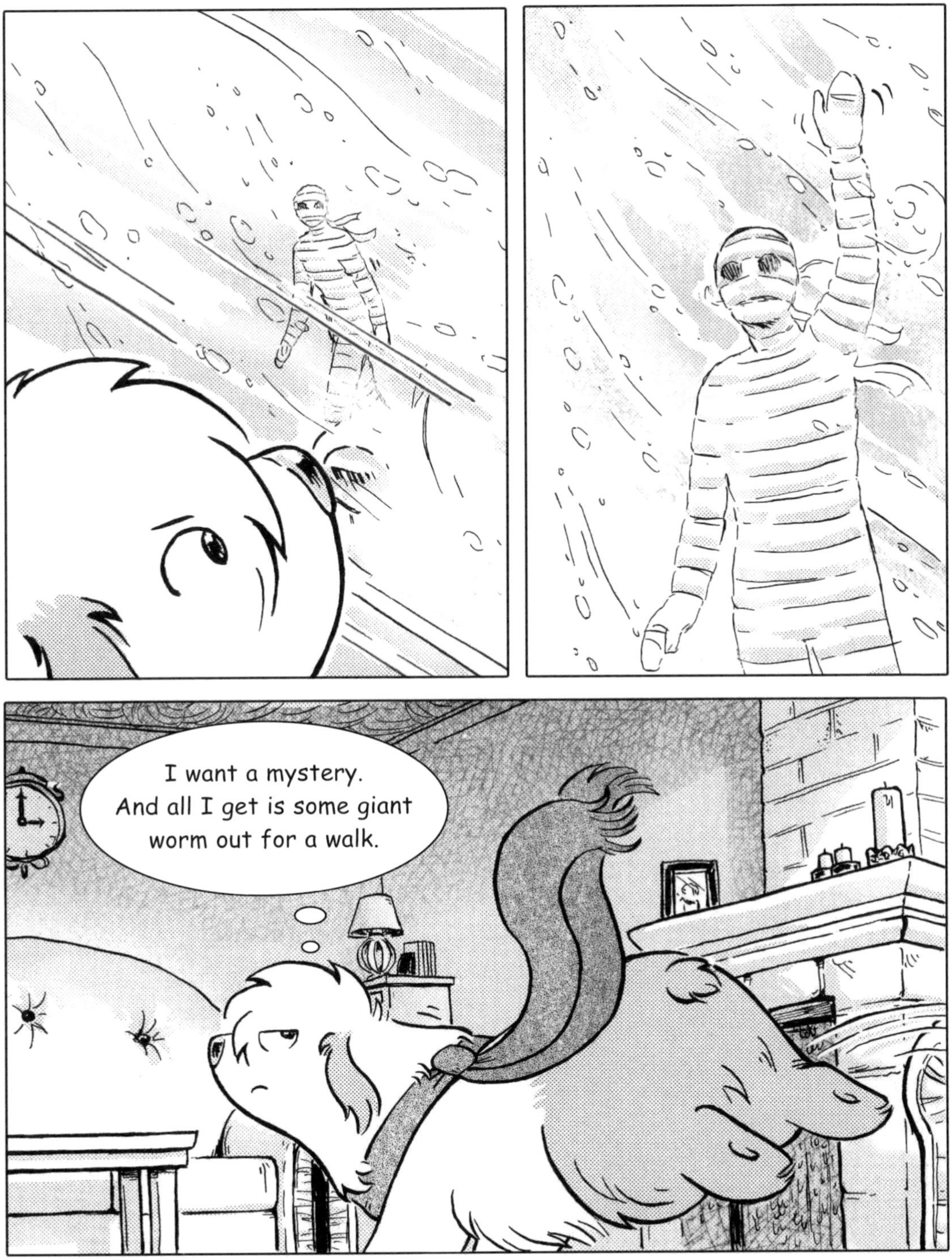
I want a mystery.
And all I get is some giant
worm out for a walk.

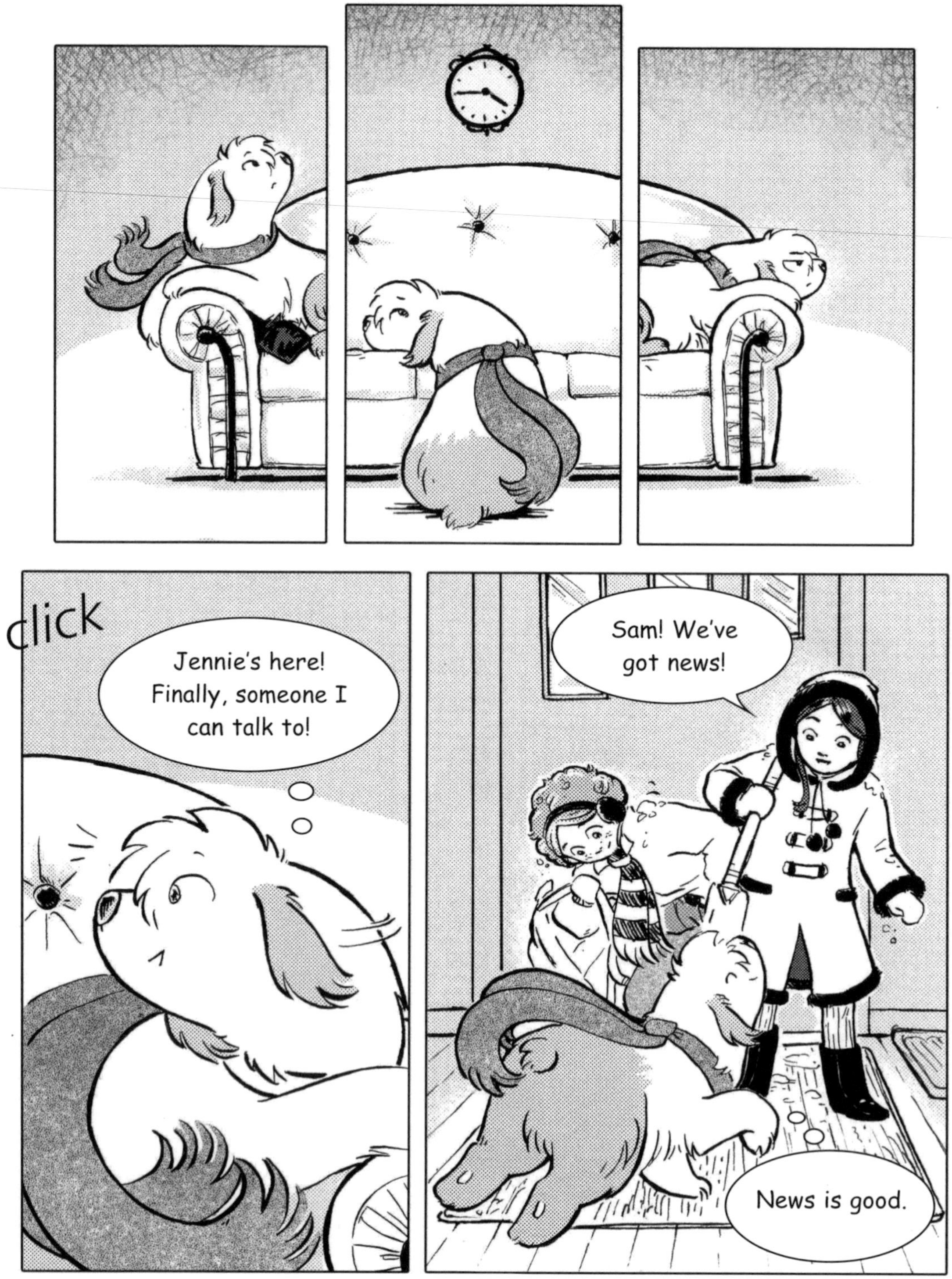

click
Jennie's here! Finally, someone I can talk to!
Sam! We've got news!
News is good.

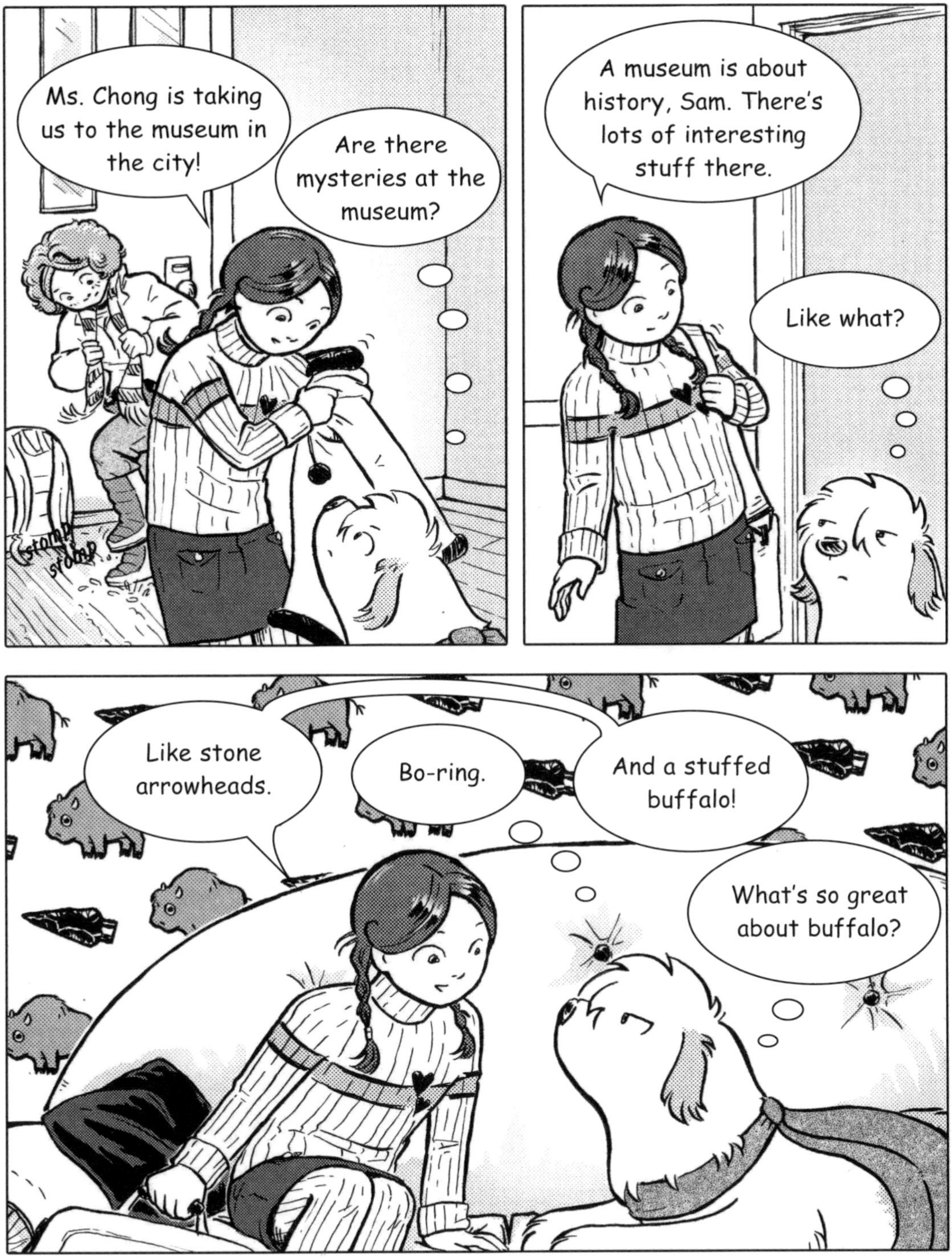
Ms. Chong is taking us to the museum in the city!
Are there mysteries at the museum?
stomp stomp
A museum is about history, Sam. There's lots of interesting stuff there.
Like what?
Like stone arrowheads.
Bo-ring.
And a stuffed buffalo!
What's so great about buffalo?

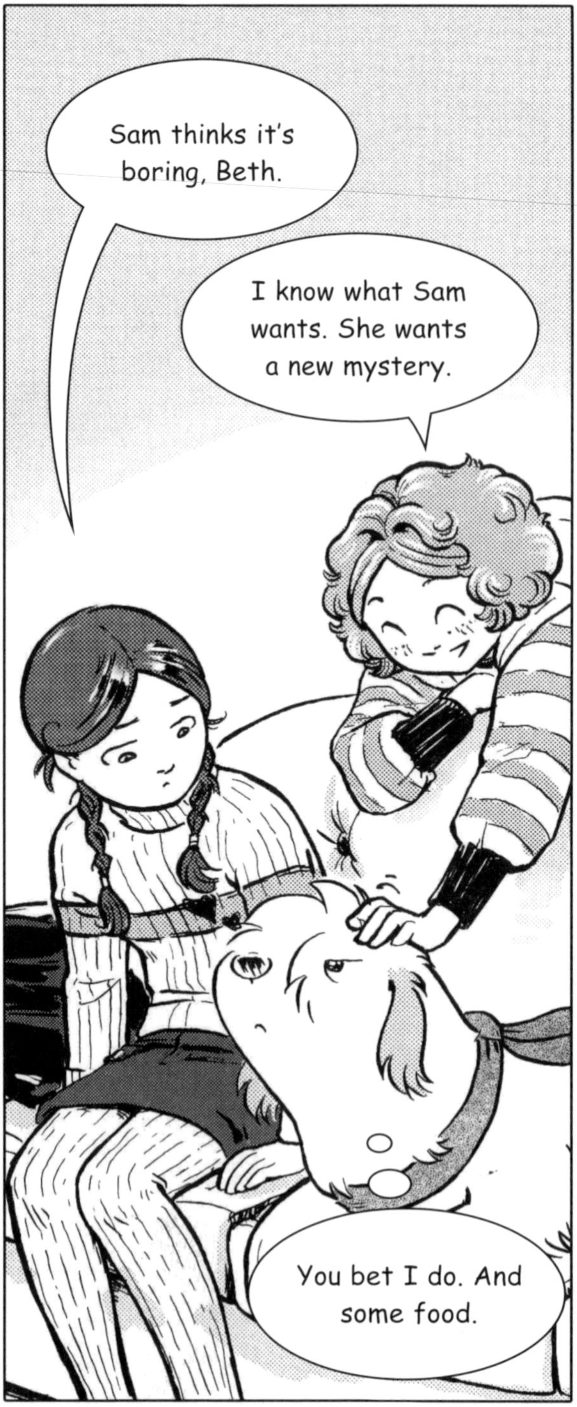
Sam thinks it's boring, Beth.
I know what Sam wants. She wants a new mystery.
You bet I do. And some food.

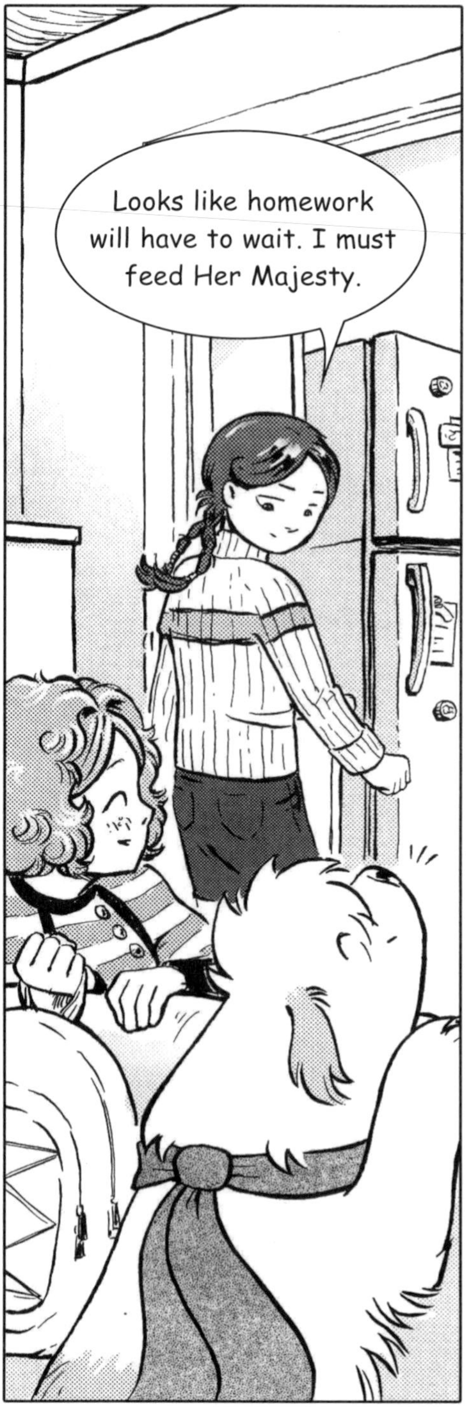
Looks like homework will have to wait. I must feed Her Majesty.

Later ...

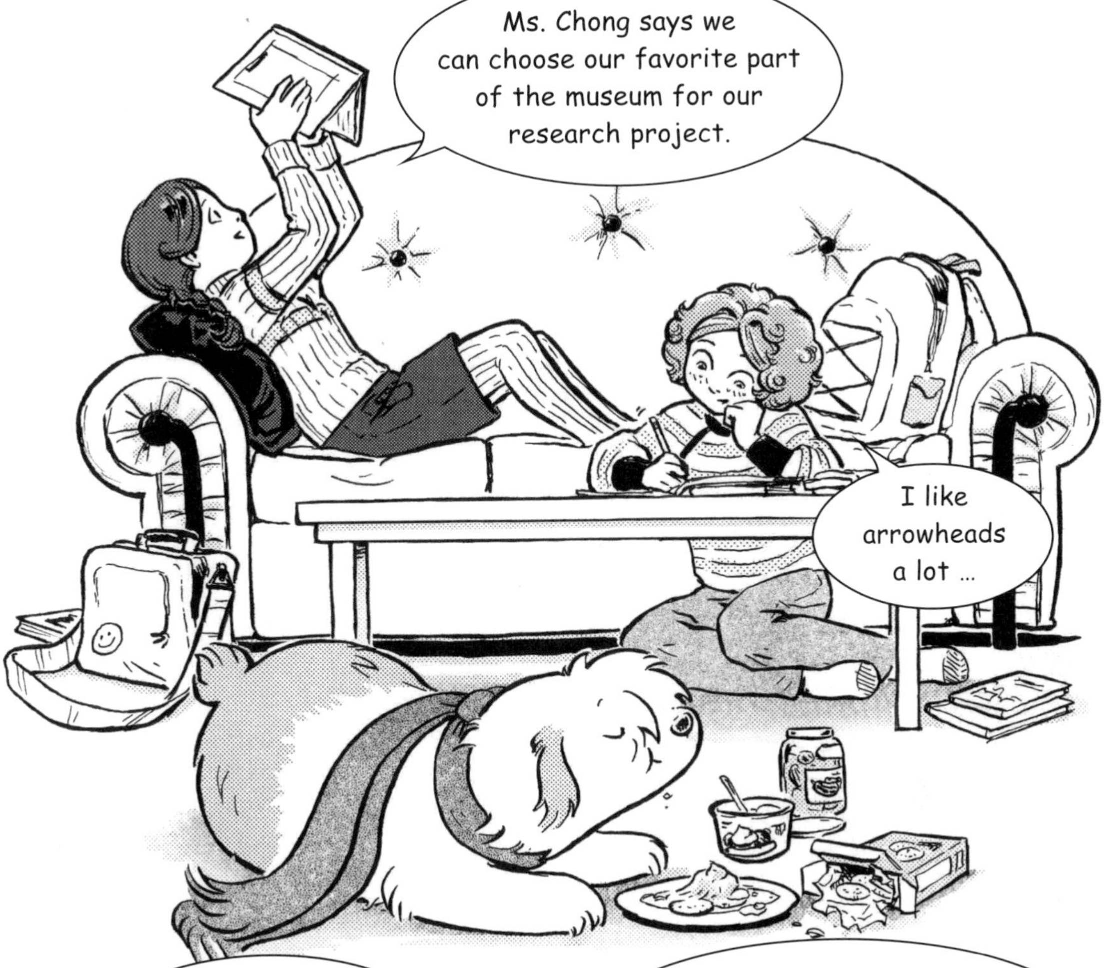
Ms. Chong says we can choose our favorite part of the museum for our research project.
I like arrowheads a lot ...

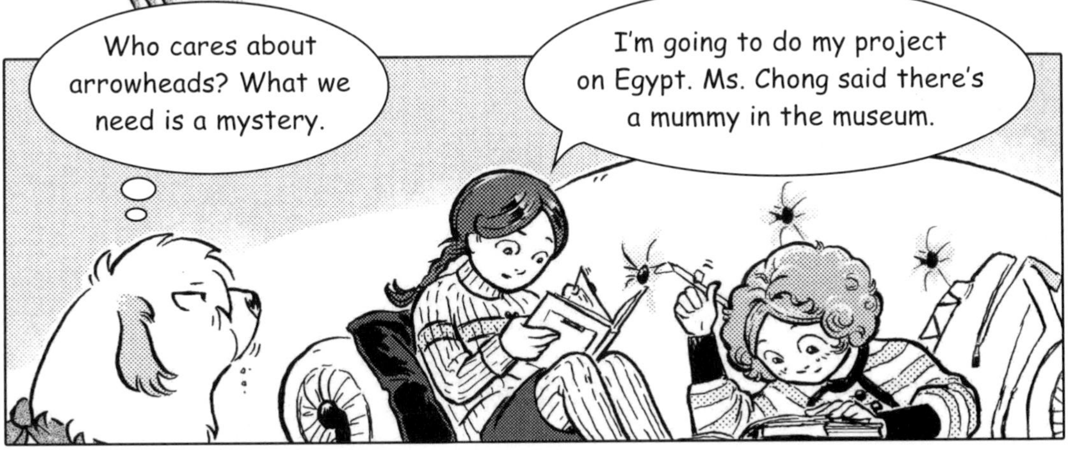
Who cares about arrowheads? What we need is a mystery.
I'm going to do my project on Egypt. Ms. Chong said there's a mummy in the museum.

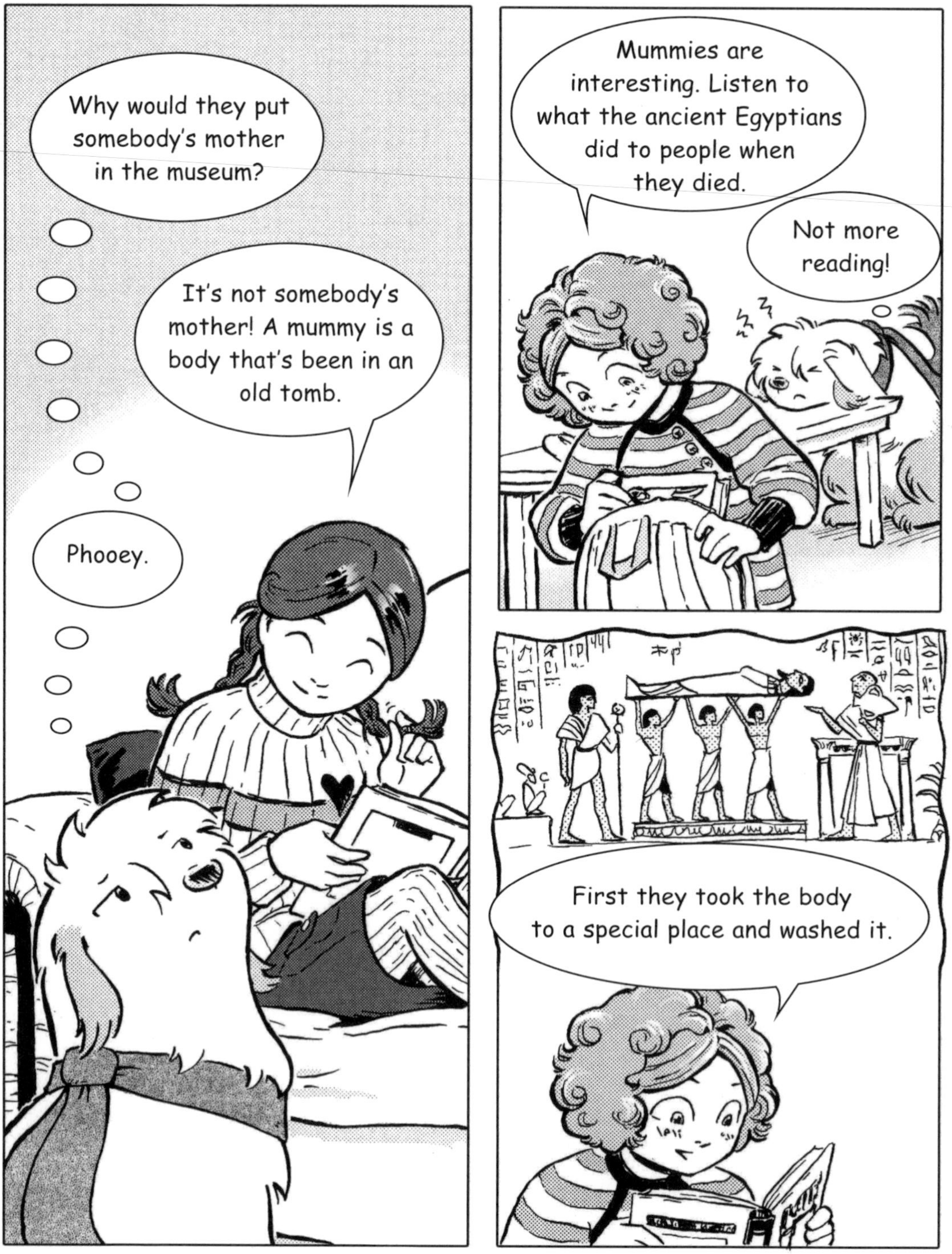
Why would they put somebody's mother in the museum?
It's not somebody's mother! A mummy is a body that's been in an old tomb.
Phooey.
Mummies are interesting. Listen to what the ancient Egyptians did to people when they died.
Not more reading!
First they took the body to a special place and washed it.

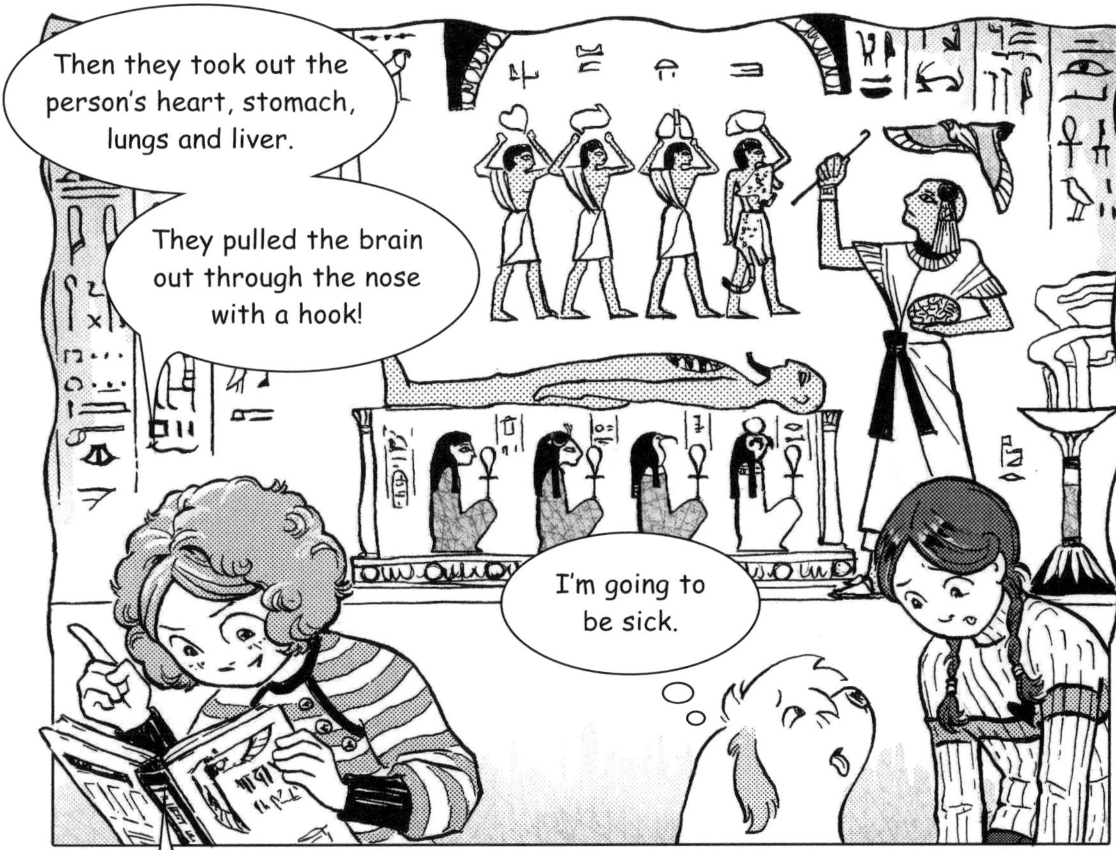
Then they took out the person's heart, stomach, lungs and liver.
They pulled the brain out through the nose with a hook!
I'm going to be sick.

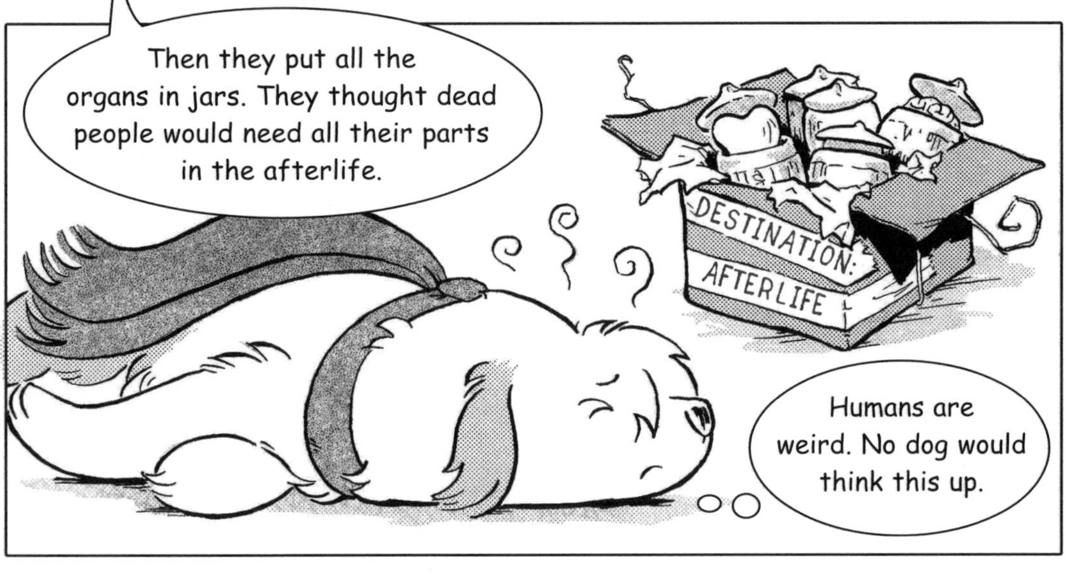
Then they put all the organs in jars. They thought dead people would need all their parts in the afterlife.
DESTINATION: AFTERLIFE
Humans are weird. No dog would think this up.

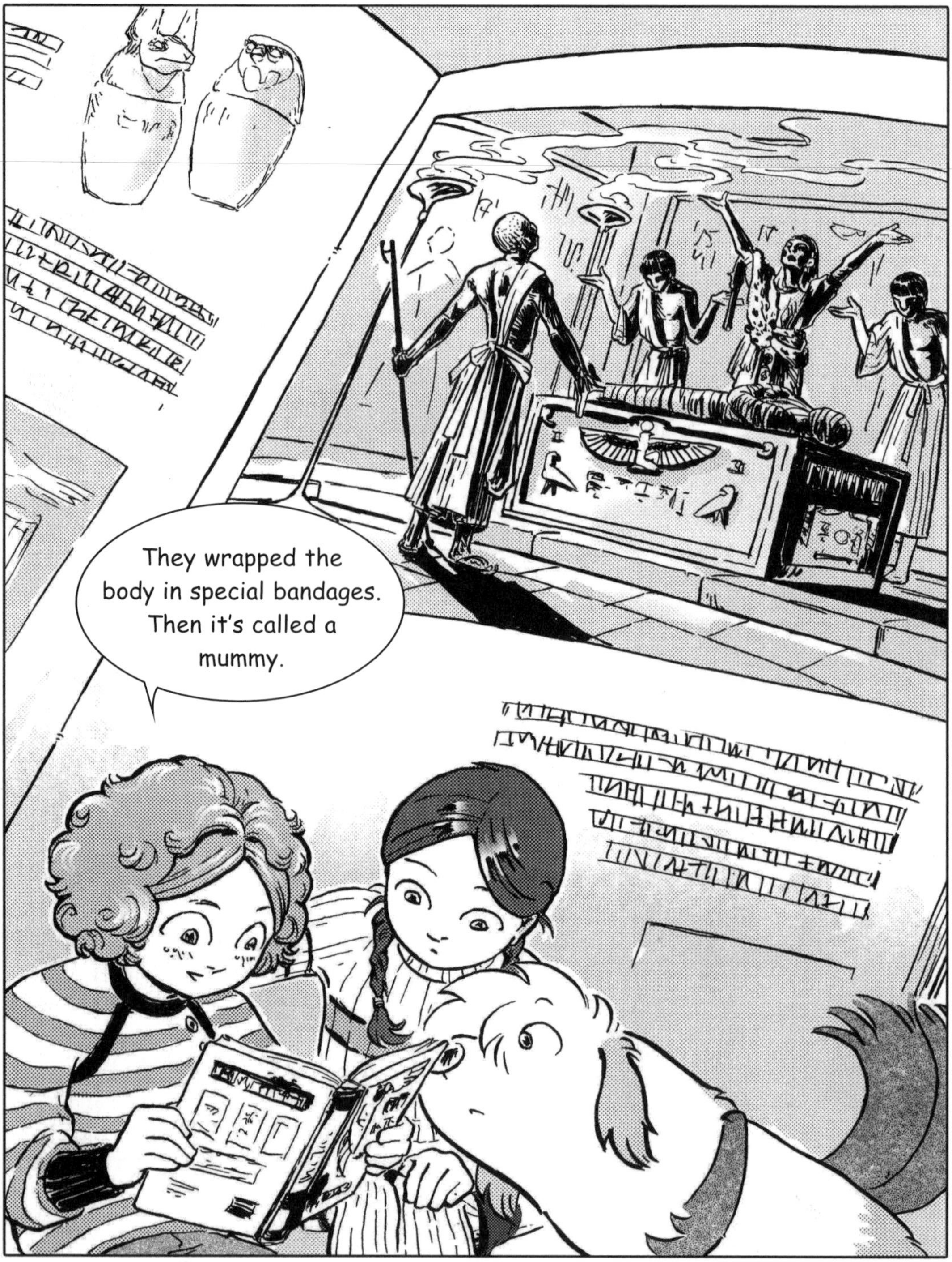
They wrapped the body in special bandages. Then it's called a mummy.

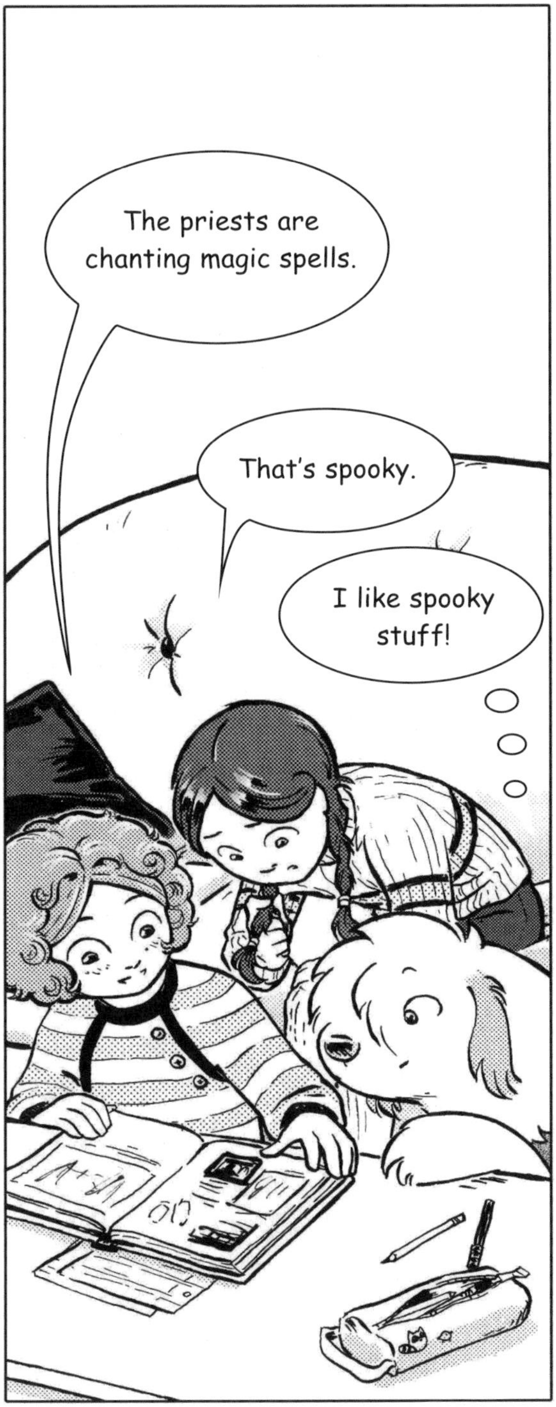
The priests are chanting magic spells.
That's spooky.
I like spooky stuff!

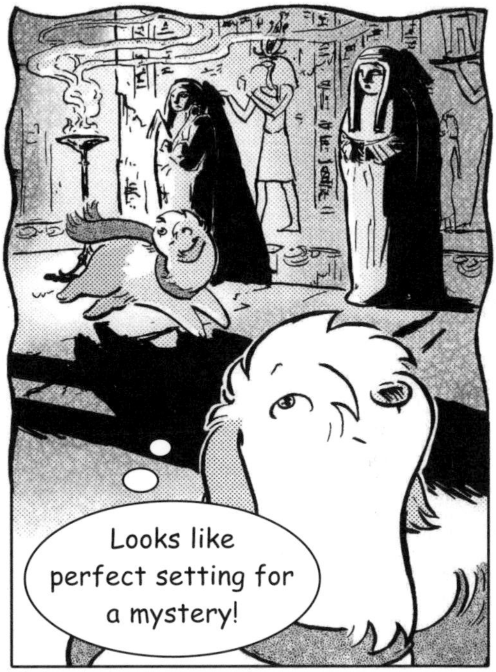
Looks like perfect setting for a mystery!

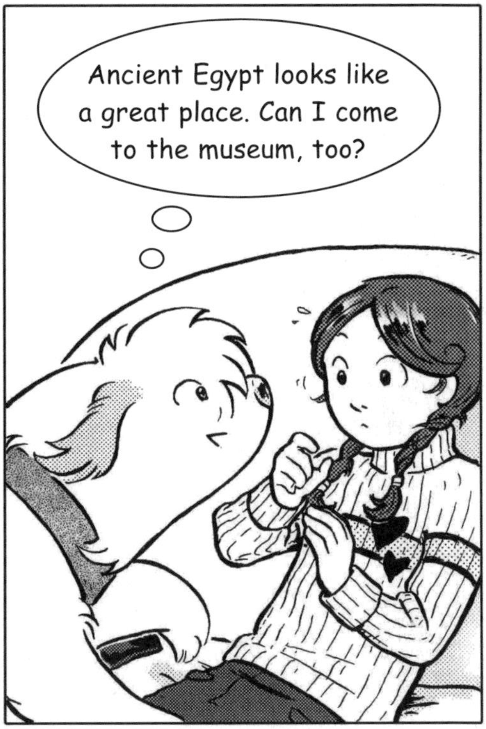
Ancient Egypt looks like a great place. Can I come to the museum, too?

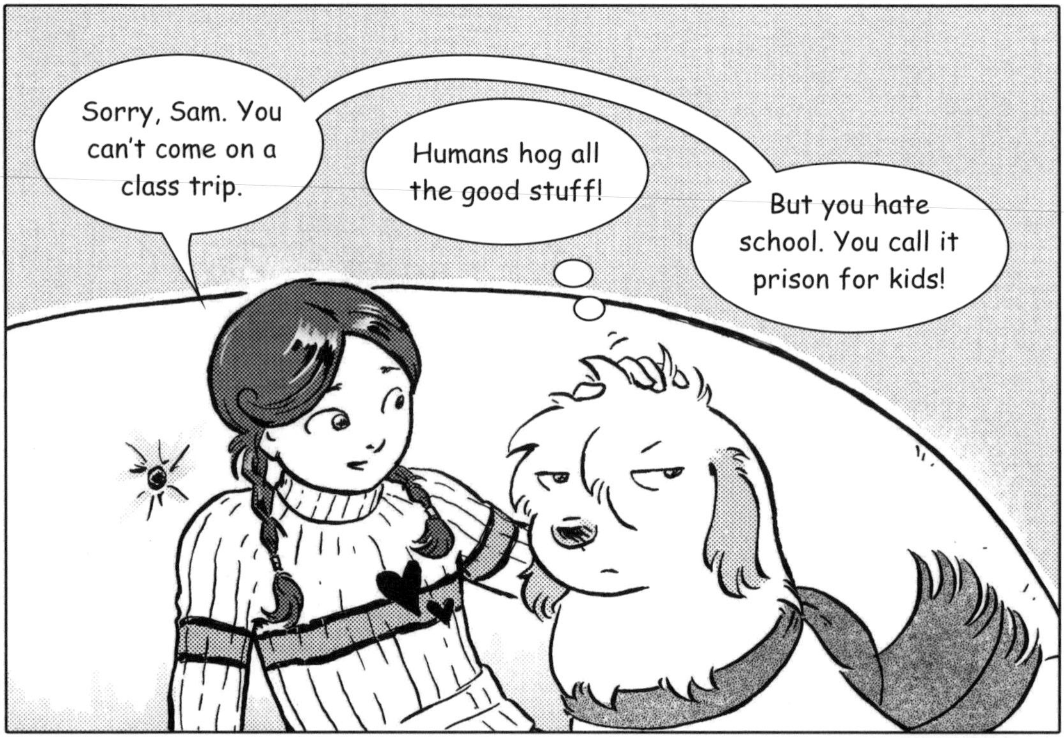
Sorry, Sam. You can't come on a class trip.
Humans hog all the good stuff!
But you hate school. You call it prison for kids!

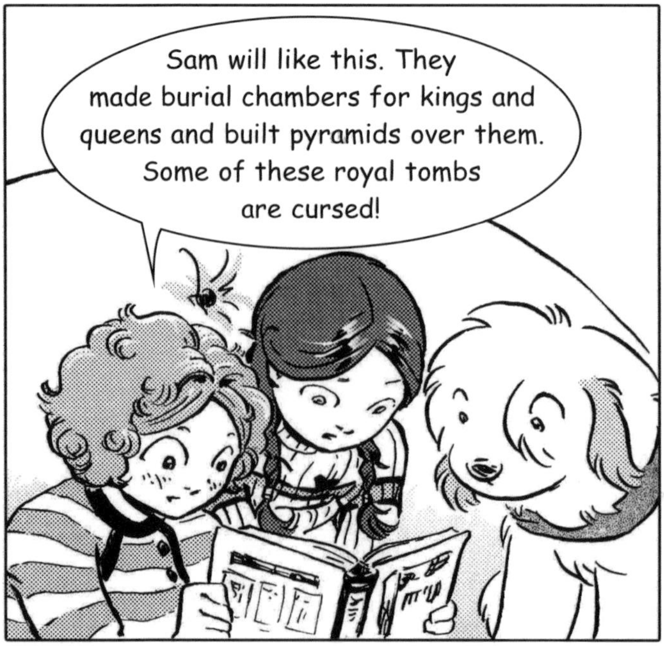
Sam will like this. They made burial chambers for kings and queens and built pyramids over them. Some of these royal tombs are cursed!

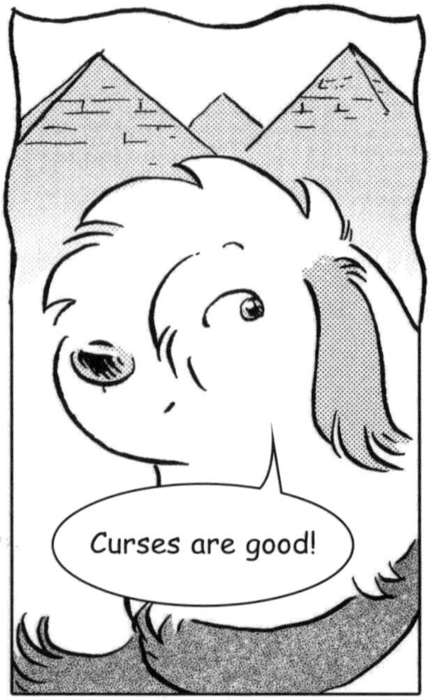
Curses are good!

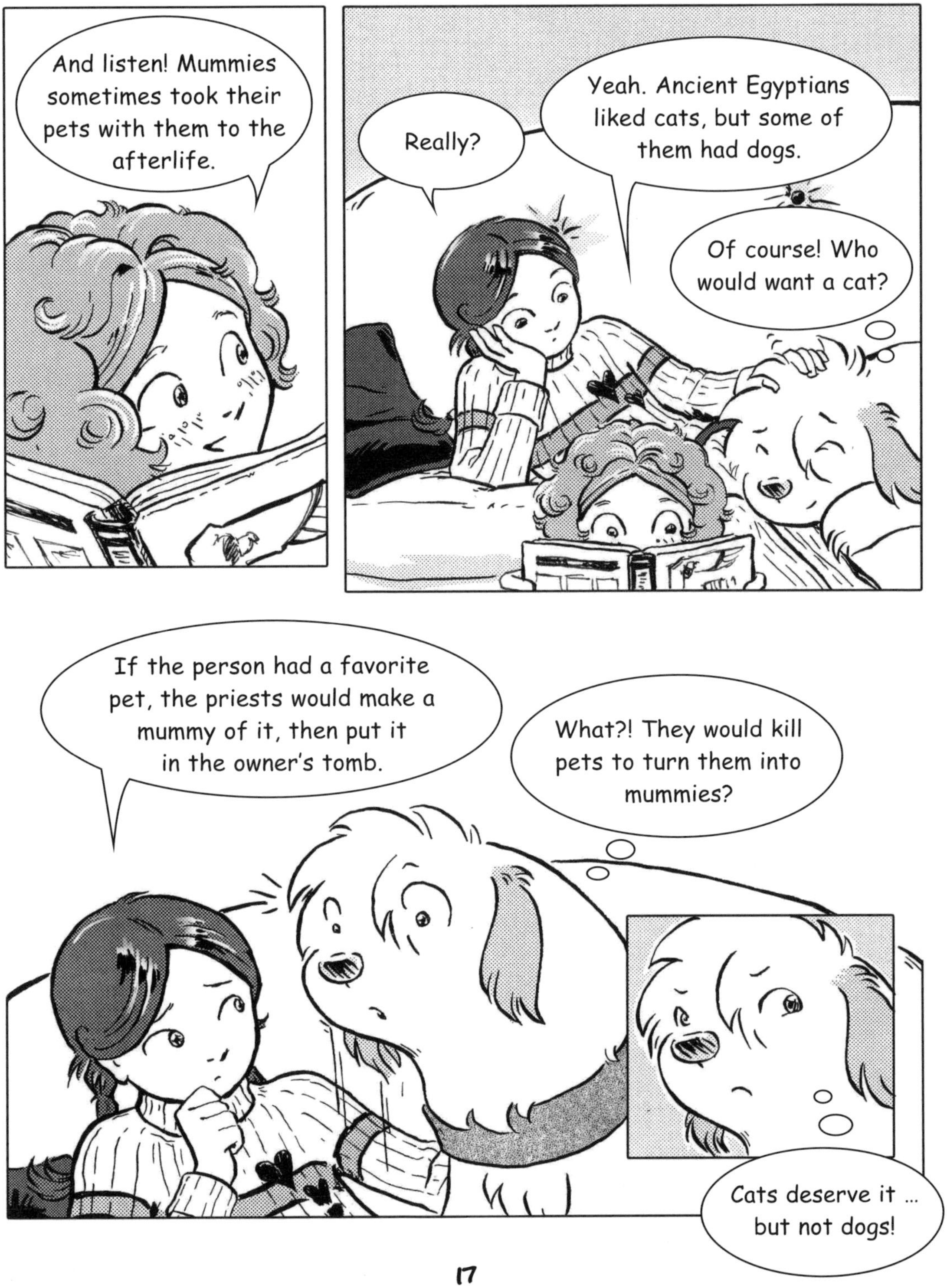

And listen! Mummies sometimes took their pets with them to the afterlife.
Really?
Yeah. Ancient Egyptians liked cats, but some of them had dogs.
Of course! Who would want a cat?
If the person had a favorite pet, the priests would make a mummy of it, then put it in the owner's tomb.
What?! They would kill pets to turn them into mummies?
Cats deserve it ... but not dogs!

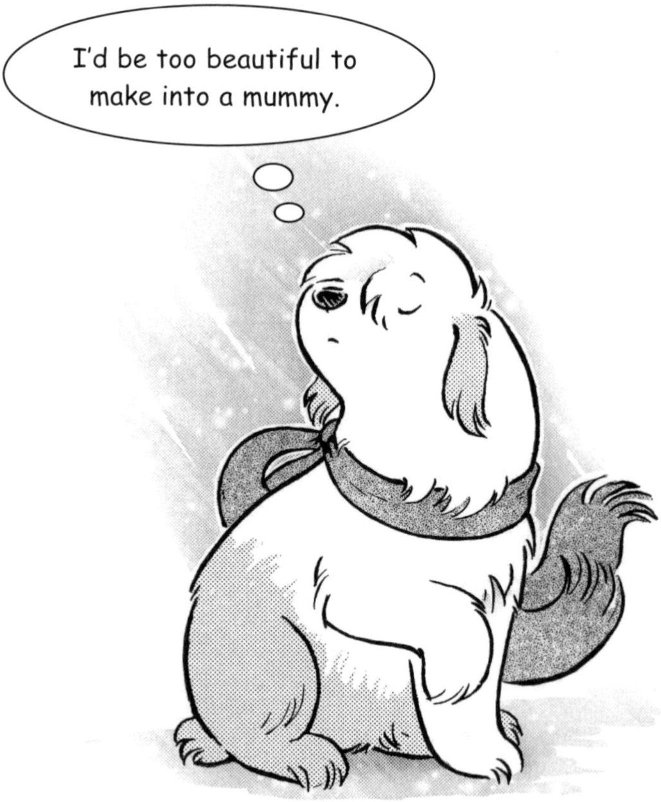
I'd be too beautiful to
make into a mummy.

The next week ...

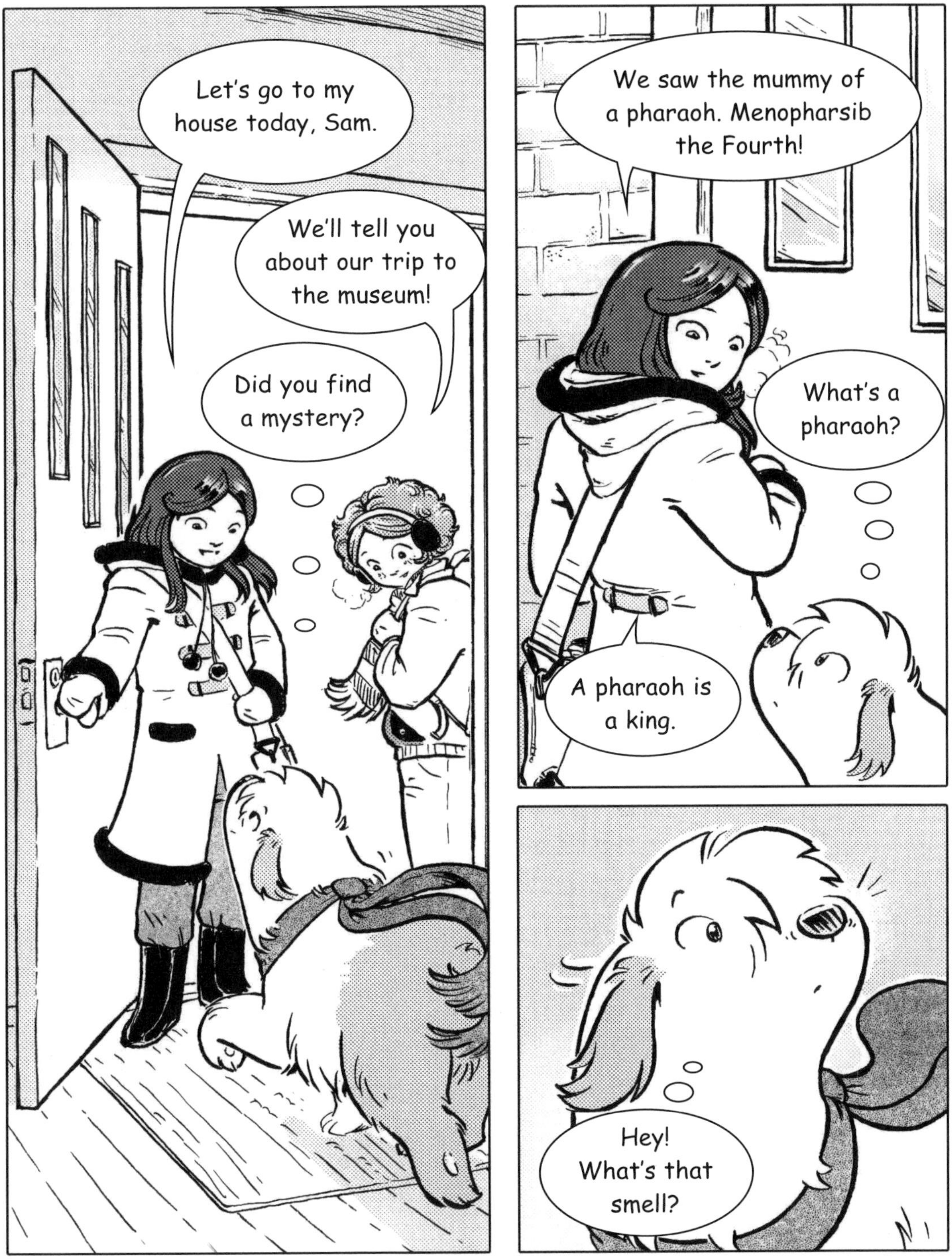
Let's go to my house today, Sam.
We'll tell you about our trip to the museum!
Did you find a mystery?
We saw the mummy of a pharaoh. Menopharsib the Fourth!
What's a pharaoh?
A pharaoh is a king.
Hey! What's that smell?

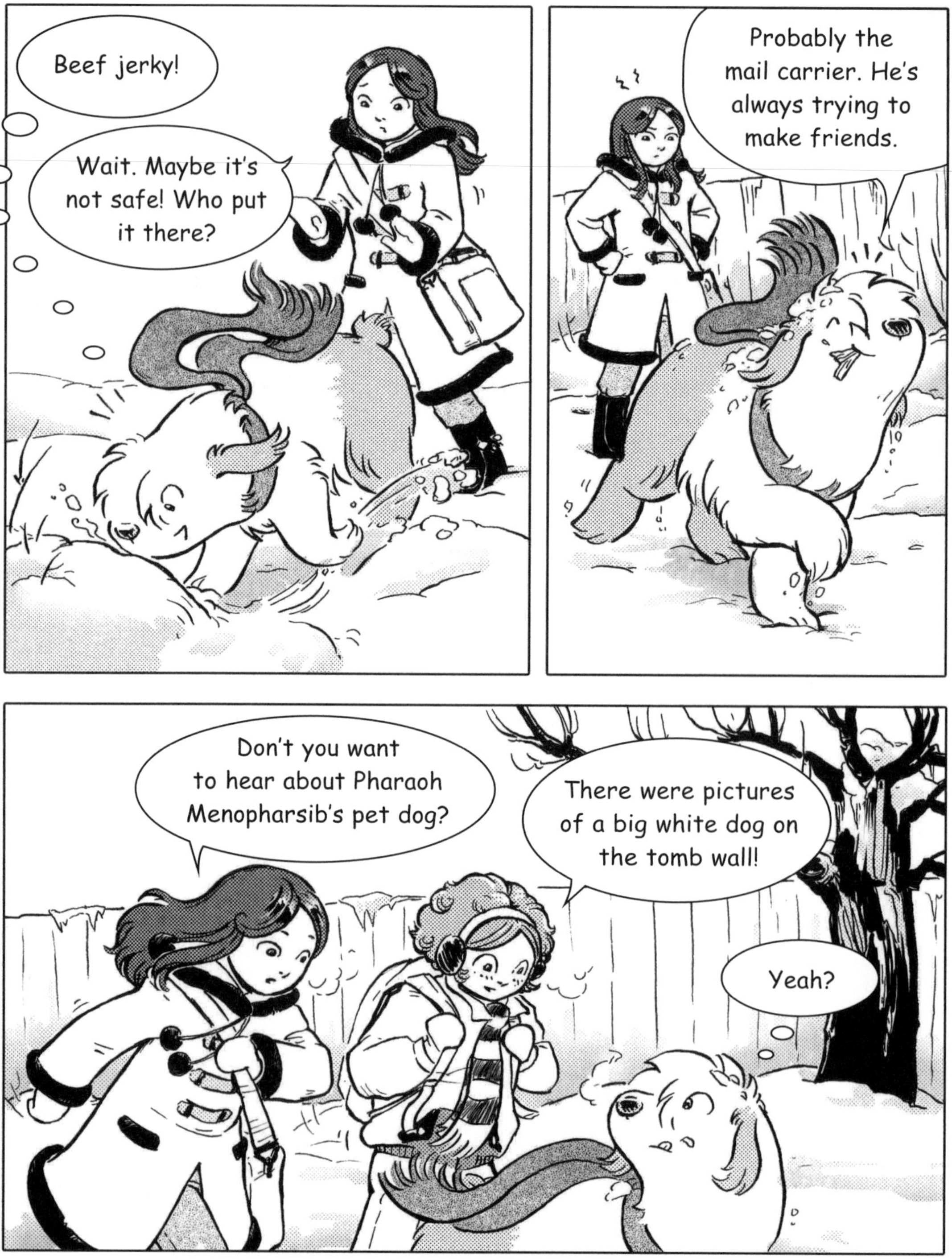
Beef jerky!
Wait. Maybe it's not safe! Who put it there?
Probably the mail carrier. He's always trying to make friends.
Don't you want to hear about Pharaoh Menopharsib's pet dog?
There were pictures of a big white dog on the tomb wall!
Yeah?

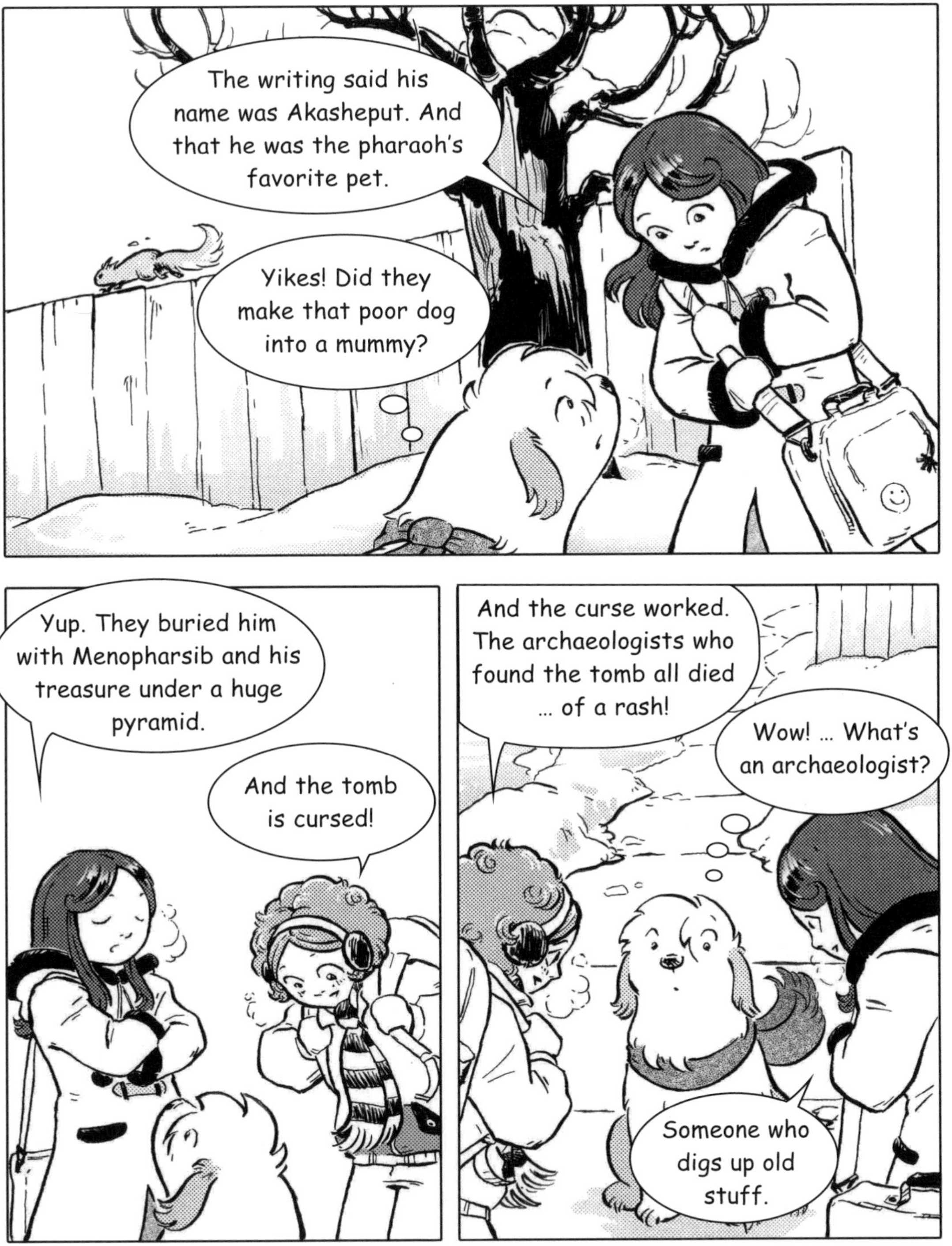
The writing said his name was Akasheput. And that he was the pharaoh's favorite pet.
Yikes! Did they make that poor dog into a mummy?
Yup. They buried him with Menopharsib and his treasure under a huge pyramid.
And the tomb is cursed!
And the curse worked. The archaeologists who found the tomb all died ... of a rash!
Wow! ... What's an archaeologist?
Someone who digs up old stuff.

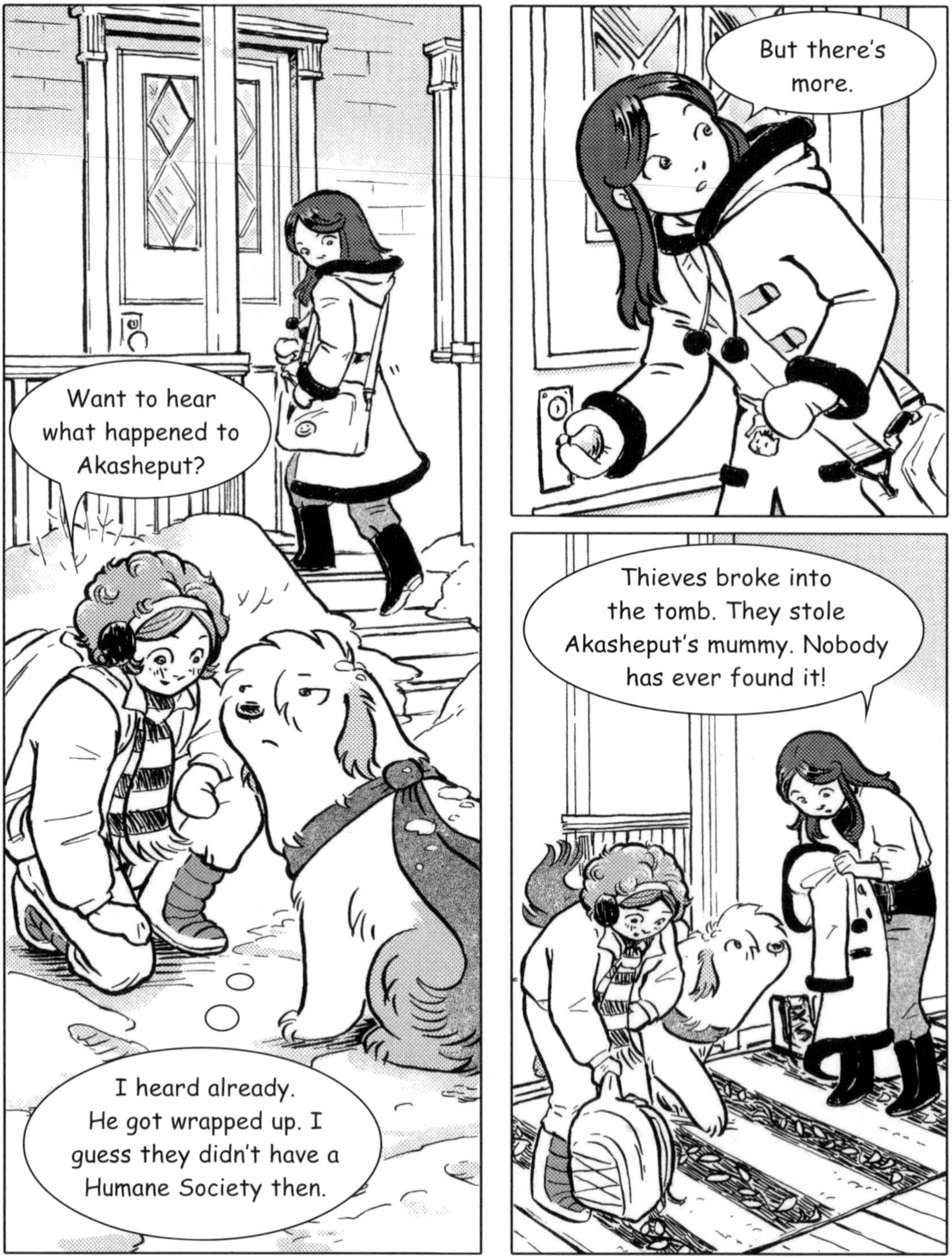
Want to hear what happened to Akasheput?
I heard already. He got wrapped up. I guess they didn't have a Humane Society then.
But there's more.
Thieves broke into the tomb. They stole Akasheput's mummy. Nobody has ever found it!

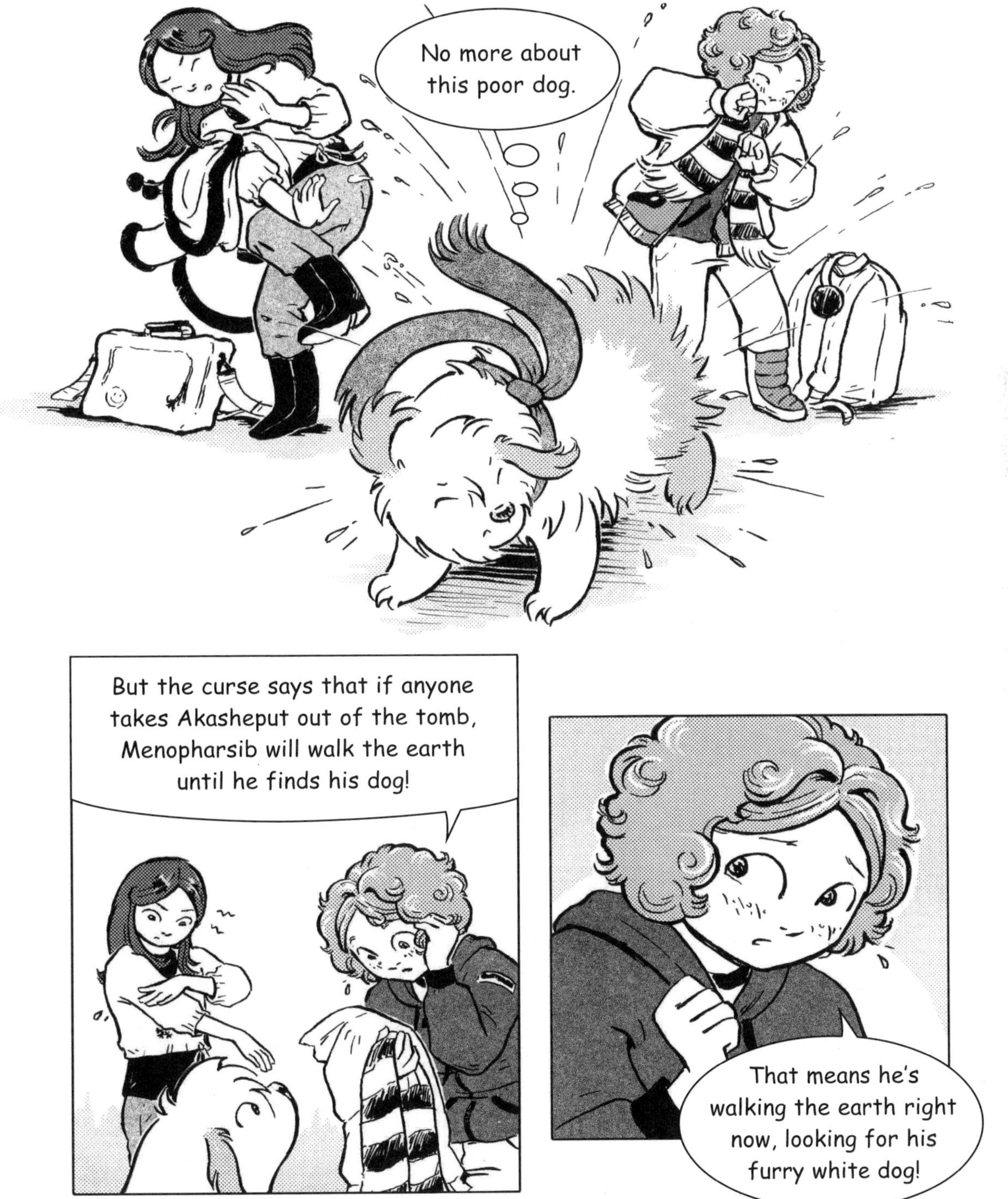
No more about this poor dog.
But the curse says that if anyone takes Akasheput out of the tomb, Menopharsib will walk the earth until he finds his dog!
That means he's walking the earth right now, looking for his furry white dog!

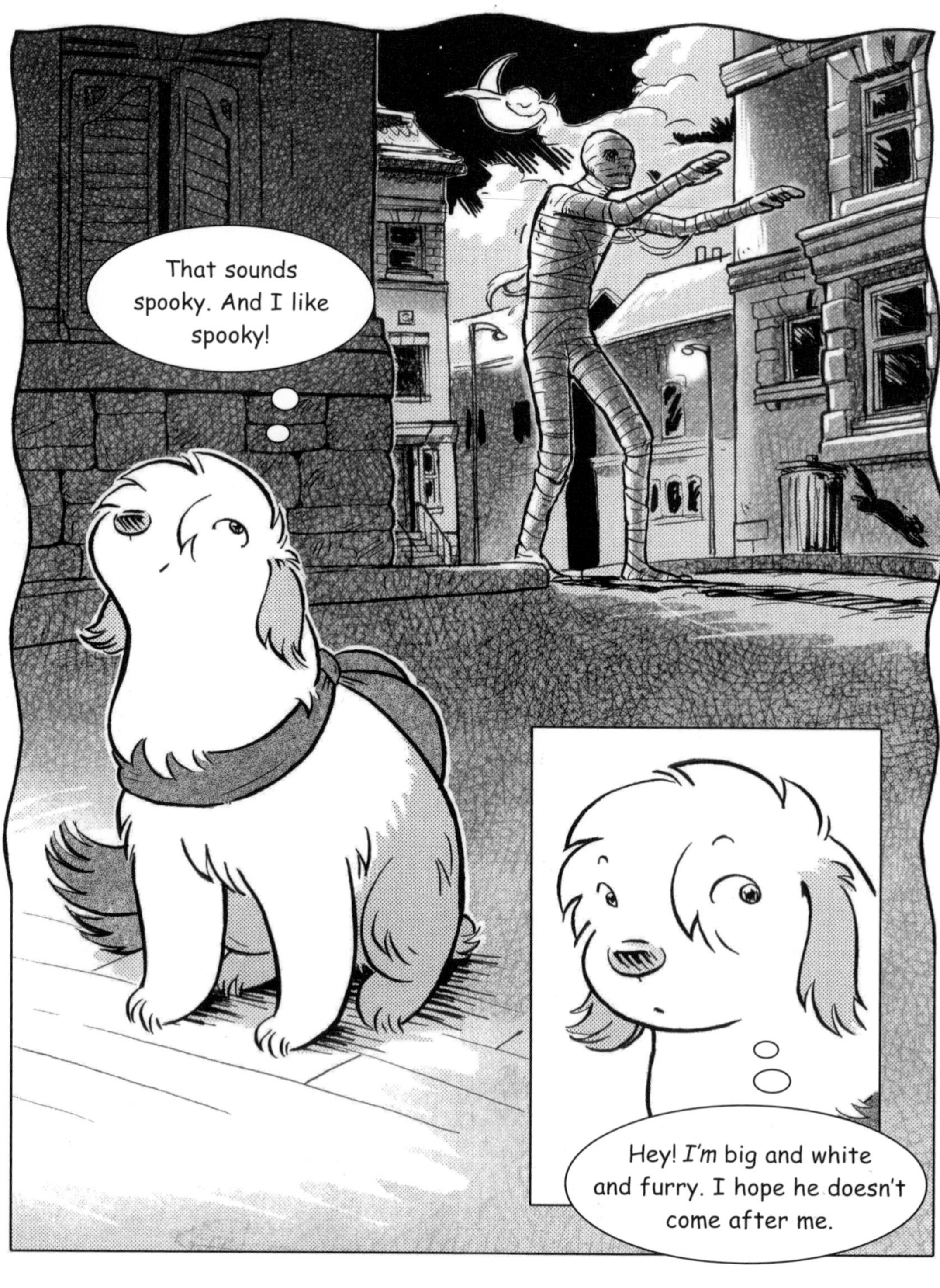
That sounds spooky. And I like spooky!
Hey! *I'm* big and white and furry. I hope he doesn't come after me.

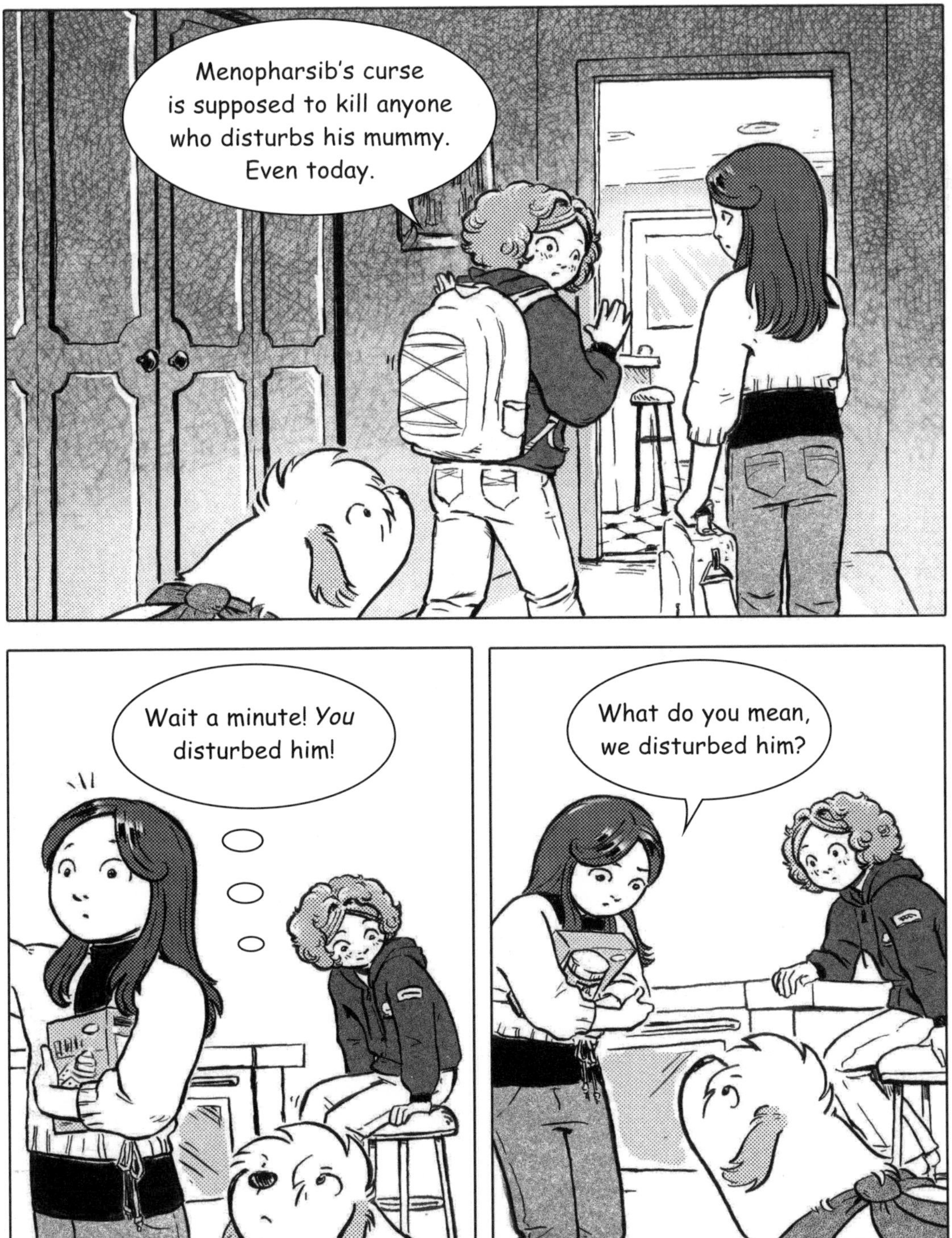
Menopharsib's curse is supposed to kill anyone who disturbs his mummy. Even today.
Wait a minute! *You* disturbed him!
What do you mean, we disturbed him?

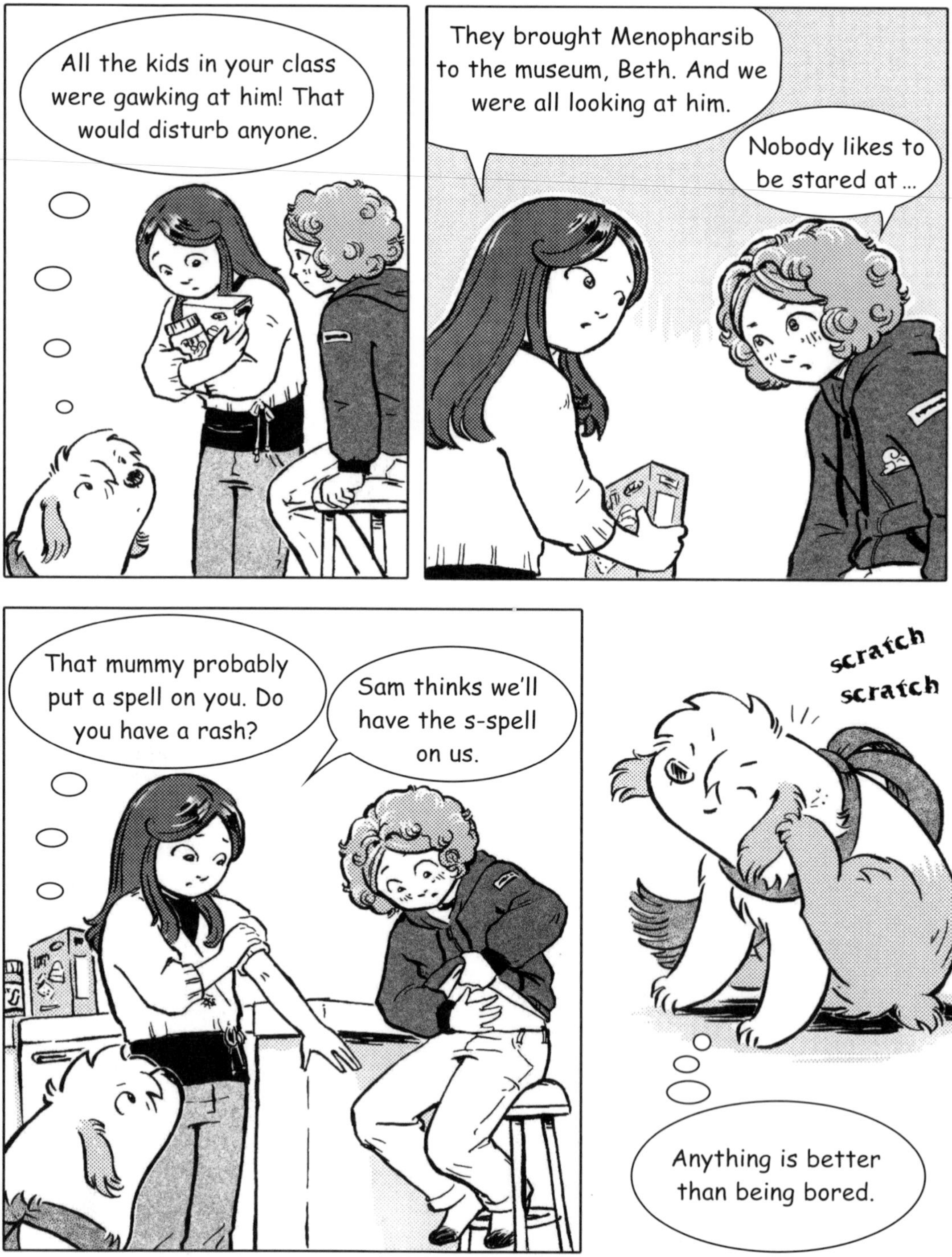
All the kids in your class were gawking at him! That would disturb anyone.
They brought Menopharsib to the museum, Beth. And we were all looking at him.
Nobody likes to be stared at ...
That mummy probably put a spell on you. Do you have a rash?
Sam thinks we'll have the s-spell on us.
scratch
scratch
Anything is better than being bored.

Later ...

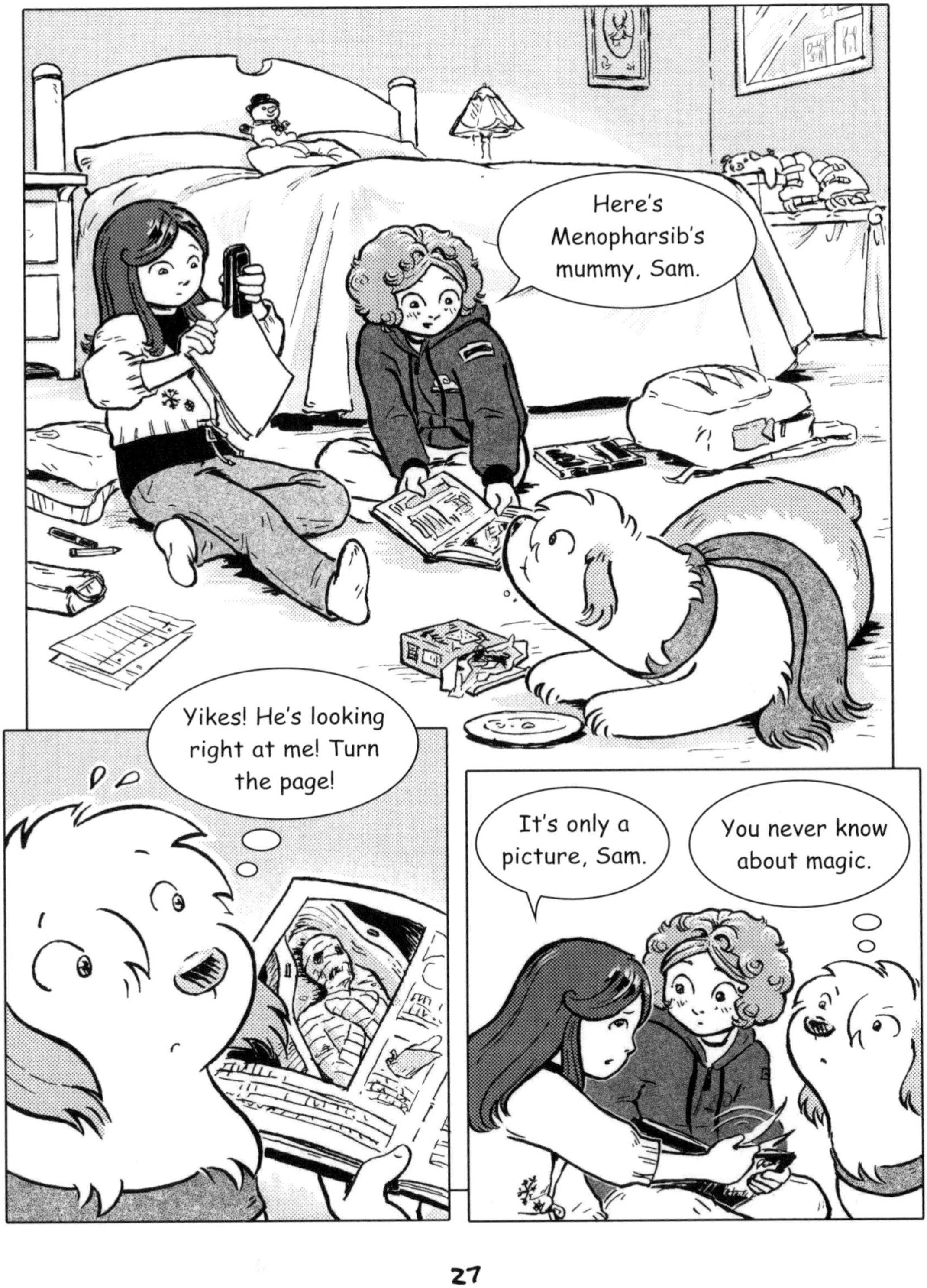

Here's Menopharsib's mummy, Sam.
Yikes! He's looking right at me! Turn the page!
It's only a picture, Sam.
You never know about magic.

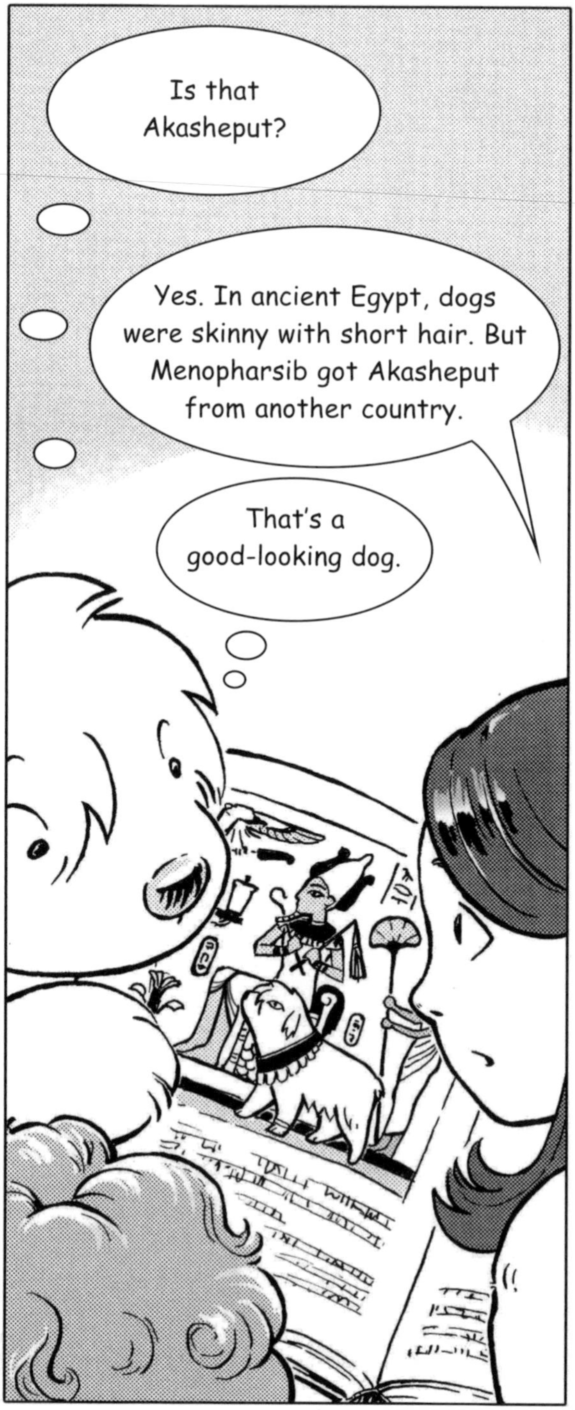
Is that Akasheput?
Yes. In ancient Egypt, dogs were skinny with short hair. But Menopharsib got Akasheput from another country.
That's a good-looking dog.

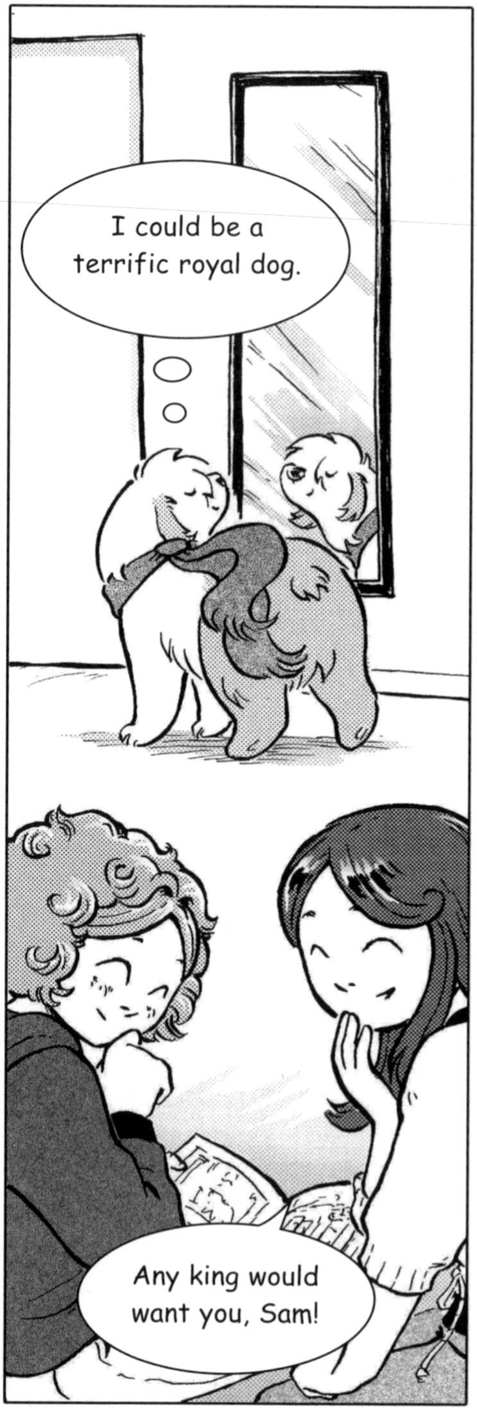
I could be a terrific royal dog.
Any king would want you, Sam!

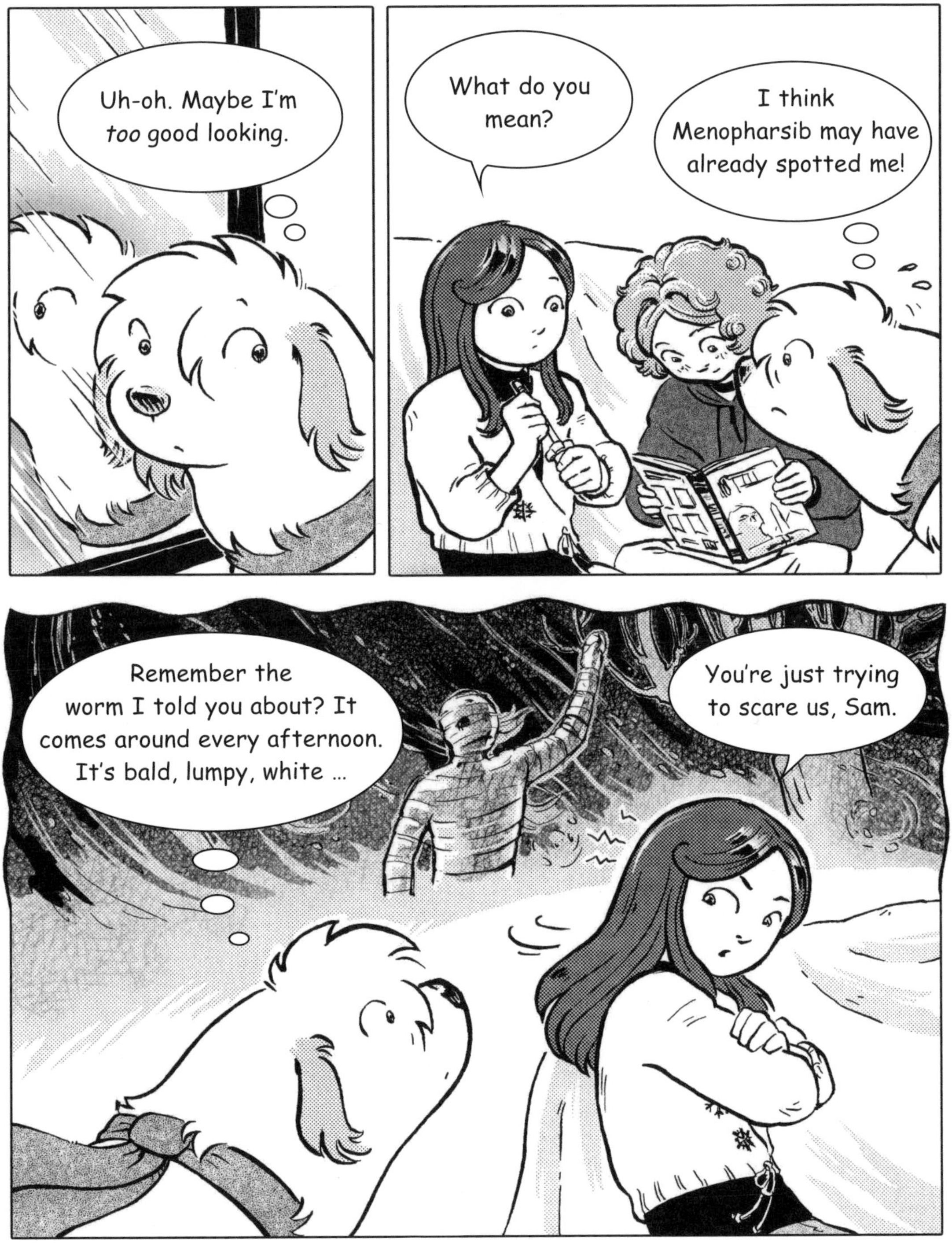
Uh-oh. Maybe I'm *too* good looking.
What do you mean?
I think Menopharsib may have already spotted me!
Remember the worm I told you about? It comes around every afternoon. It's bald, lumpy, white ...
You're just trying to scare us, Sam.

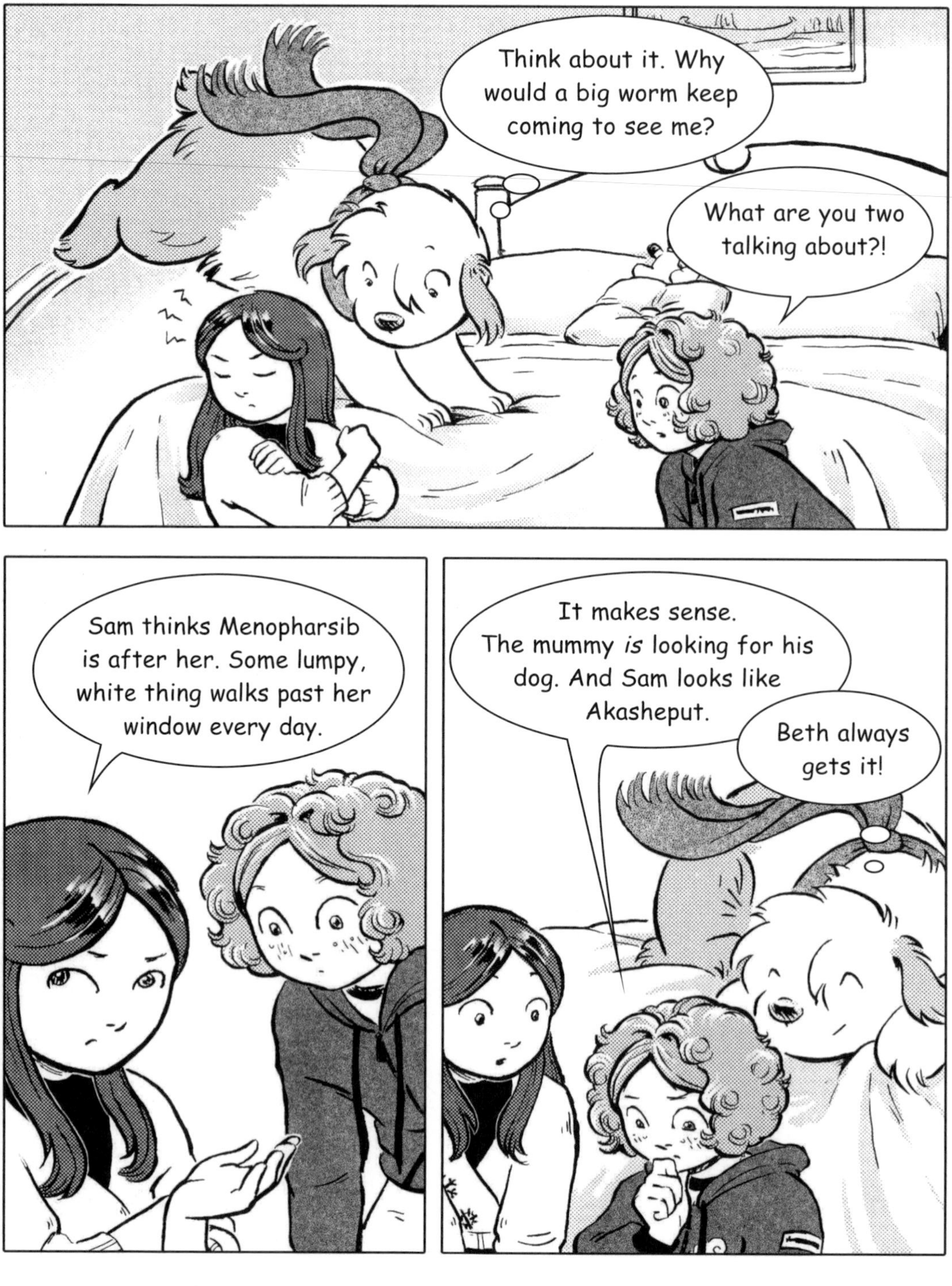
Think about it. Why would a big worm keep coming to see me?
What are you two talking about?!
Sam thinks Menopharsib is after her. Some lumpy, white thing walks past her window every day.
It makes sense. The mummy *is* looking for his dog. And Sam looks like Akasheput.
Beth always gets it!

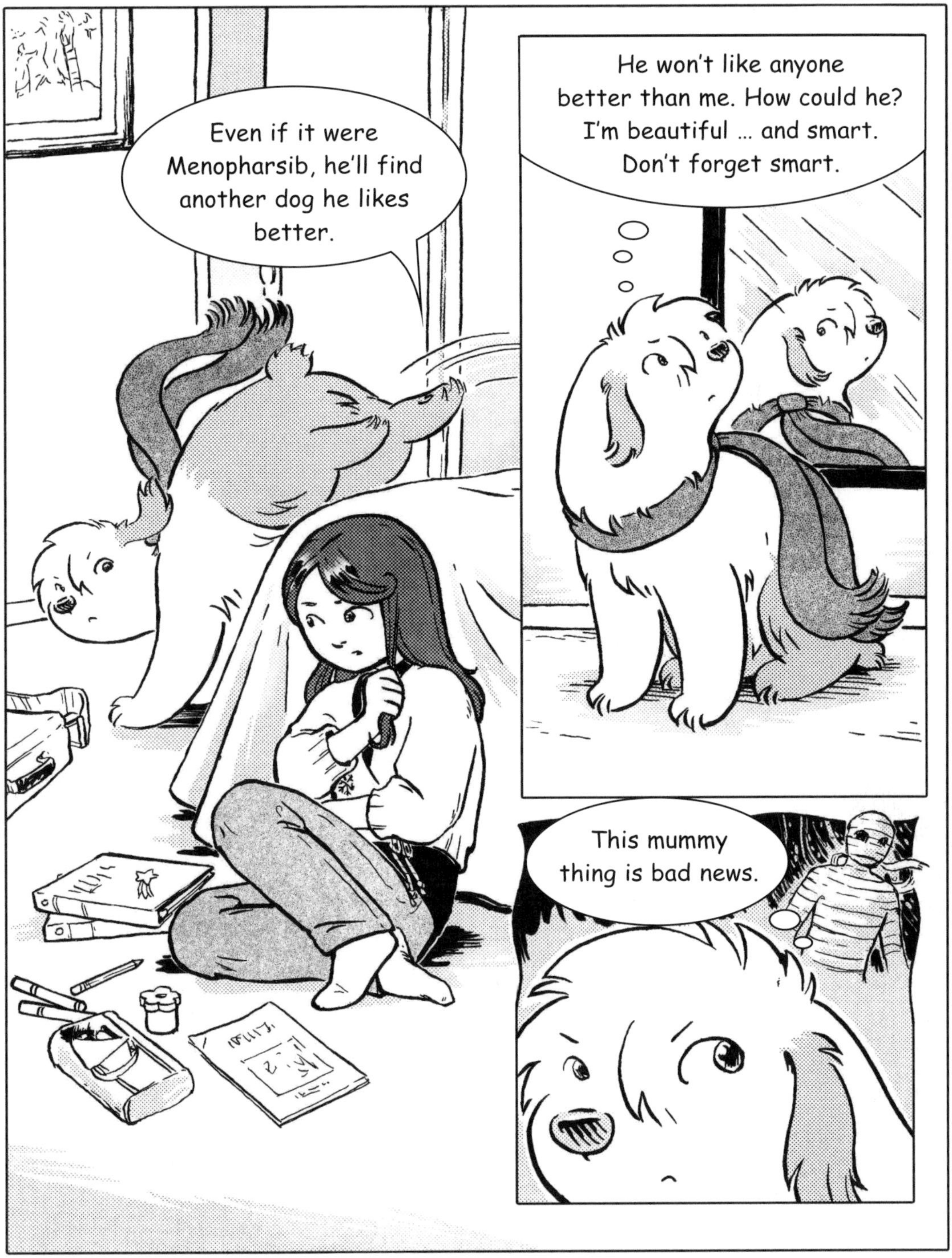
Even if it were Menopharsib, he'll find another dog he likes better.
He won't like anyone better than me. How could he? I'm beautiful ... and smart. Don't forget smart.
This mummy thing is bad news.

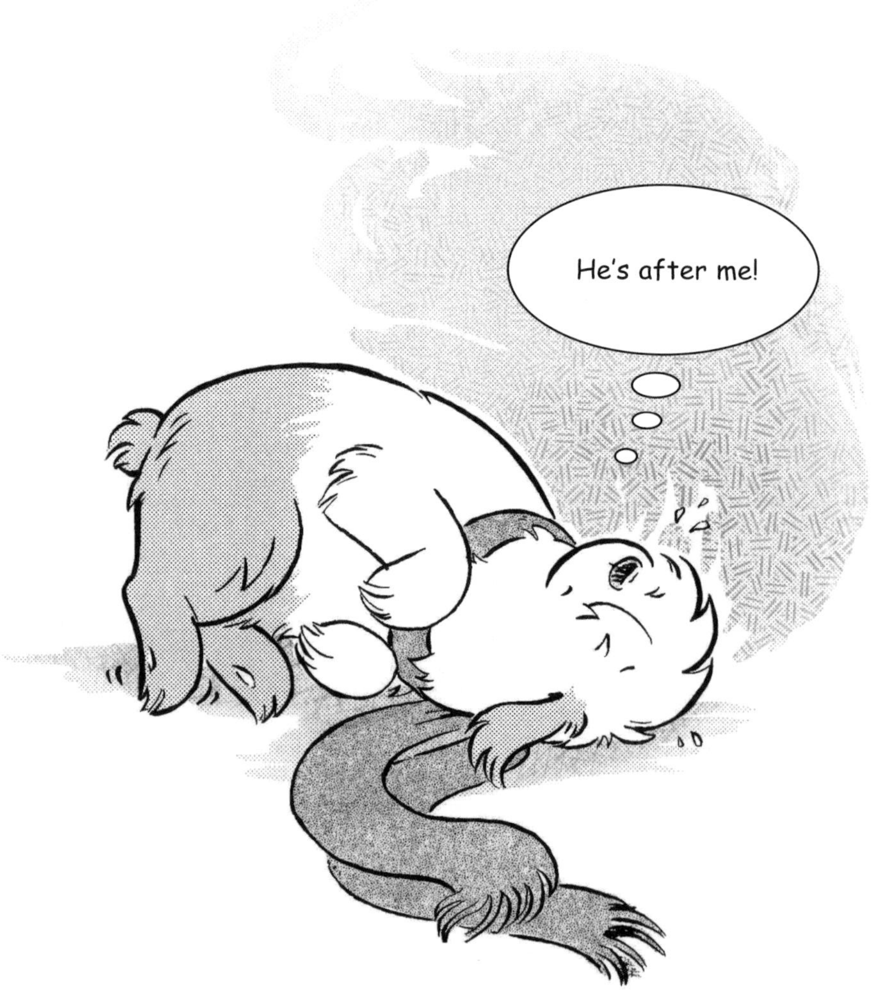
He's after me!

That night ...

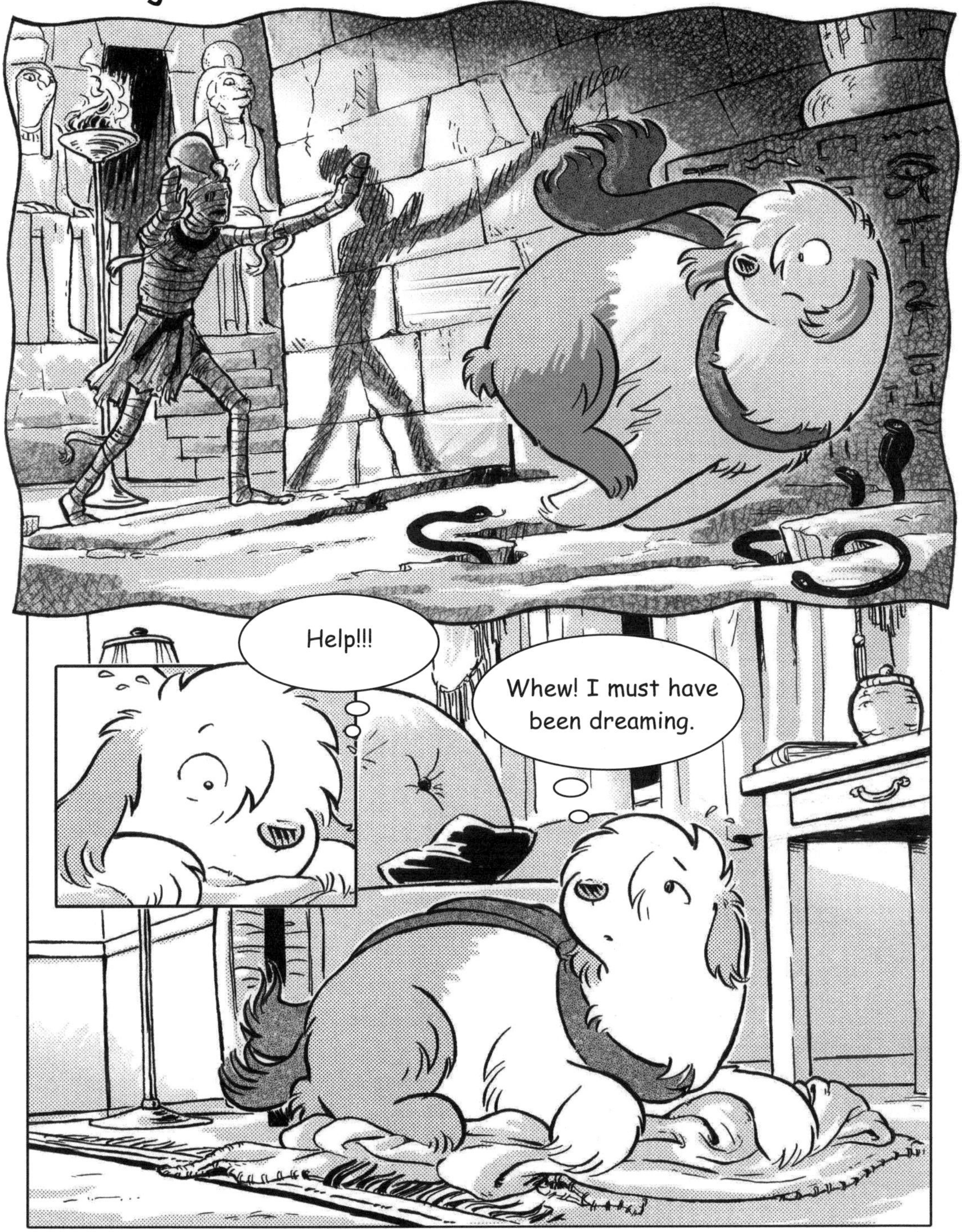

Help!!!
Whew! I must have been dreaming.

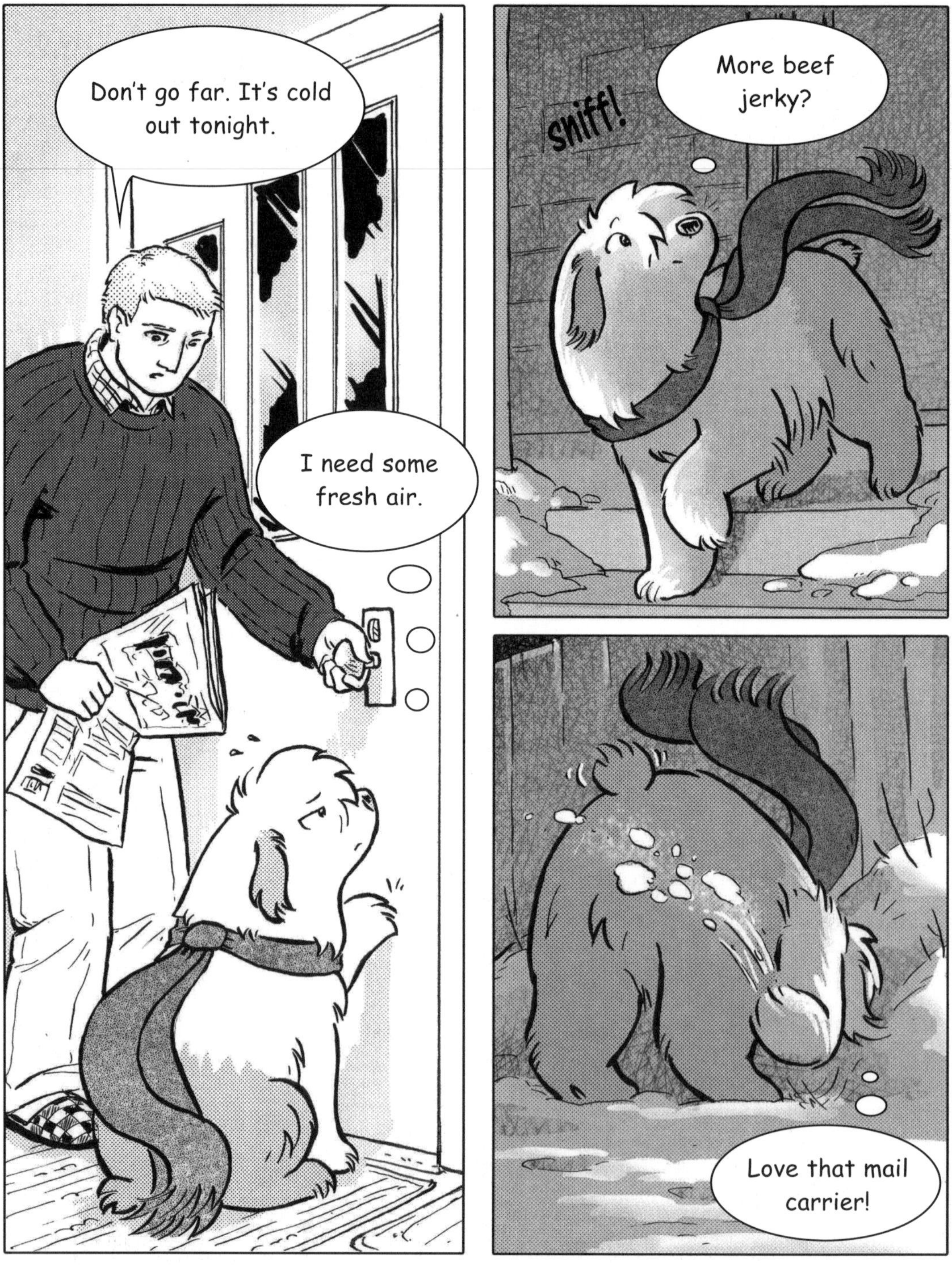
Don't go far. It's cold out tonight.
I need some fresh air.
sniff!
More beef jerky?
Love that mail carrier!

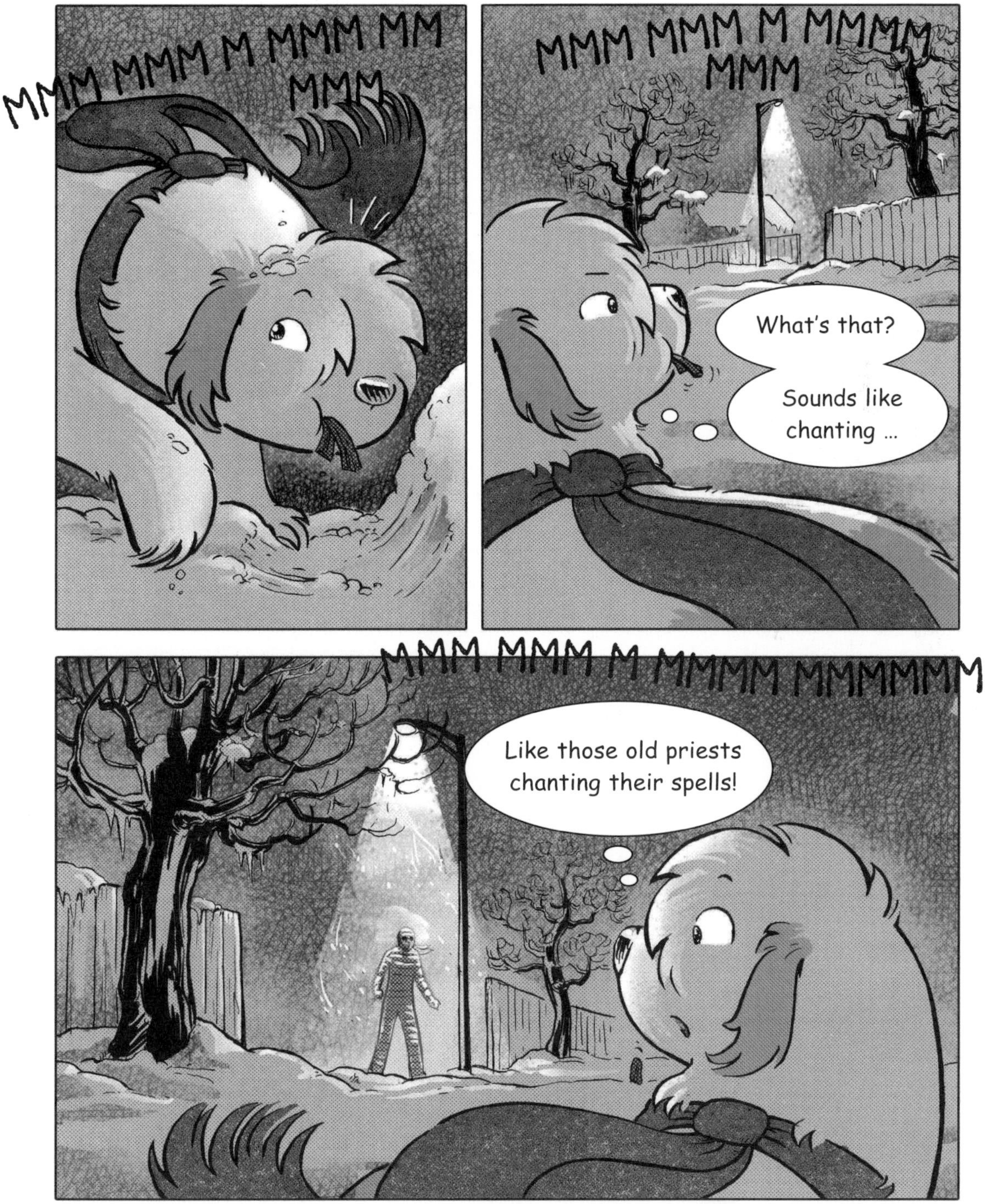

MMM MMM M MMM MM
MMM
MMM MMM M MMMM
MMM
What's that?
Sounds like chanting ...
MMM MMM M MMMM MMMMMM
Like those old priests chanting their spells!

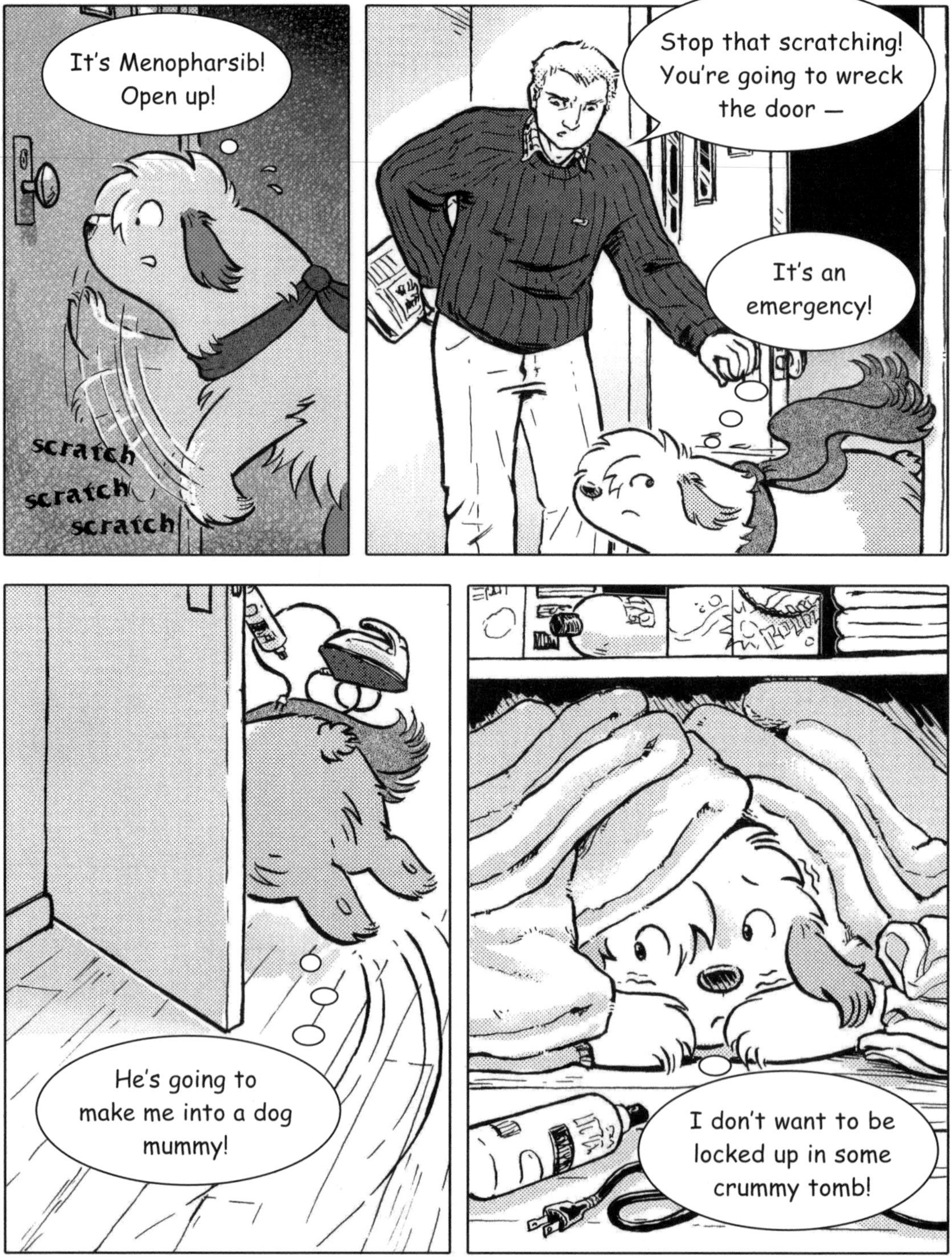
It's Menopharsib! Open up!
scratch
scratch
scratch
Stop that scratching! You're going to wreck the door —
It's an emergency!
He's going to make me into a dog mummy!
I don't want to be locked up in some crummy tomb!

The next afternoon ...

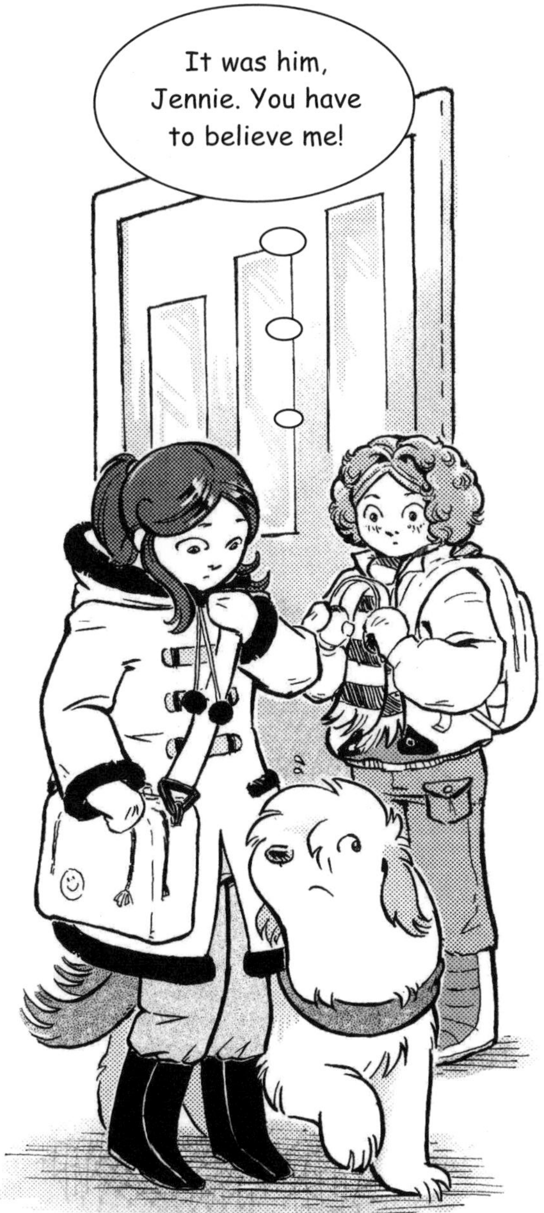
It was him, Jennie. You have to believe me!

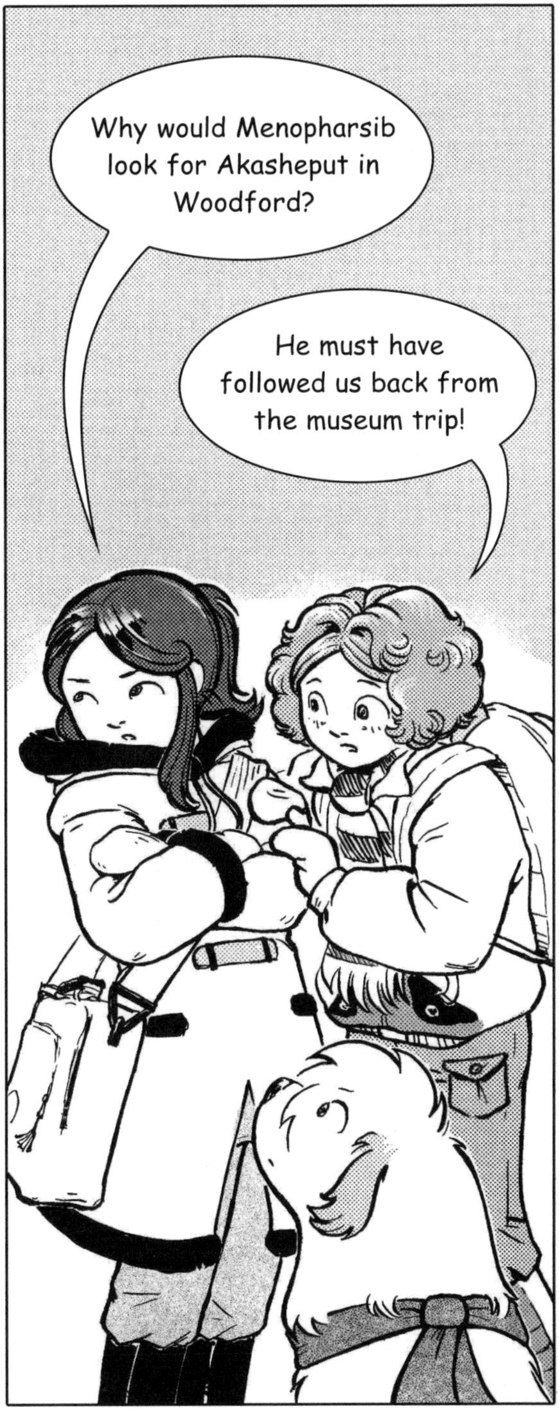
Why would Menopharsib look for Akasheput in Woodford?
He must have followed us back from the museum trip!

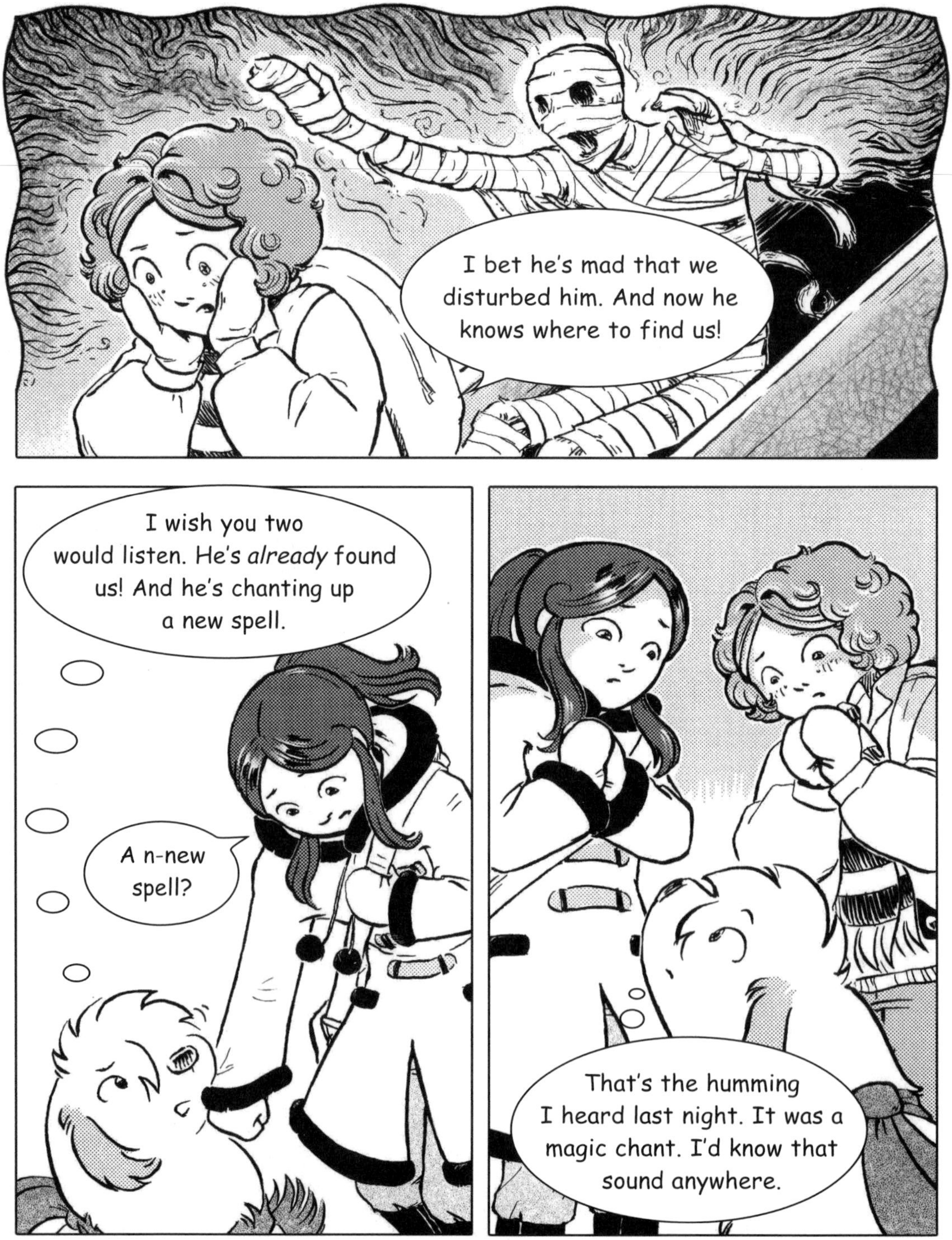
I bet he's mad that we disturbed him. And now he knows where to find us!
I wish you two would listen. He's *already* found us! And he's chanting up a new spell.
A n-new spell?
That's the humming I heard last night. It was a magic chant. I'd know that sound anywhere.

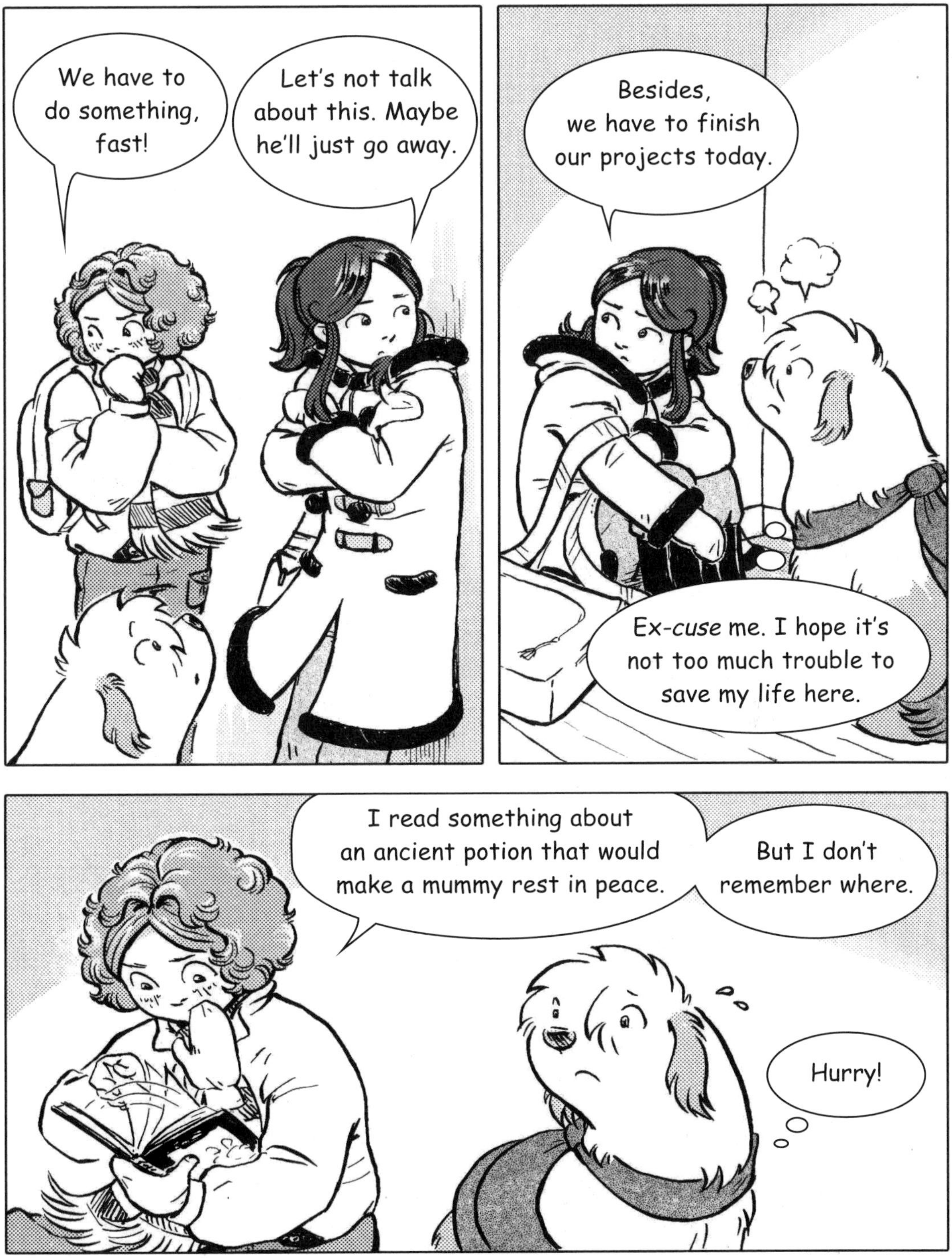
We have to do something, fast!
Let's not talk about this. Maybe he'll just go away.
Besides, we have to finish our projects today.
Ex-*cuse* me. I hope it's not too much trouble to save my life here.
I read something about an ancient potion that would make a mummy rest in peace.
But I don't remember where.
Hurry!

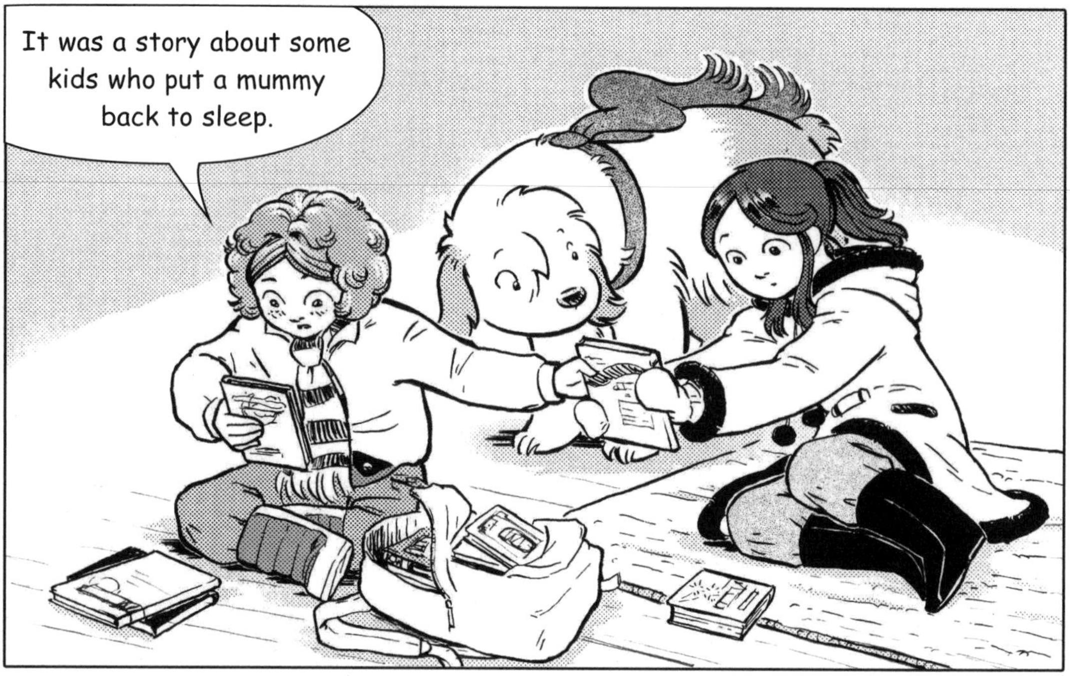
It was a story about some kids who put a mummy back to sleep.

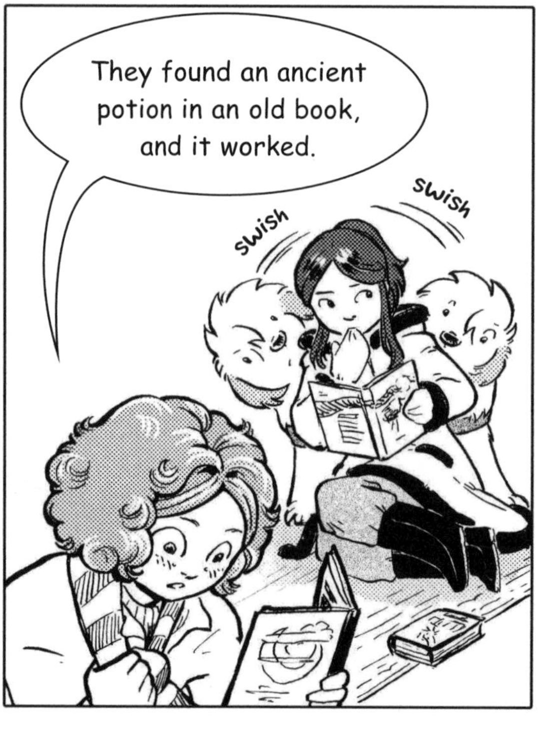
They found an ancient potion in an old book, and it worked.
swish
swish

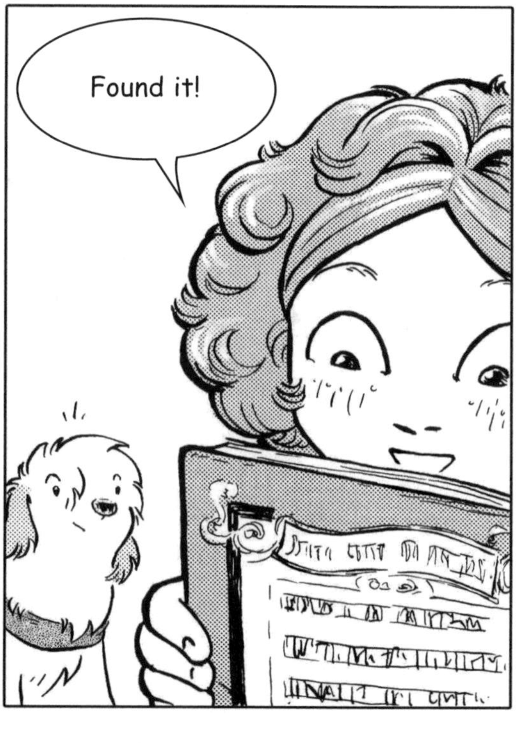
Found it!

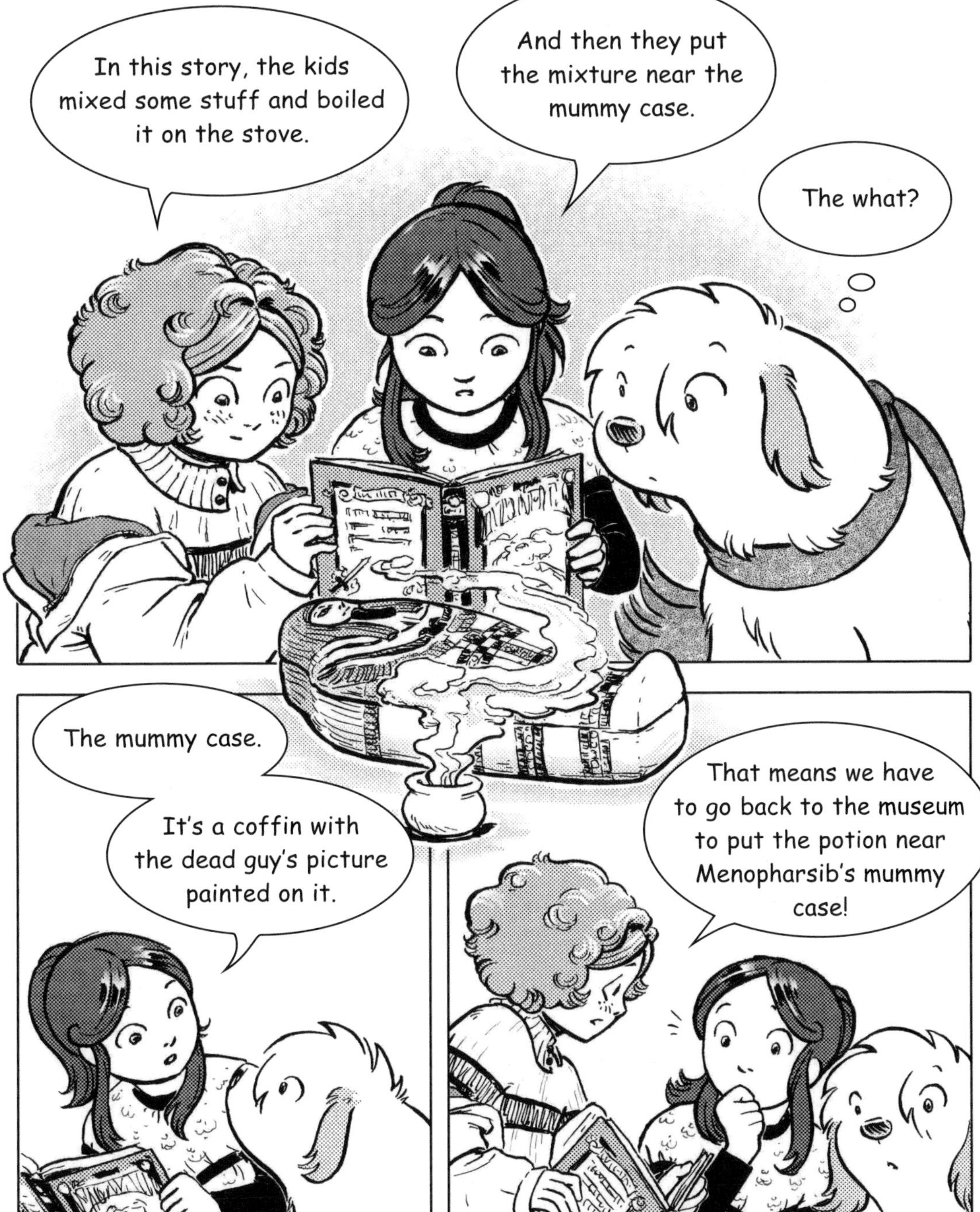
In this story, the kids mixed some stuff and boiled it on the stove.
And then they put the mixture near the mummy case.
The what?
The mummy case.
It's a coffin with the dead guy's picture painted on it.
That means we have to go back to the museum to put the potion near Menopharsib's mummy case!

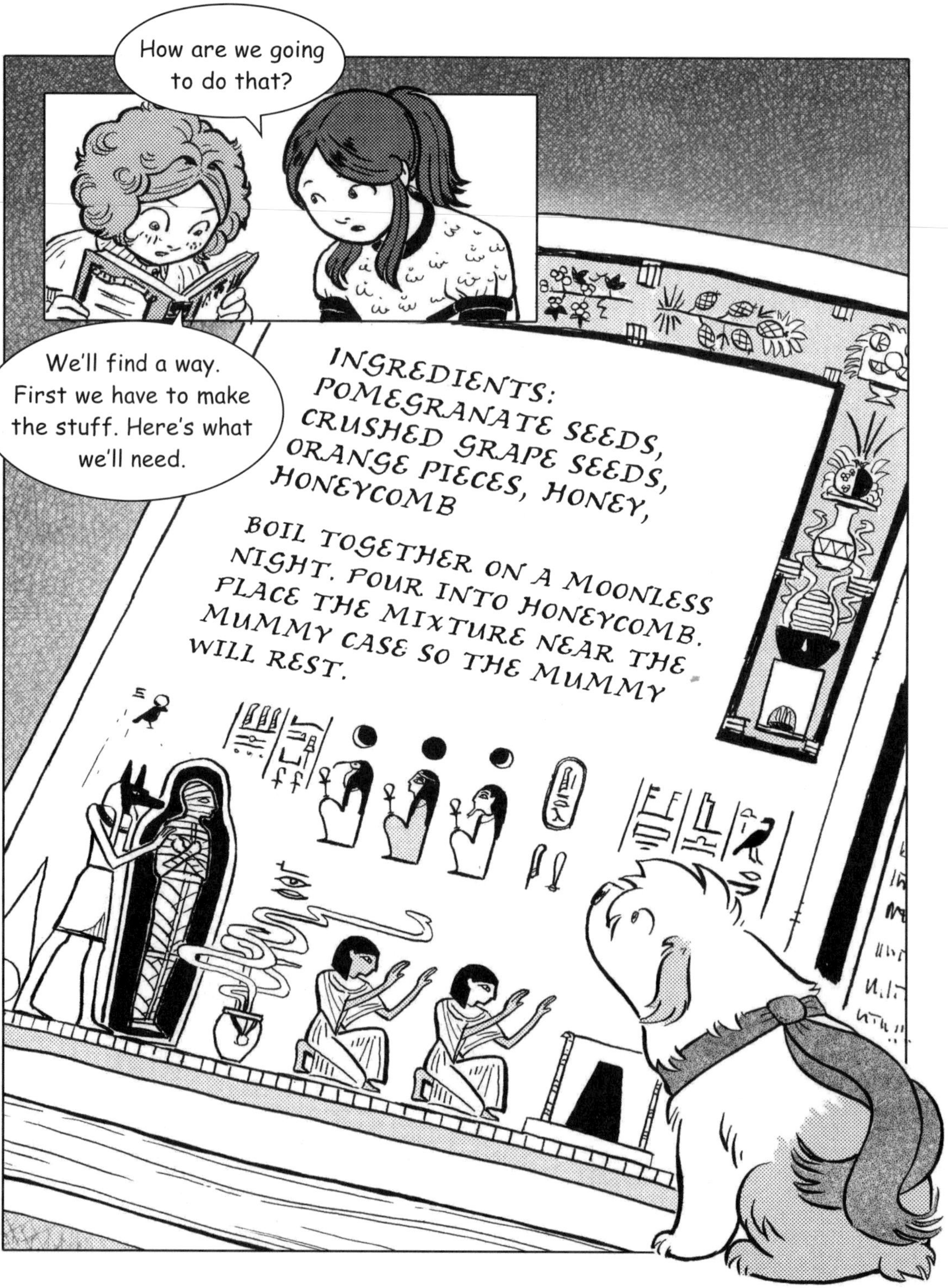
How are we going to do that?
We'll find a way. First we have to make the stuff. Here's what we'll need.
INGREDIENTS: POMEGRANATE SEEDS, CRUSHED GRAPE SEEDS, ORANGE PIECES, HONEY, HONEYCOMB
BOIL TOGETHER ON A MOONLESS NIGHT. POUR INTO HONEYCOMB. PLACE THE MIXTURE NEAR THE MUMMY CASE SO THE MUMMY WILL REST.

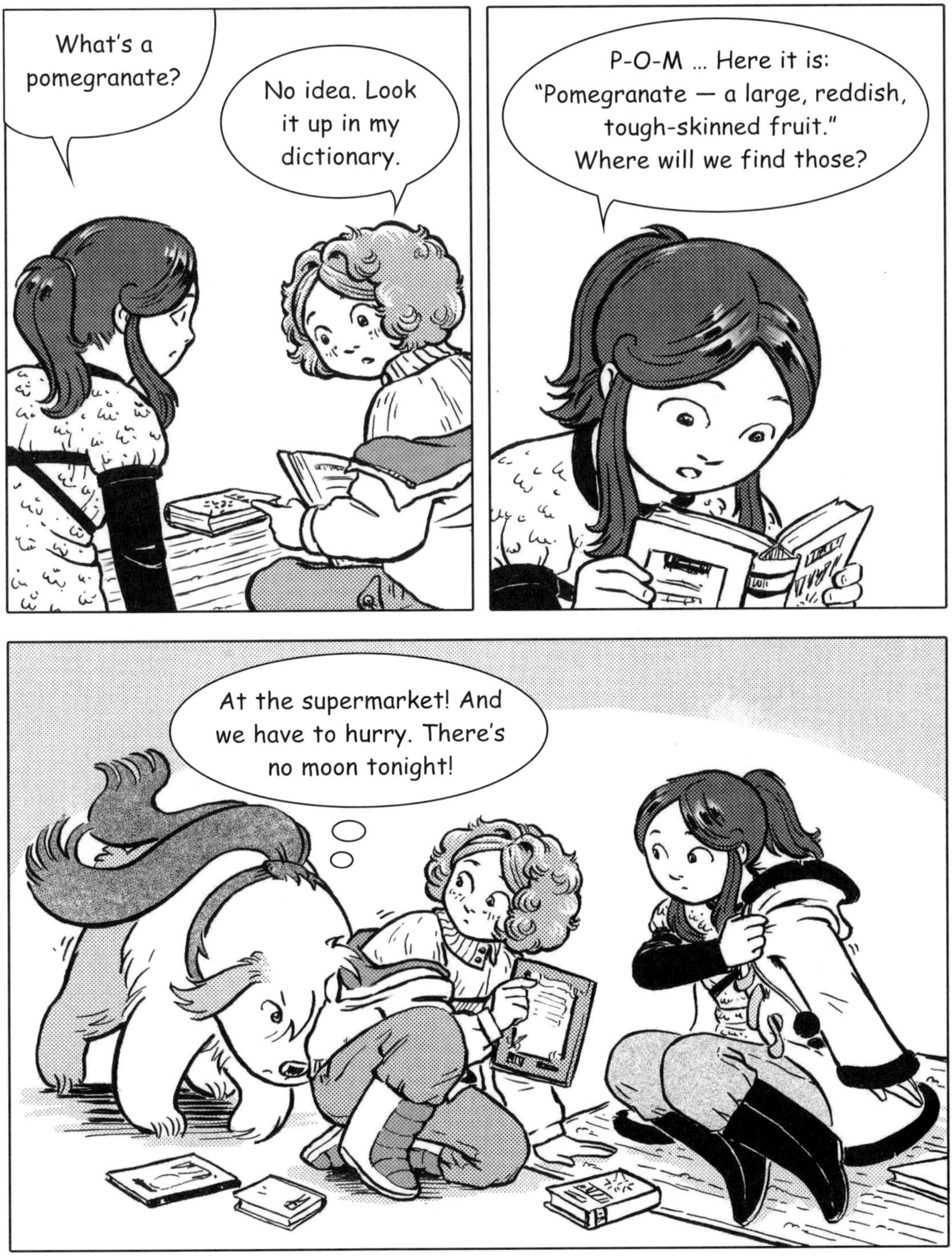
What's a pomegranate?
No idea. Look it up in my dictionary.
P-O-M ... Here it is: "Pomegranate — a large, reddish, tough-skinned fruit." Where will we find those?
At the supermarket! And we have to hurry. There's no moon tonight!

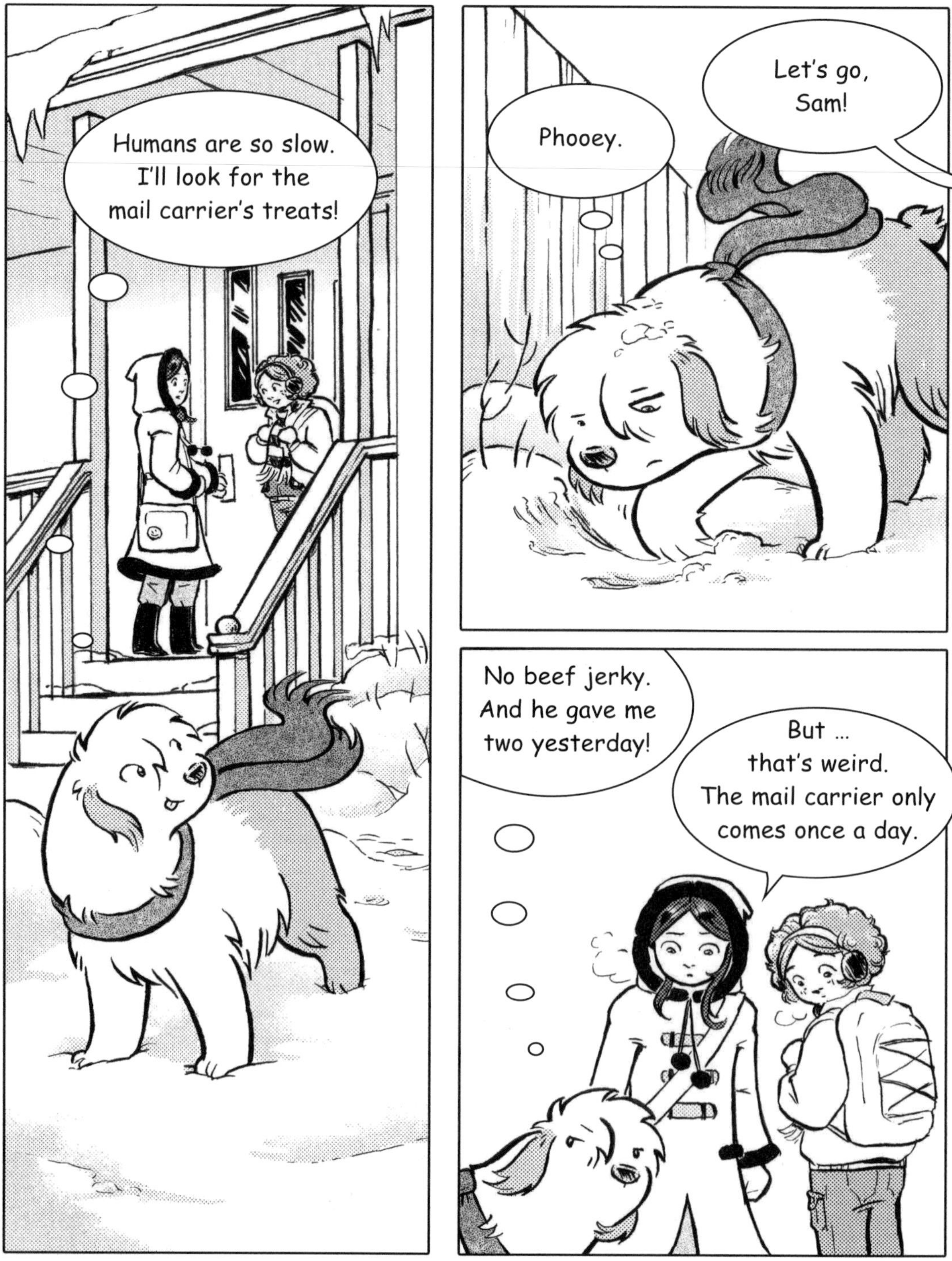
Humans are so slow. I'll look for the mail carrier's treats!
Let's go, Sam!
Phooey.
No beef jerky. And he gave me two yesterday!
But ... that's weird. The mail carrier only comes once a day.

Soon ...

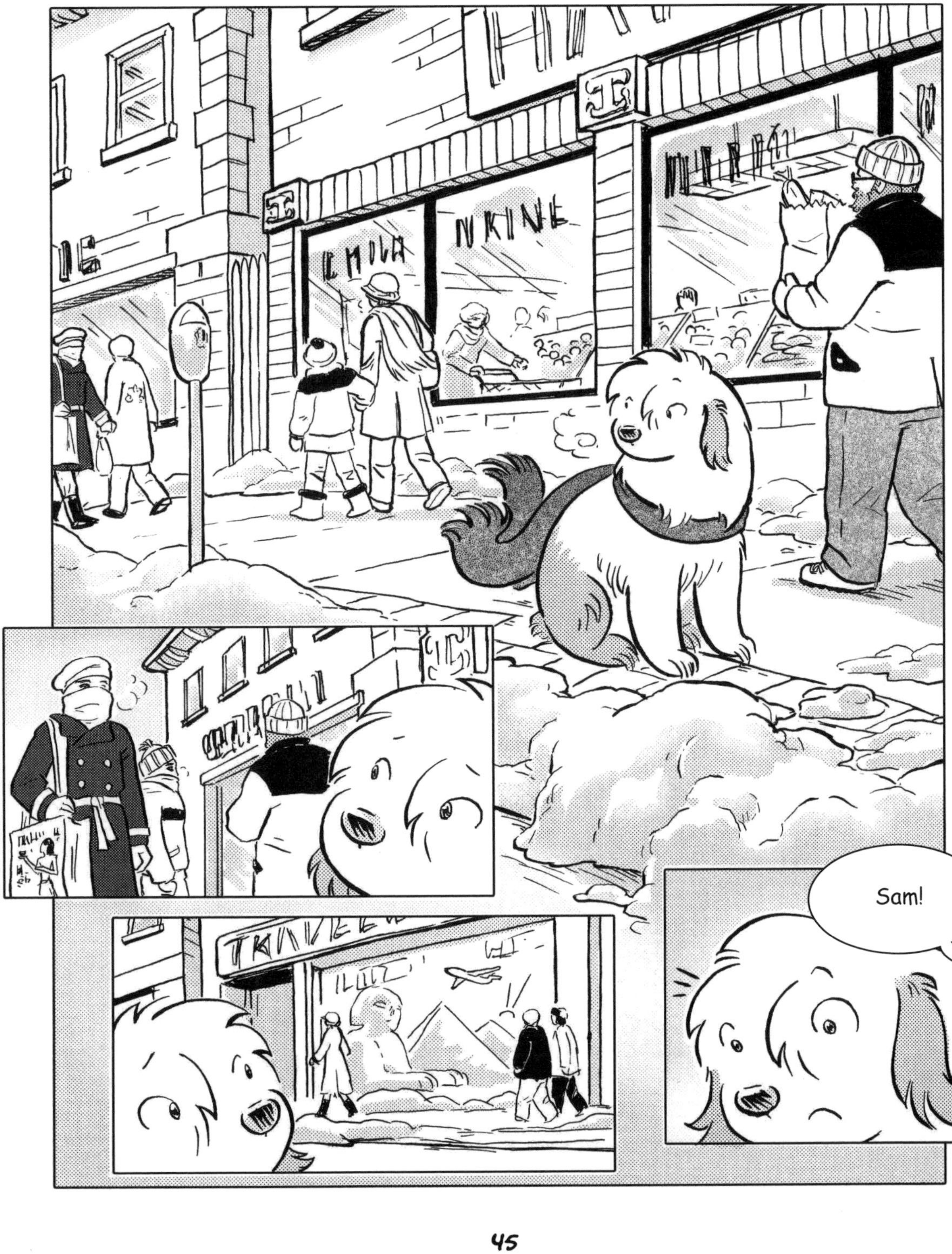
Sam!

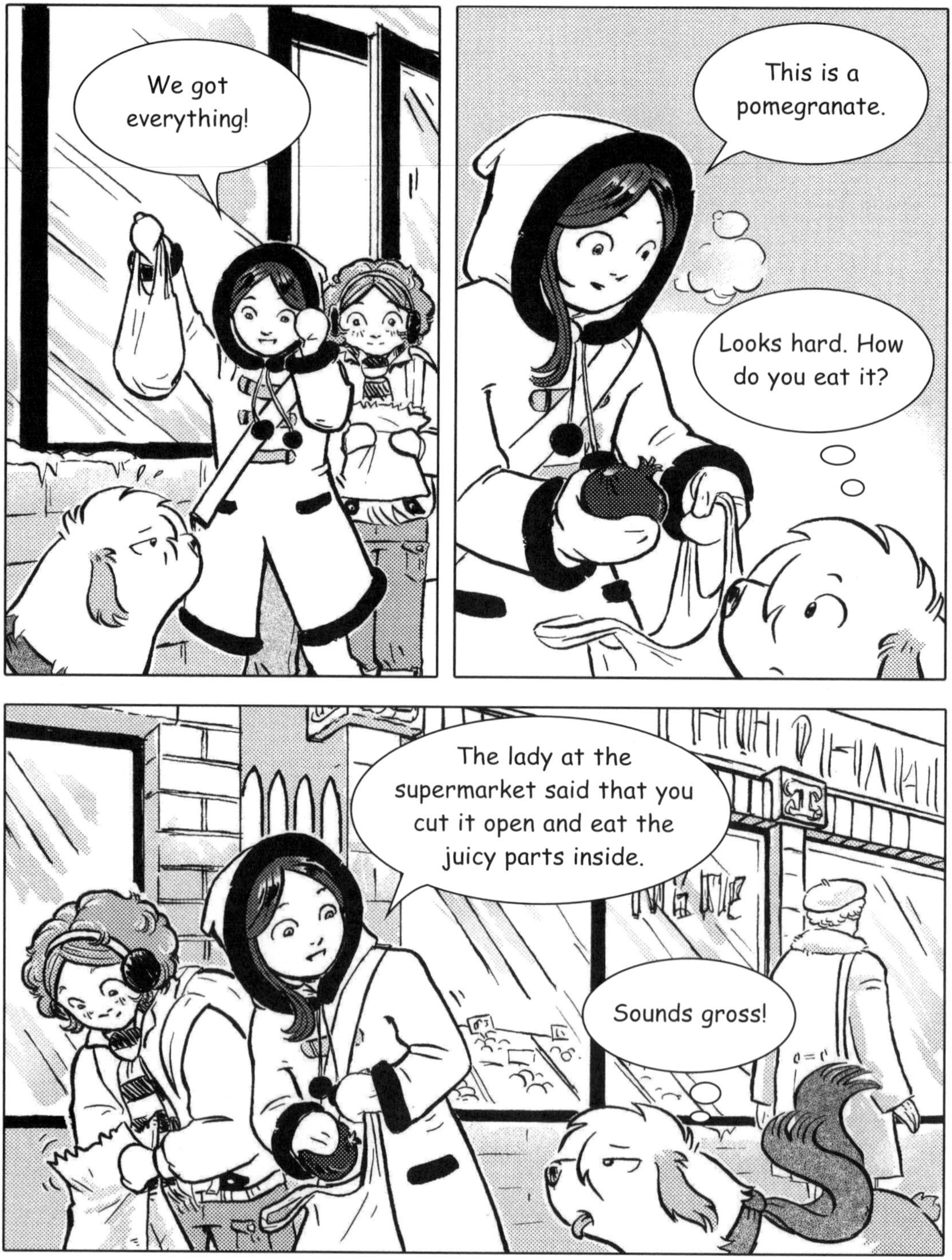
We got everything!
This is a pomegranate.
Looks hard. How do you eat it?
The lady at the supermarket said that you cut it open and eat the juicy parts inside.
Sounds gross!

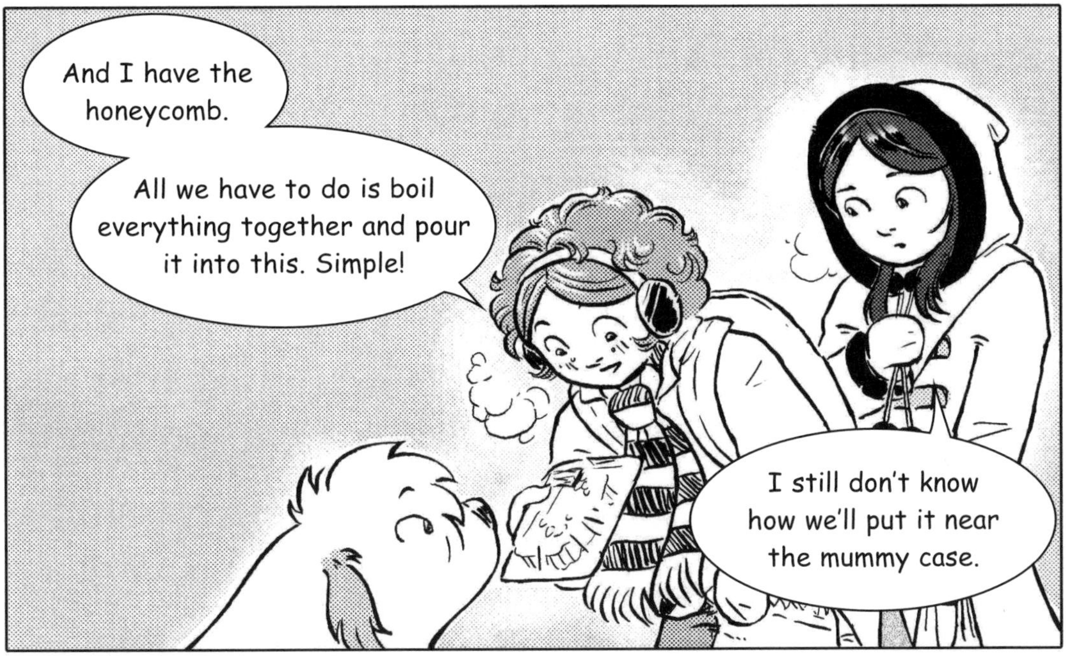
And I have the honeycomb.
All we have to do is boil everything together and pour it into this. Simple!
I still don't know how we'll put it near the mummy case.

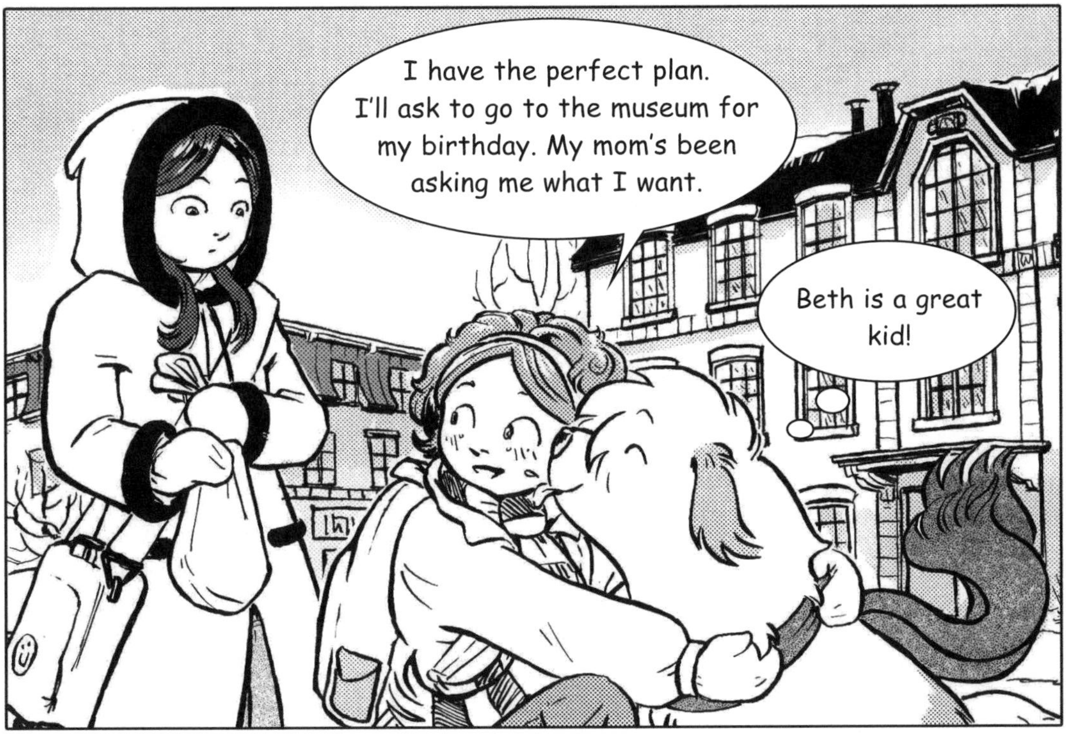
I have the perfect plan. I'll ask to go to the museum for my birthday. My mom's been asking me what I want.
Beth is a great kid!

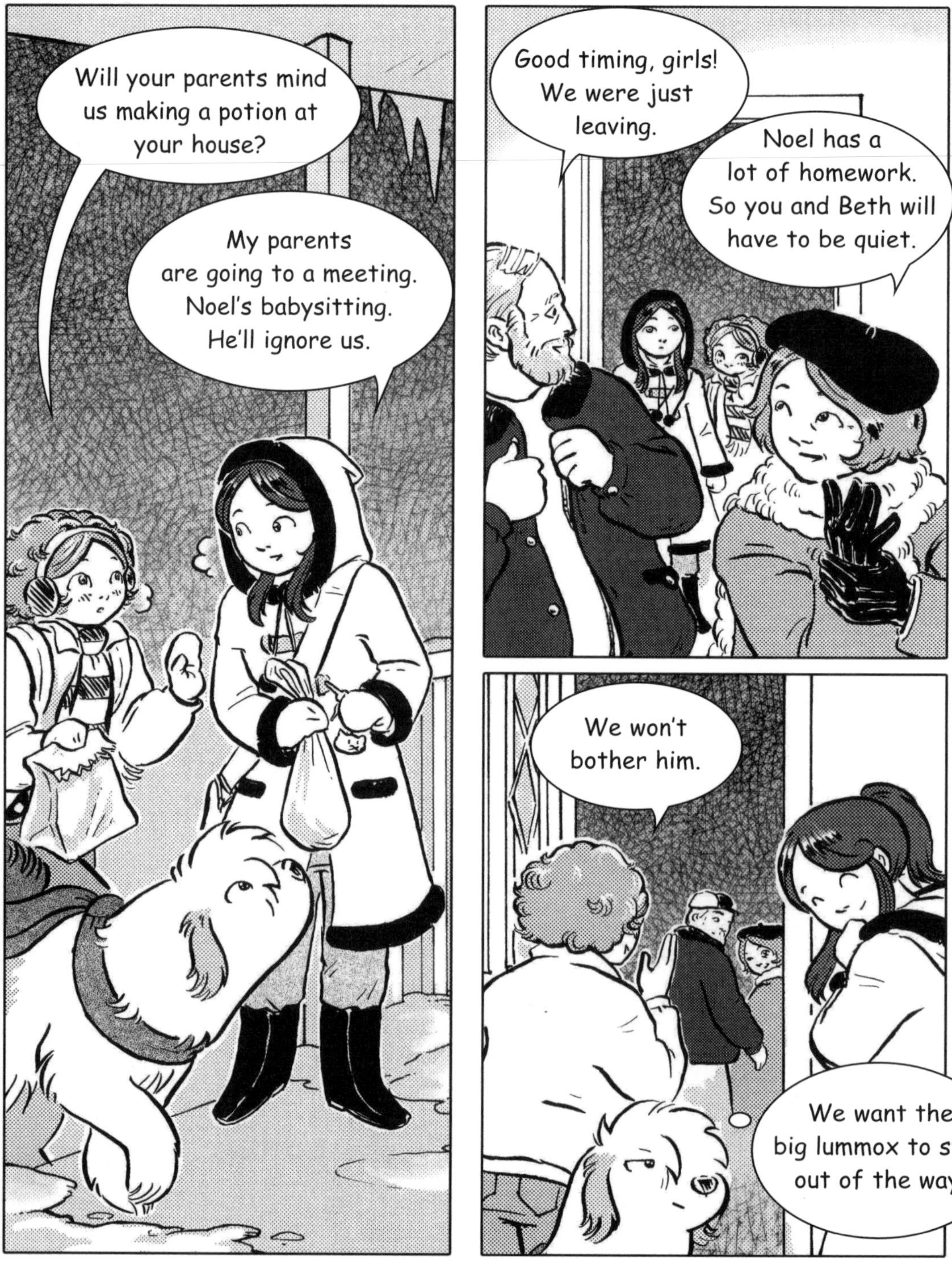
Will your parents mind us making a potion at your house?
My parents are going to a meeting. Noel's babysitting. He'll ignore us.
Good timing, girls! We were just leaving.
Noel has a lot of homework. So you and Beth will have to be quiet.
We won't bother him.
We want the big lummox to stay out of the way!

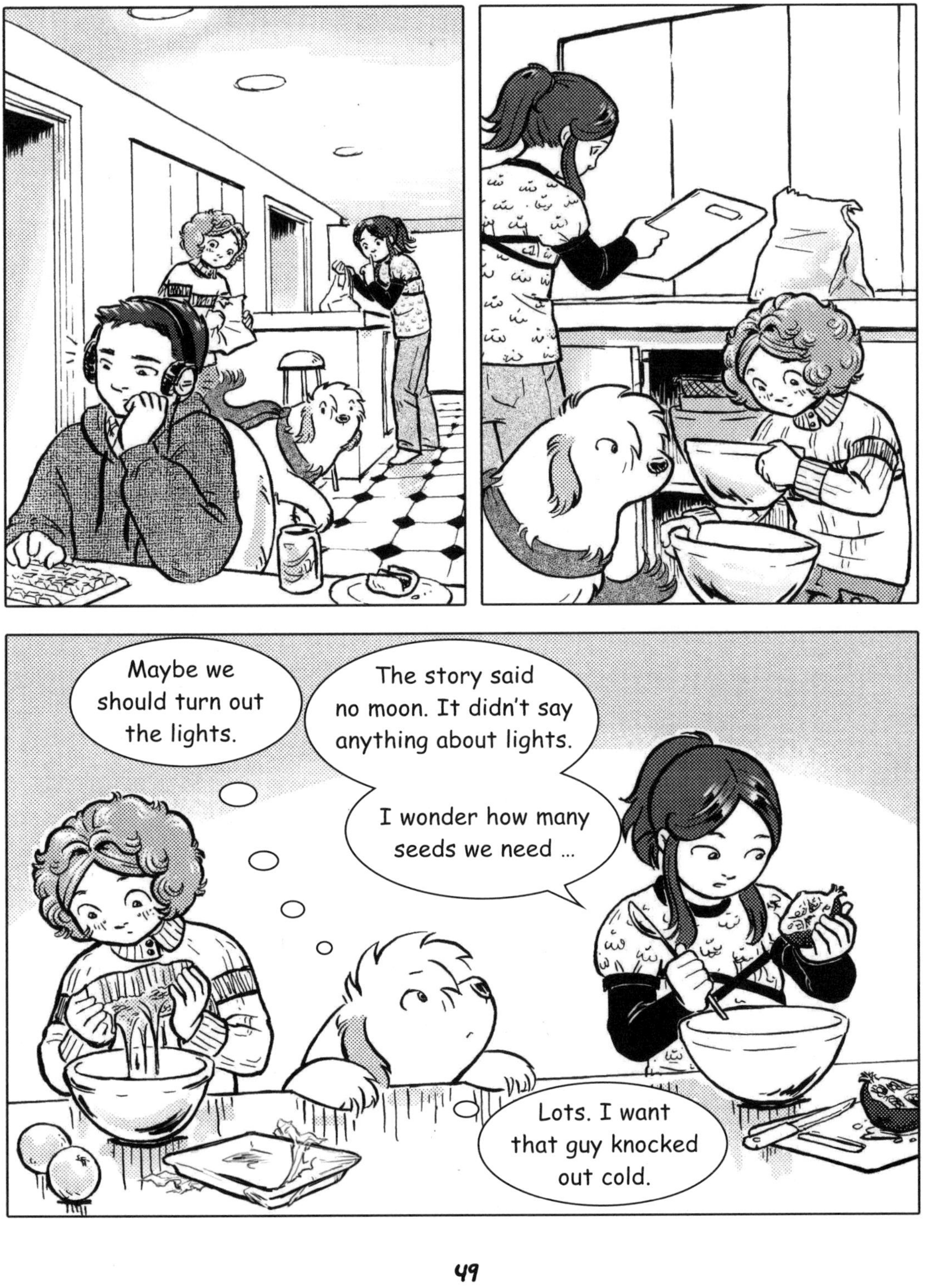
Maybe we should turn out the lights.
The story said no moon. It didn't say anything about lights.
I wonder how many seeds we need ...
Lots. I want that guy knocked out cold.

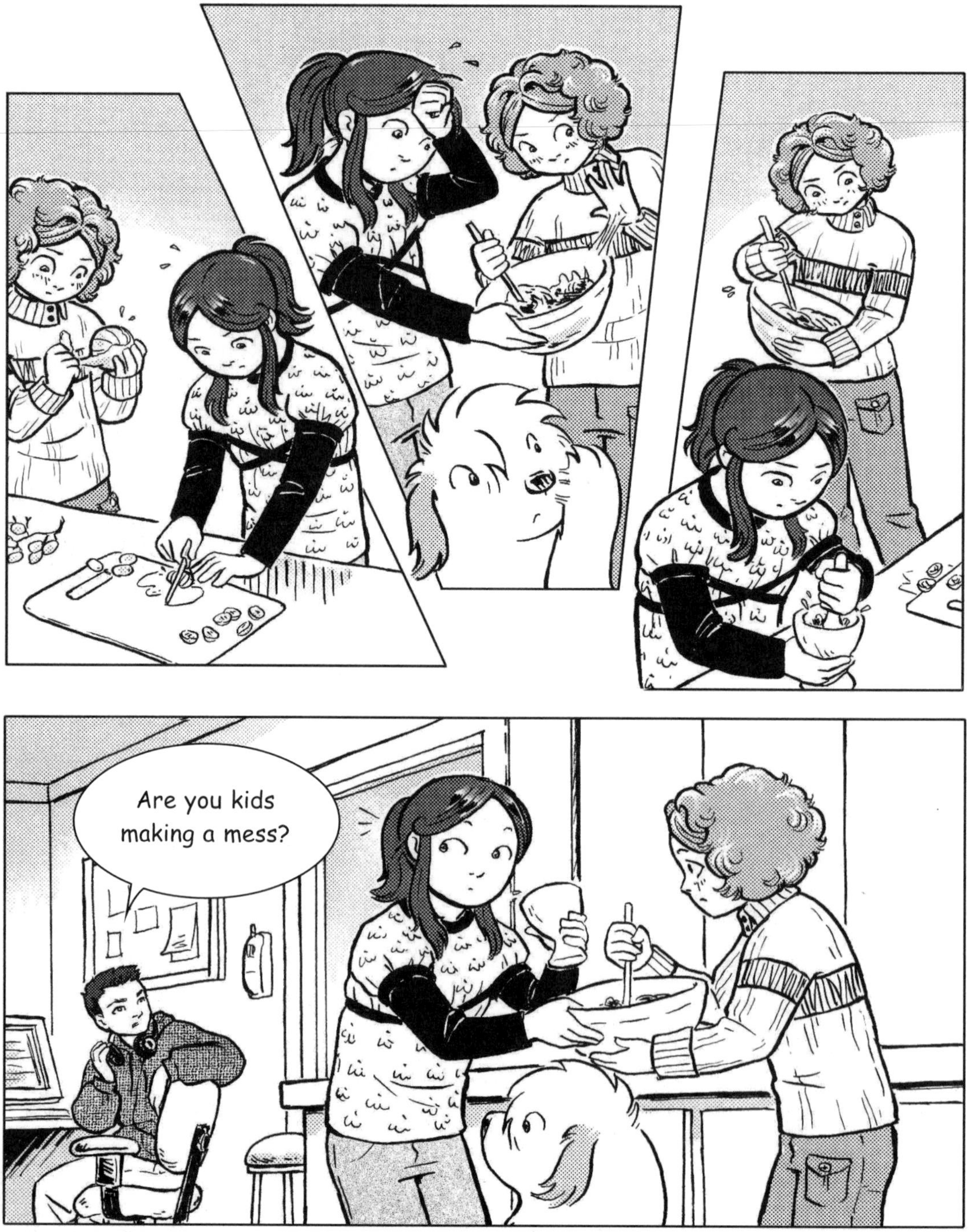
Are you kids making a mess?

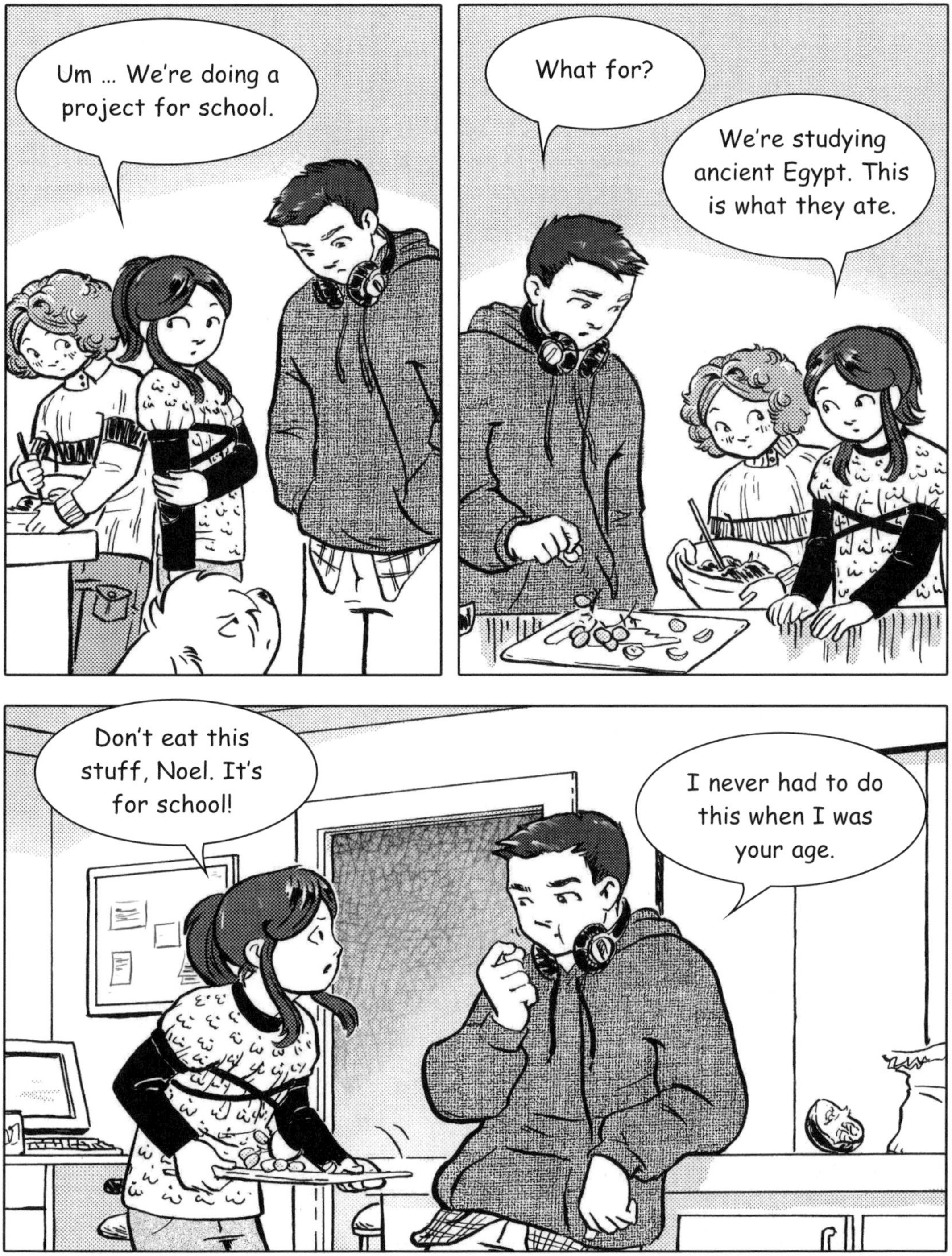
Um ... We're doing a project for school.
What for?
We're studying ancient Egypt. This is what they ate.
Don't eat this stuff, Noel. It's for school!
I never had to do this when I was your age.

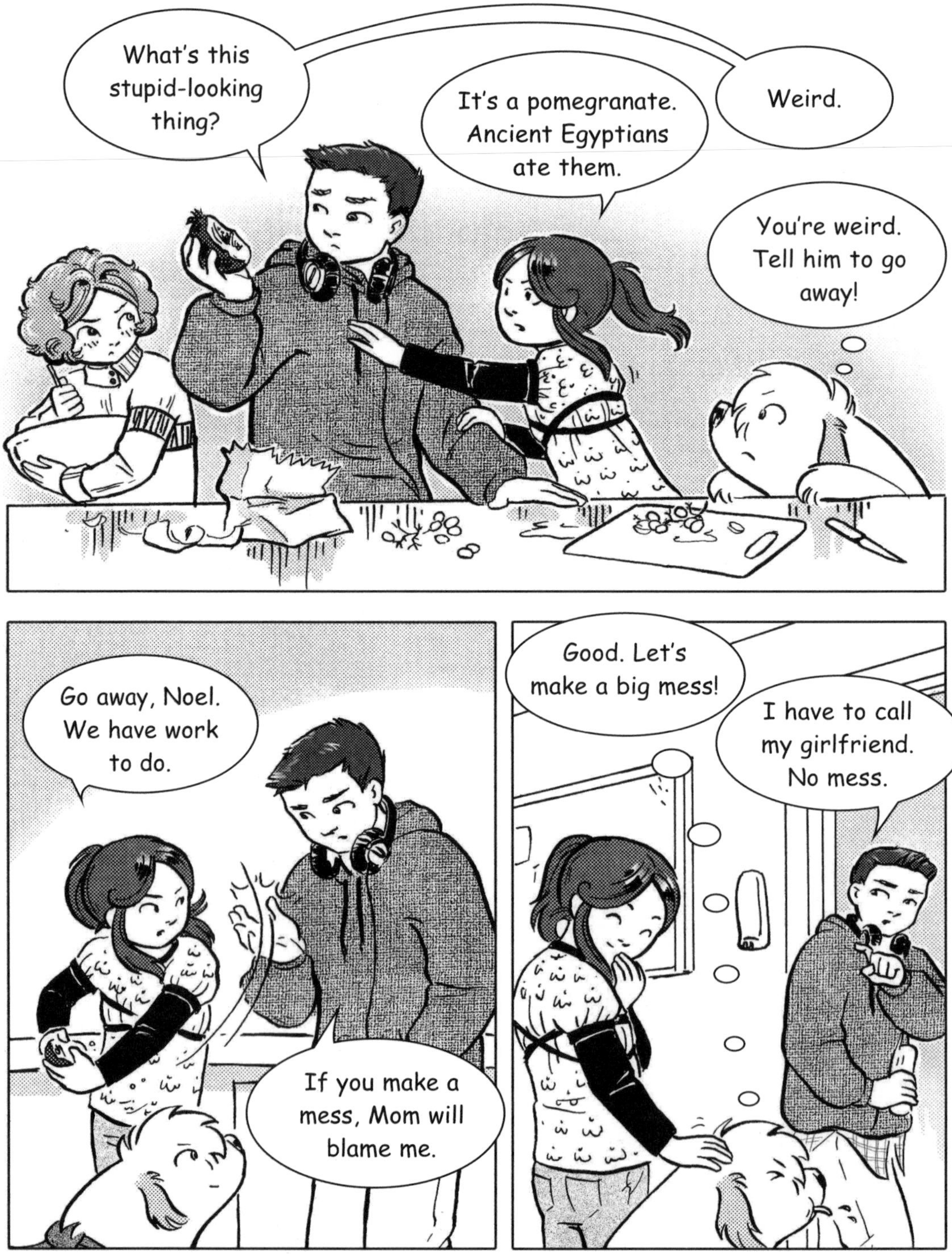
What's this stupid-looking thing?
It's a pomegranate. Ancient Egyptians ate them.
Weird.
You're weird. Tell him to go away!
Go away, Noel. We have work to do.
If you make a mess, Mom will blame me.
Good. Let's make a big mess!
I have to call my girlfriend. No mess.

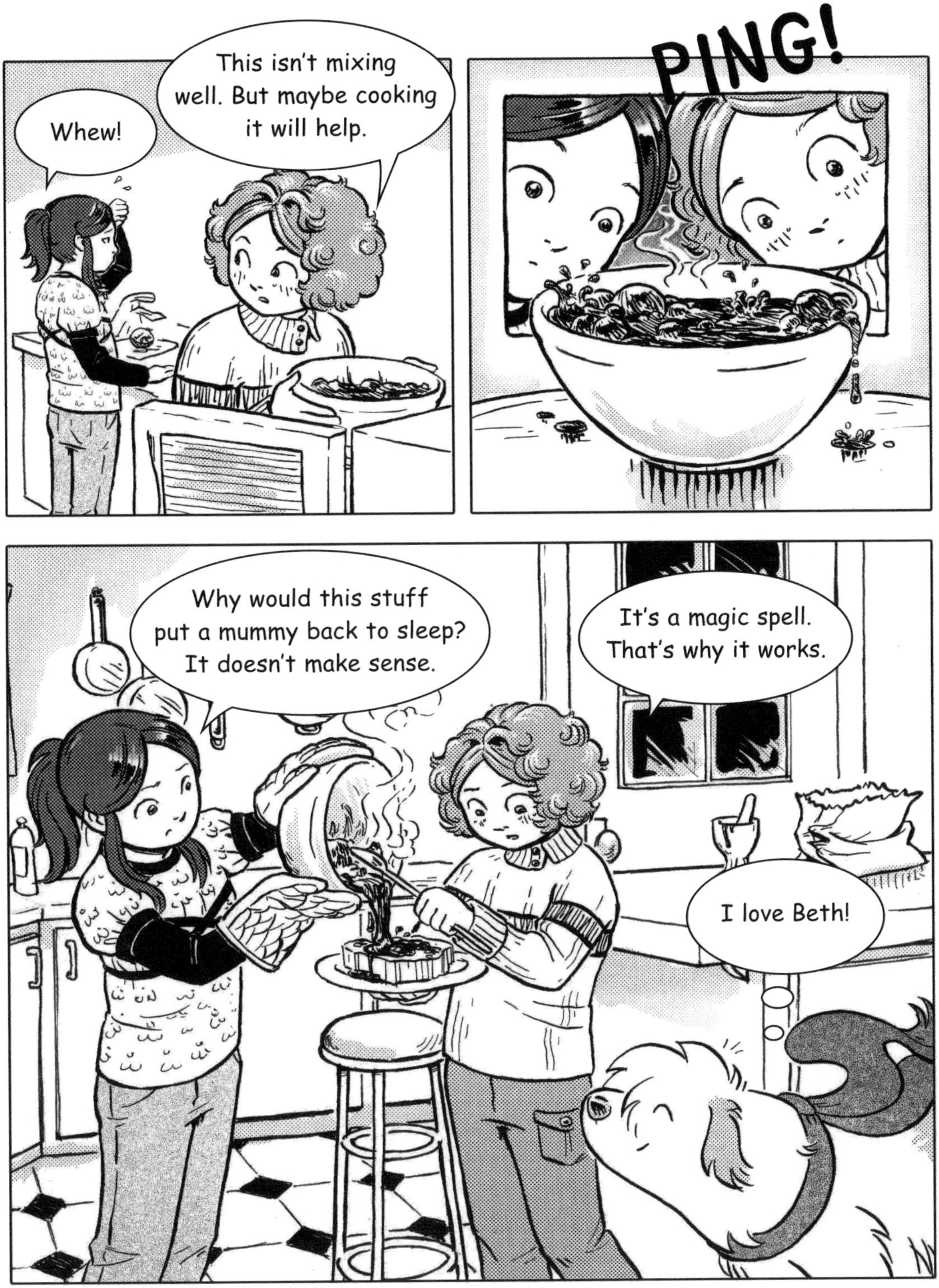
Whew!
This isn't mixing well. But maybe cooking it will help.
PING!
Why would this stuff put a mummy back to sleep? It doesn't make sense.
It's a magic spell. That's why it works.
I love Beth!

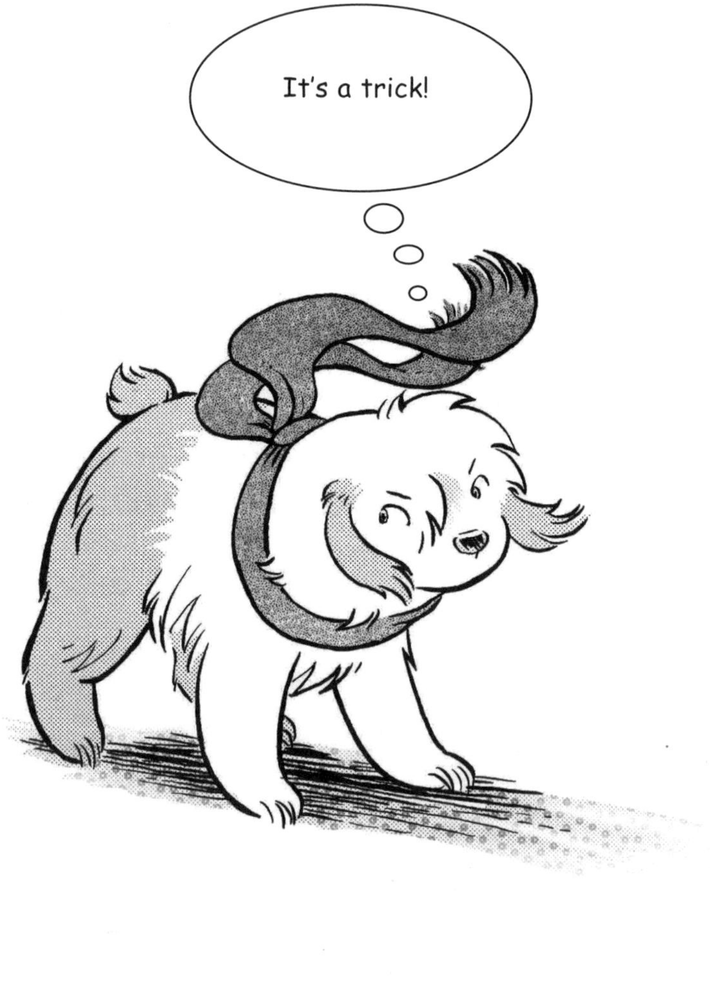
It's a trick!

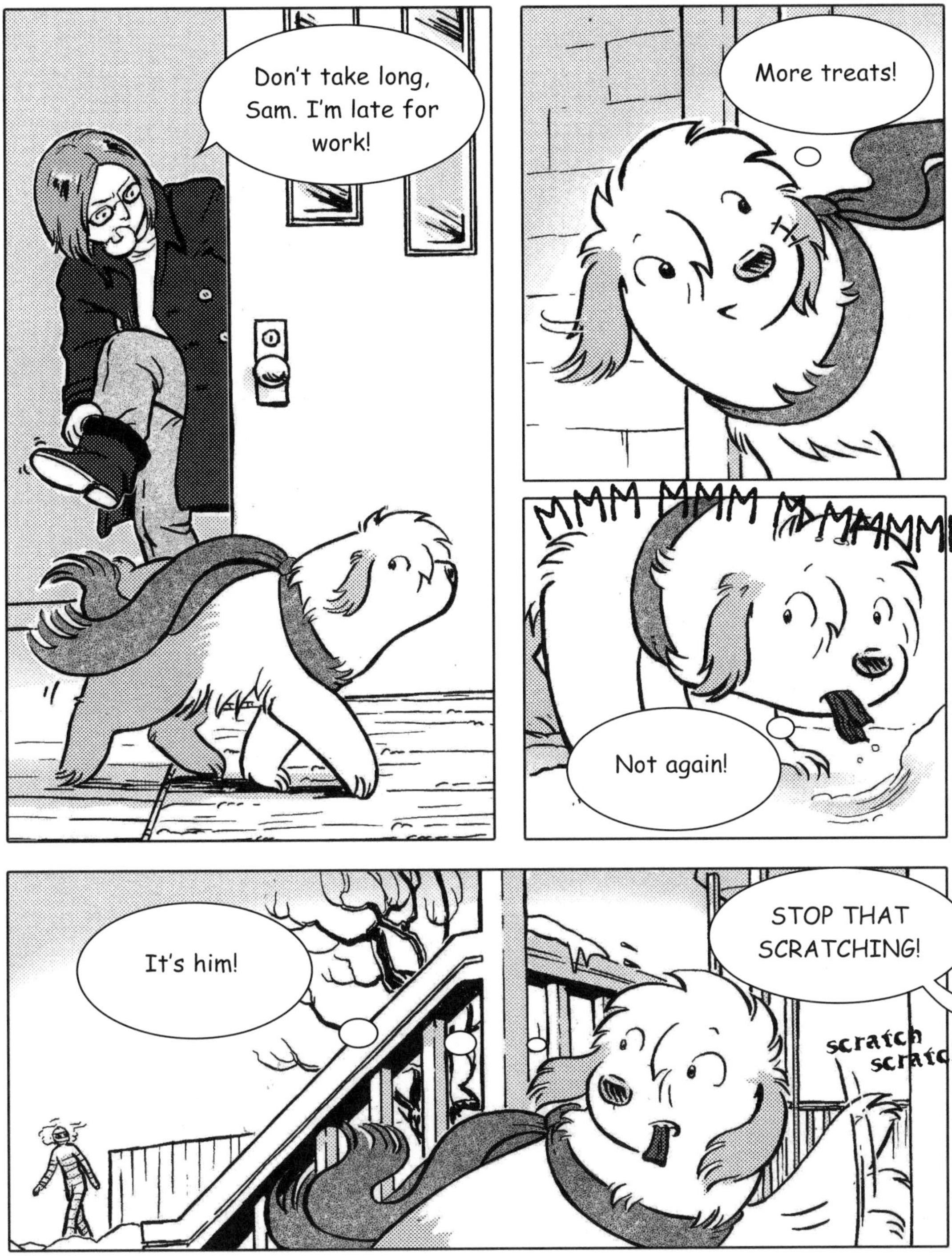
Don't take long, Sam. I'm late for work!
More treats!
MMM MMM MMMMMM
Not again!
It's him!
STOP THAT SCRATCHING!
scratch scratch

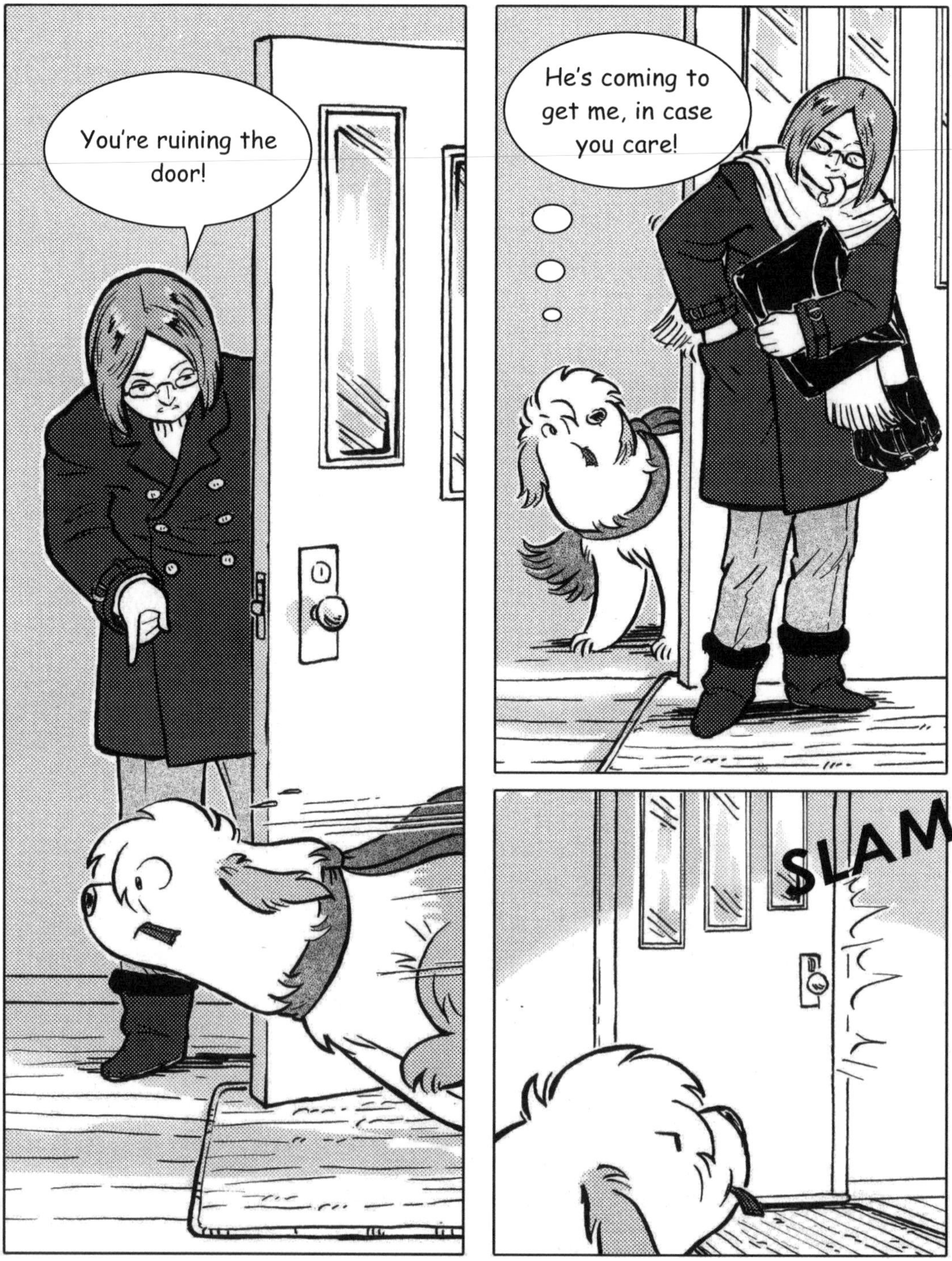
You're ruining the door!
He's coming to get me, in case you care!
SLAM!

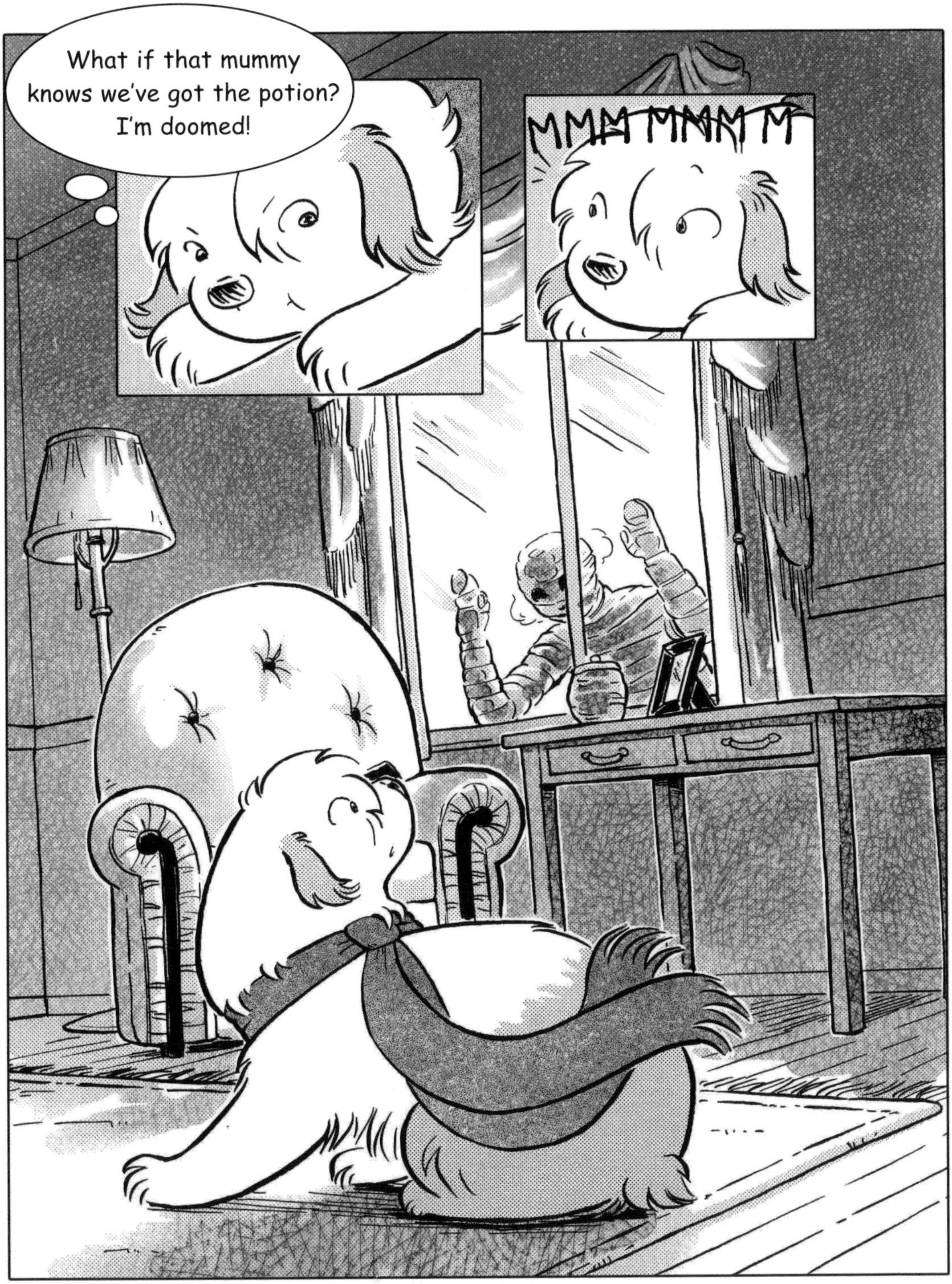
What if that mummy knows we've got the potion? I'm doomed!
MMM MMM M

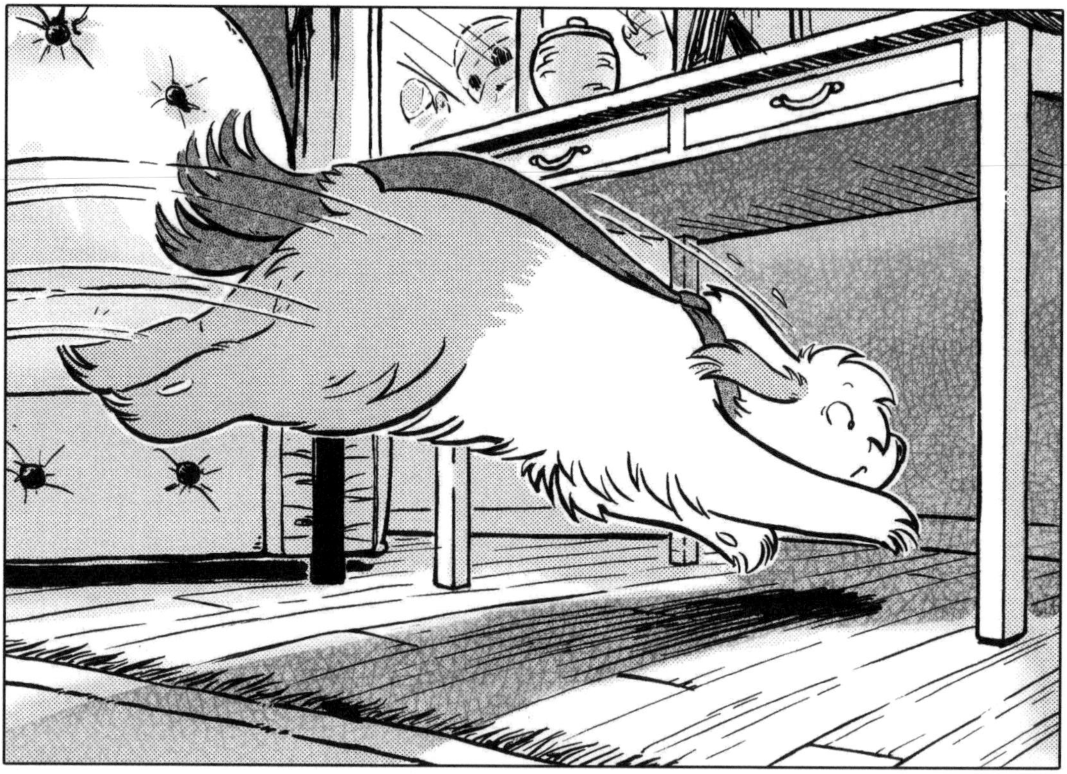

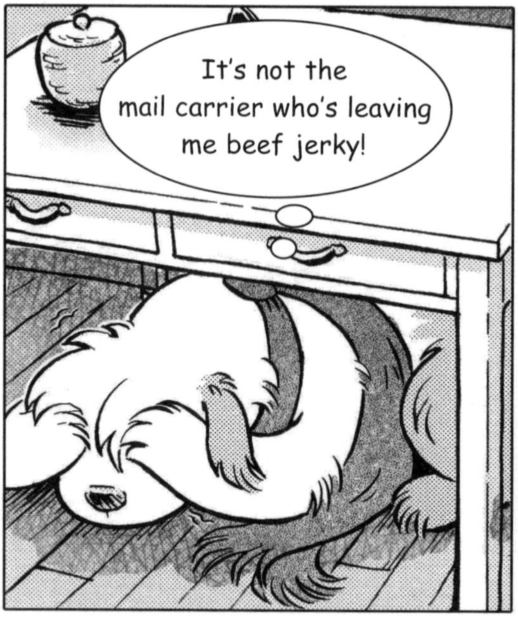
It's not the mail carrier who's leaving me beef jerky!

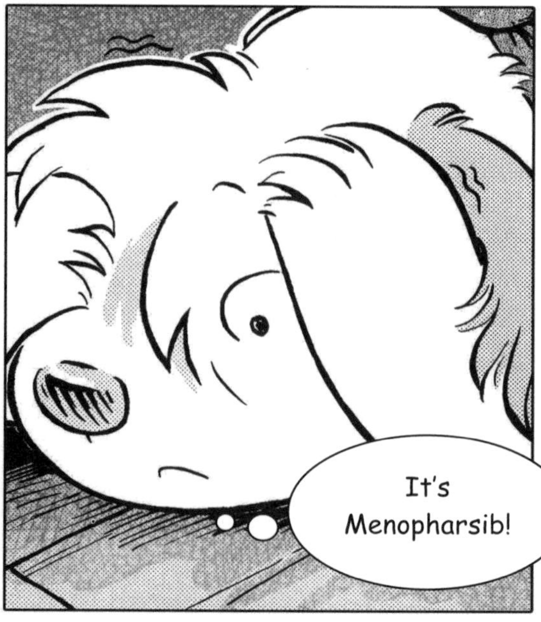
It's Menopharsib!

That afternoon ...

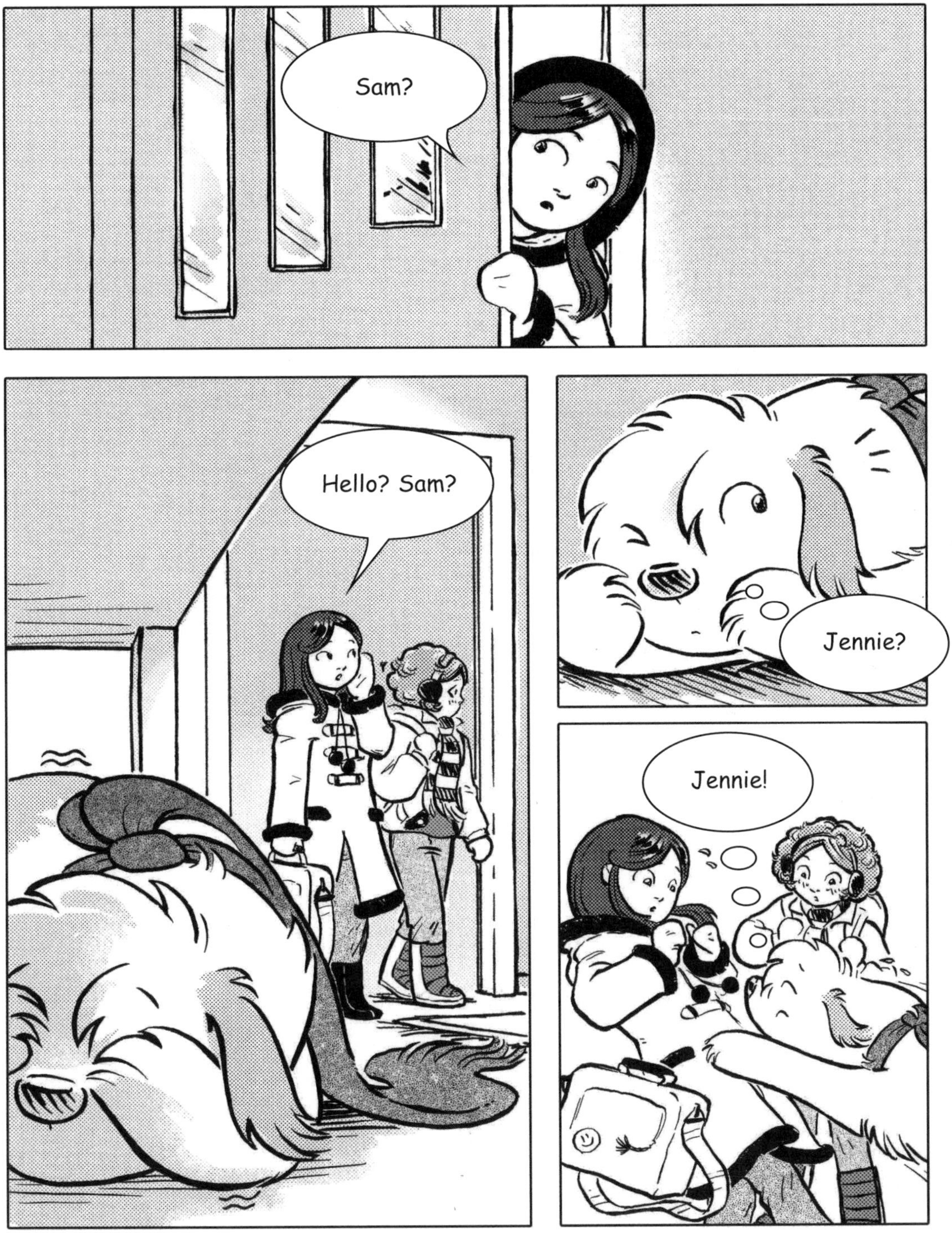
Sam?
Hello? Sam?
Jennie?
Jennie!

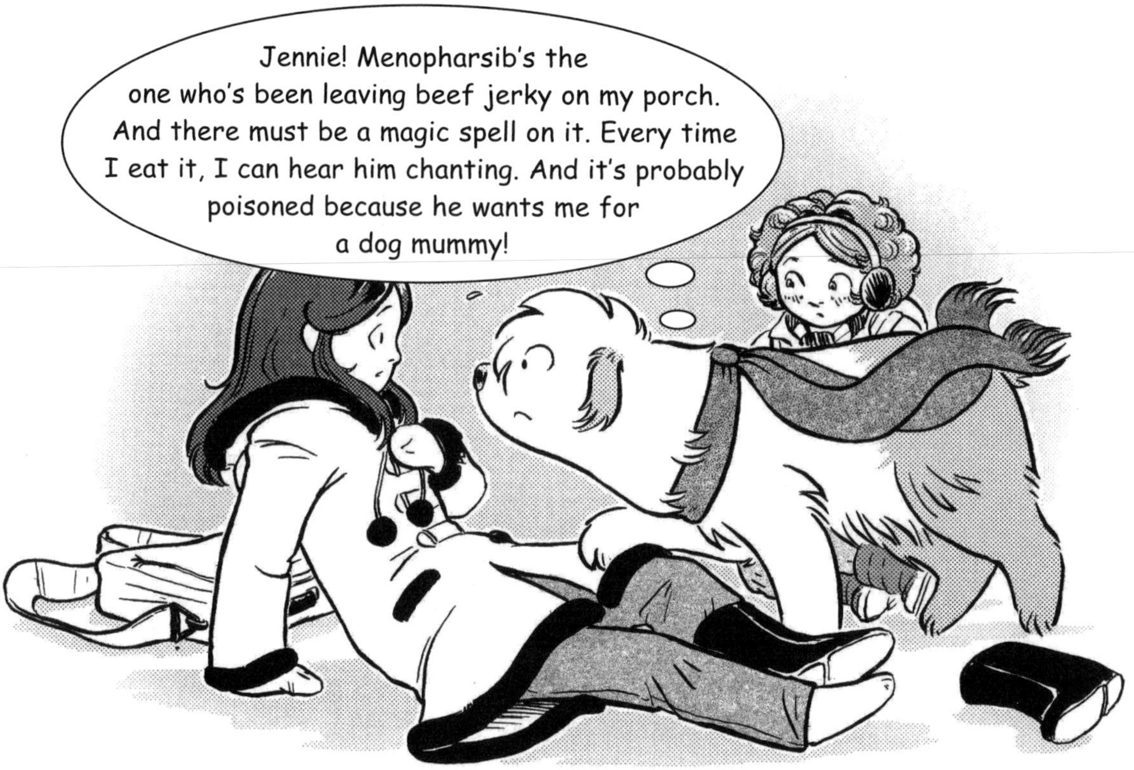
Jennie! Menopharsib's the one who's been leaving beef jerky on my porch. And there must be a magic spell on it. Every time I eat it, I can hear him chanting. And it's probably poisoned because he wants me for a dog mummy!

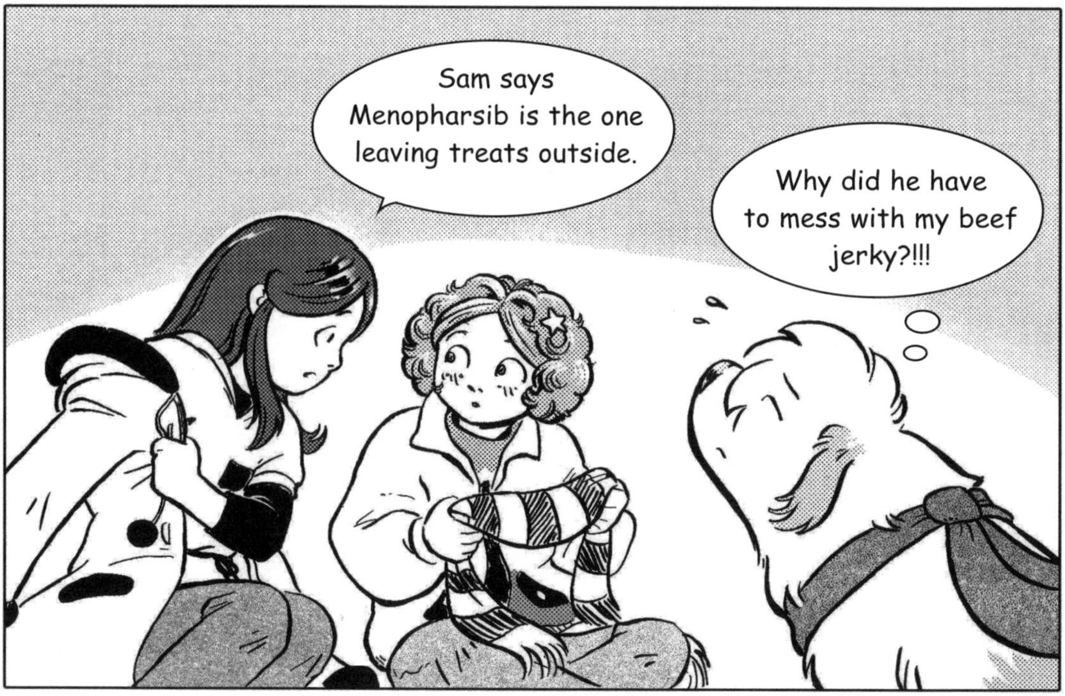
Sam says Menopharsib is the one leaving treats outside.
Why did he have to mess with my beef jerky?!!!

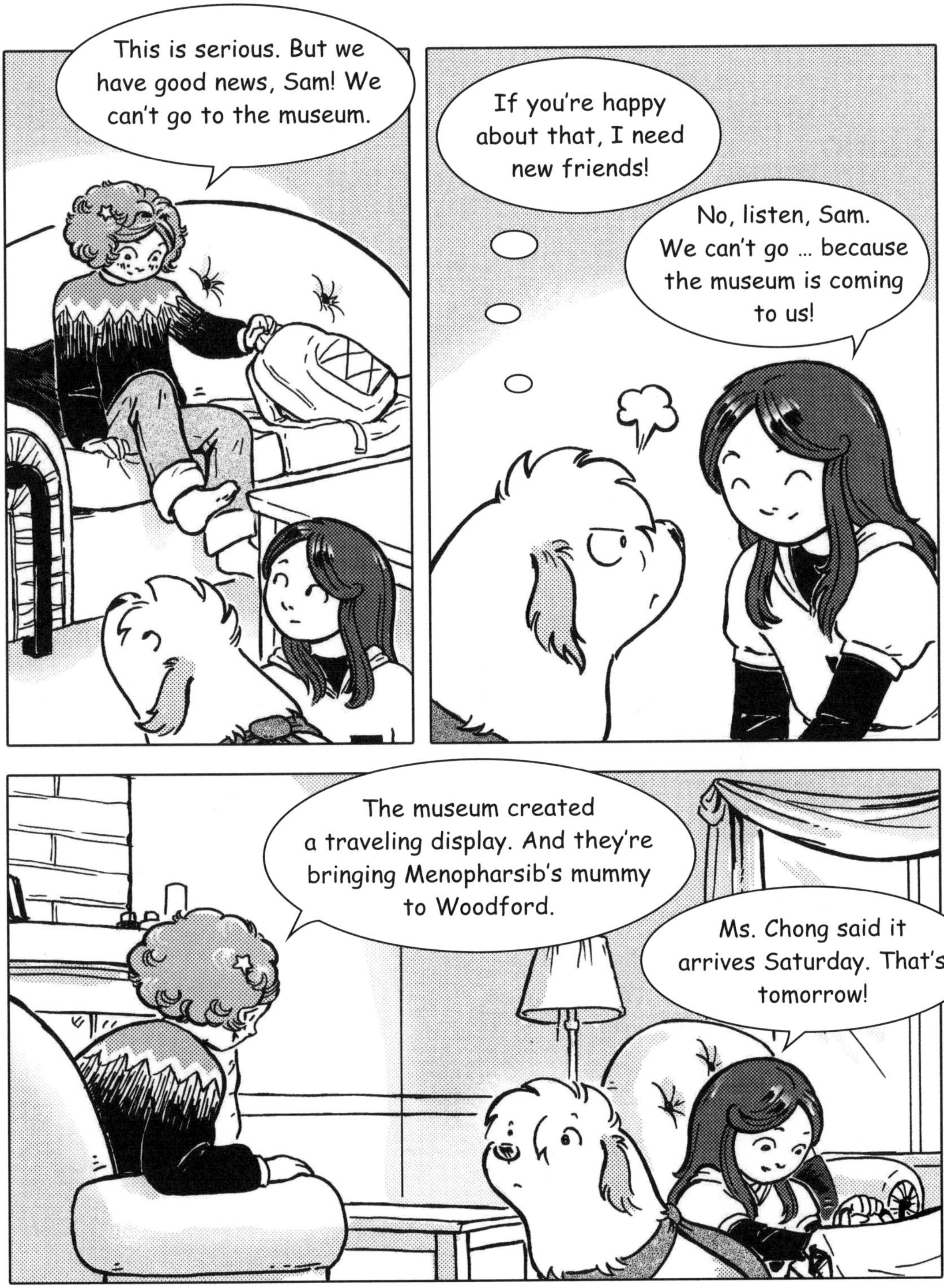
This is serious. But we have good news, Sam! We can't go to the museum.
If you're happy about that, I need new friends!
No, listen, Sam. We can't go ... because the museum is coming to us!
The museum created a traveling display. And they're bringing Menopharsib's mummy to Woodford.
Ms. Chong said it arrives Saturday. That's tomorrow!

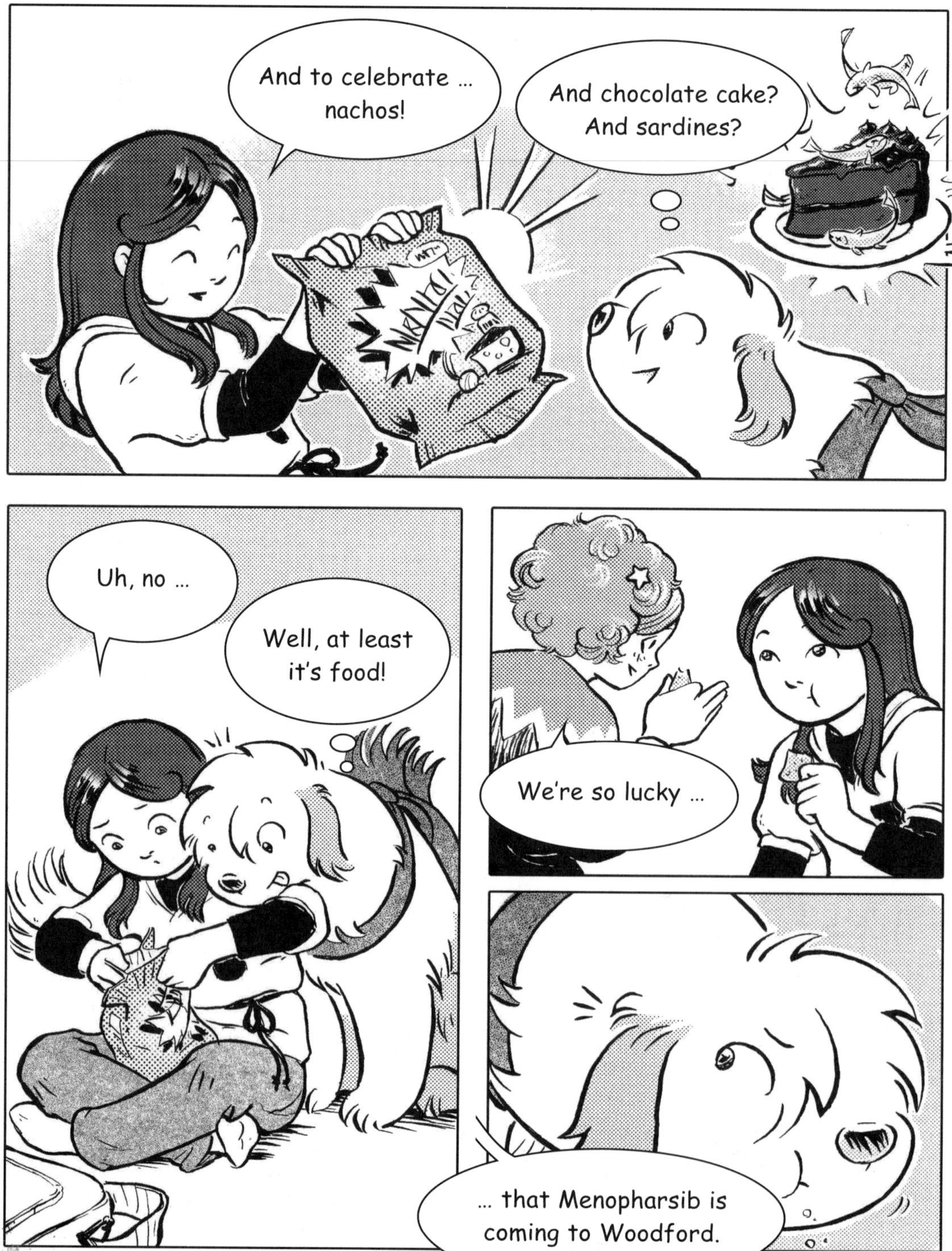
And to celebrate ... nachos!
And chocolate cake? And sardines?
Uh, no ...
Well, at least it's food!
We're so lucky ...
... that Menopharsib is coming to Woodford.

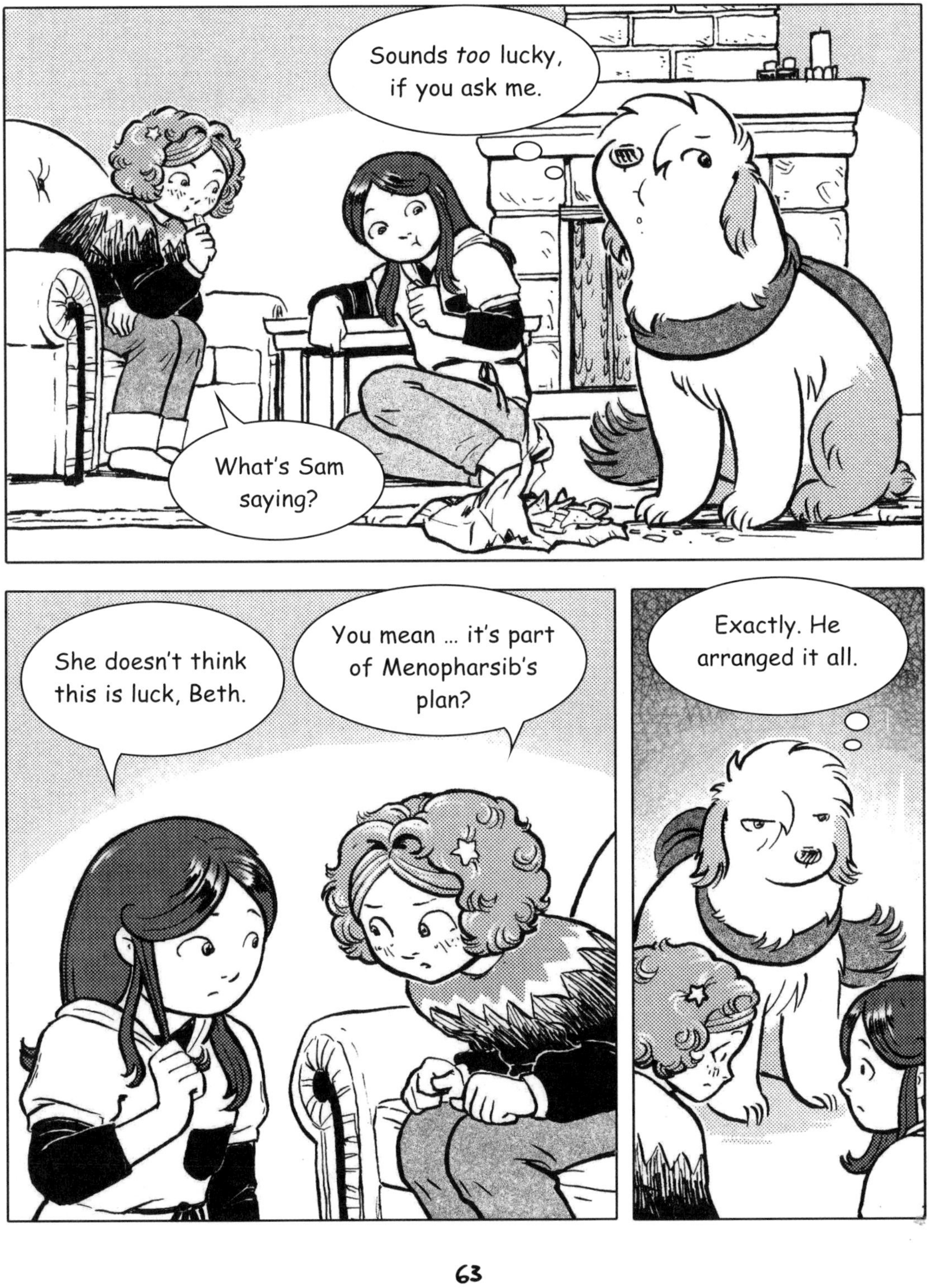

Sounds *too* lucky, if you ask me.
What's Sam saying?
She doesn't think this is luck, Beth.
You mean … it's part of Menopharsib's plan?
Exactly. He arranged it all.

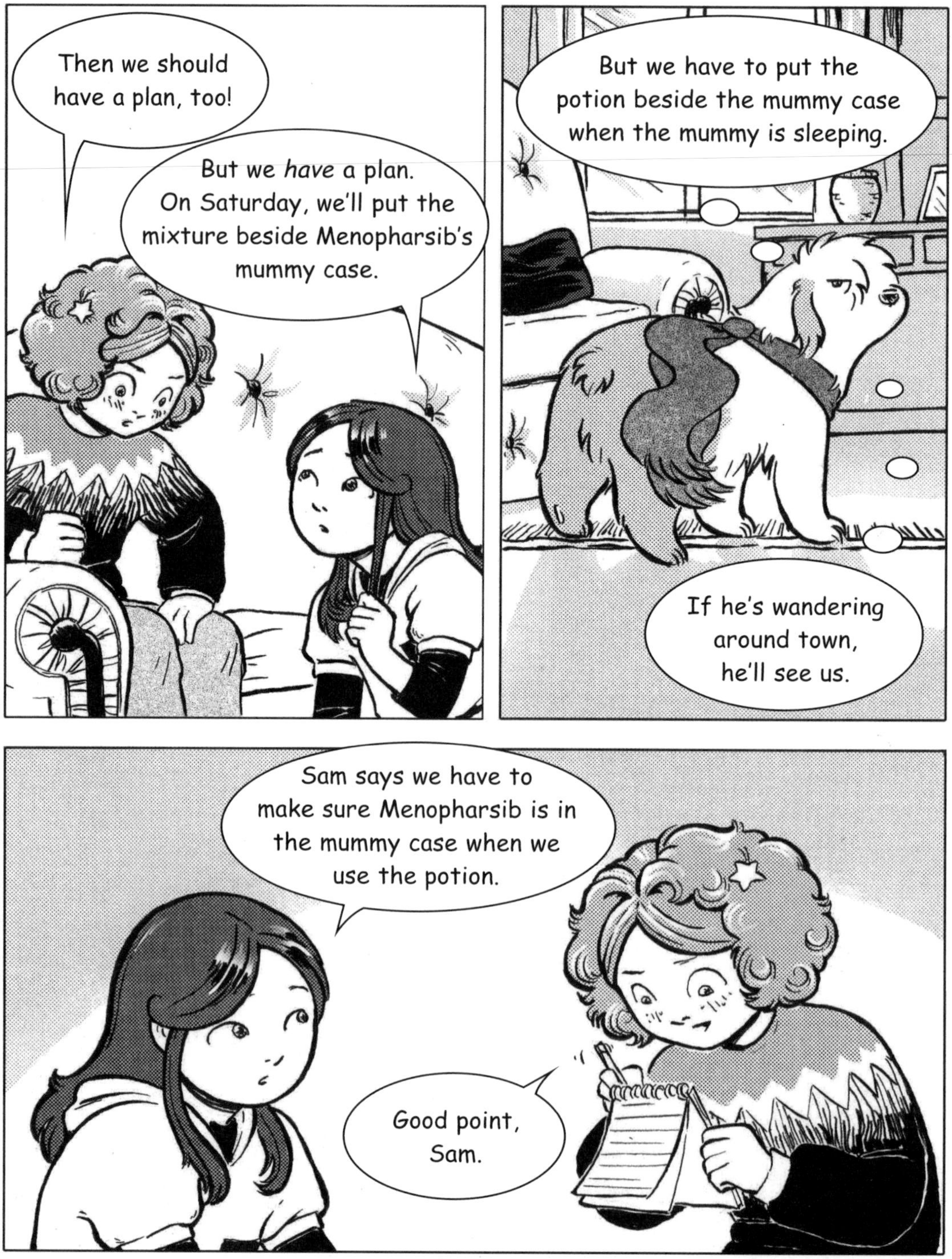
Then we should have a plan, too!
But we *have* a plan. On Saturday, we'll put the mixture beside Menopharsib's mummy case.
But we have to put the potion beside the mummy case when the mummy is sleeping.
If he's wandering around town, he'll see us.
Sam says we have to make sure Menopharsib is in the mummy case when we use the potion.
Good point, Sam.

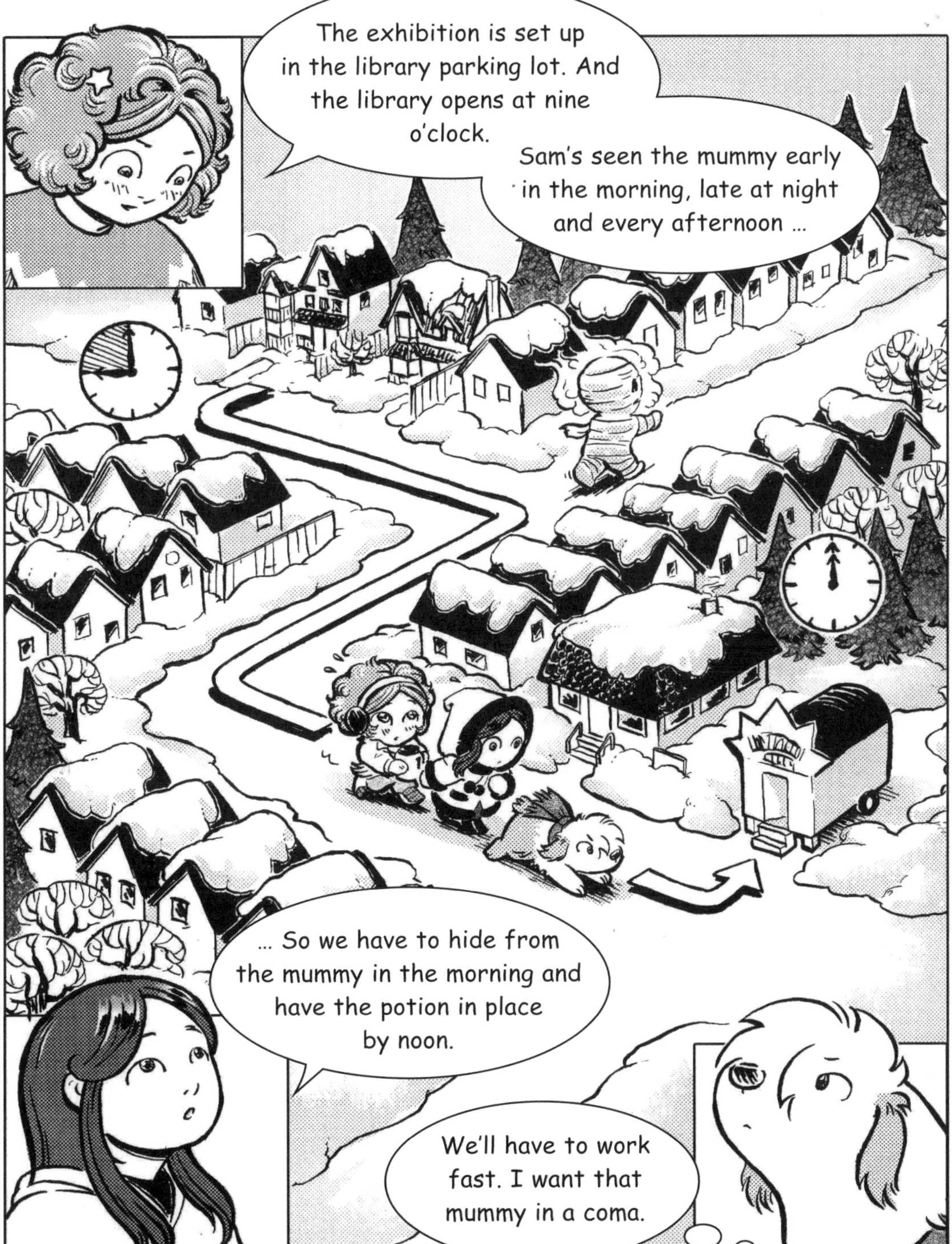
The exhibition is set up in the library parking lot. And the library opens at nine o'clock.
Sam's seen the mummy early in the morning, late at night and every afternoon ...
... So we have to hide from the mummy in the morning and have the potion in place by noon.
We'll have to work fast. I want that mummy in a coma.

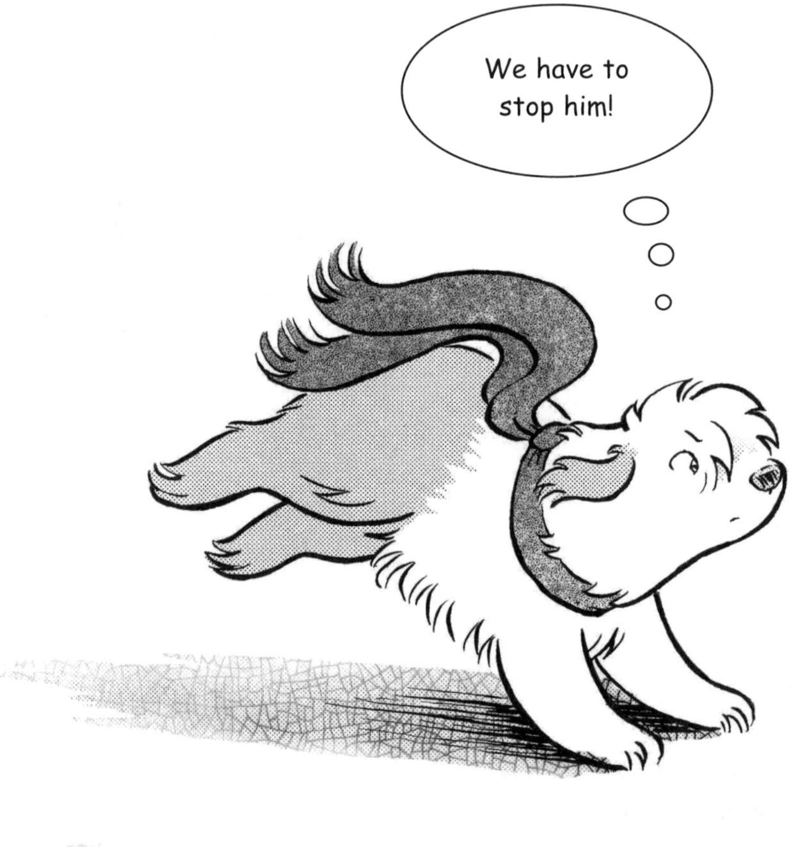
We have to stop him!

The next morning ...

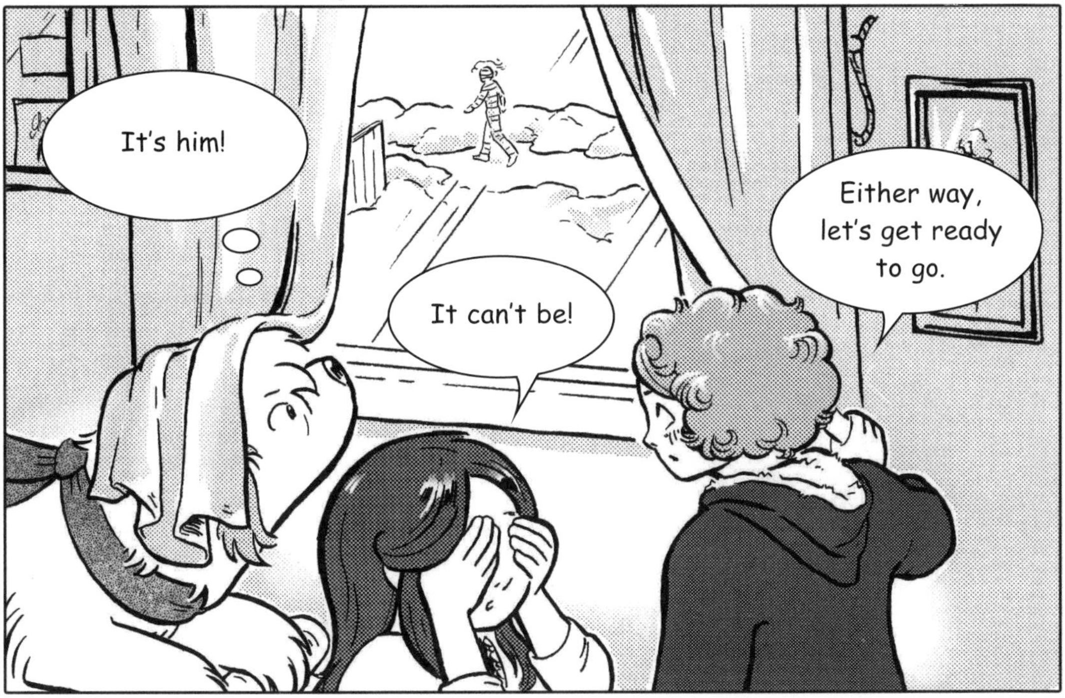
It's him!
It can't be!
Either way, let's get ready to go.

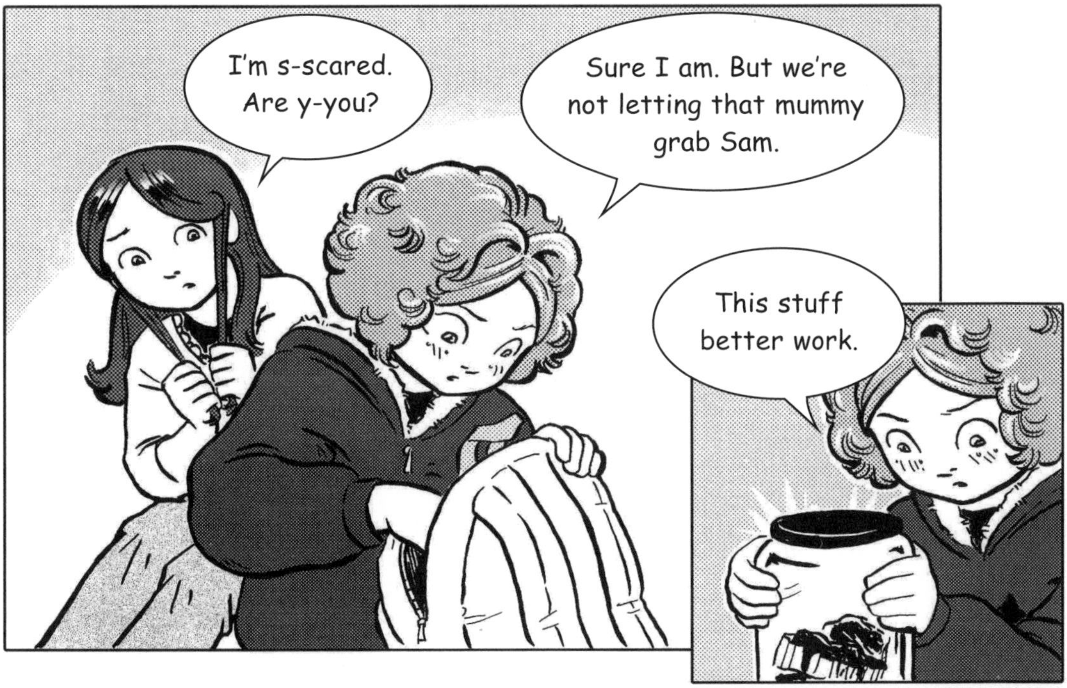
I'm s-scared. Are y-you?
Sure I am. But we're not letting that mummy grab Sam.
This stuff better work.

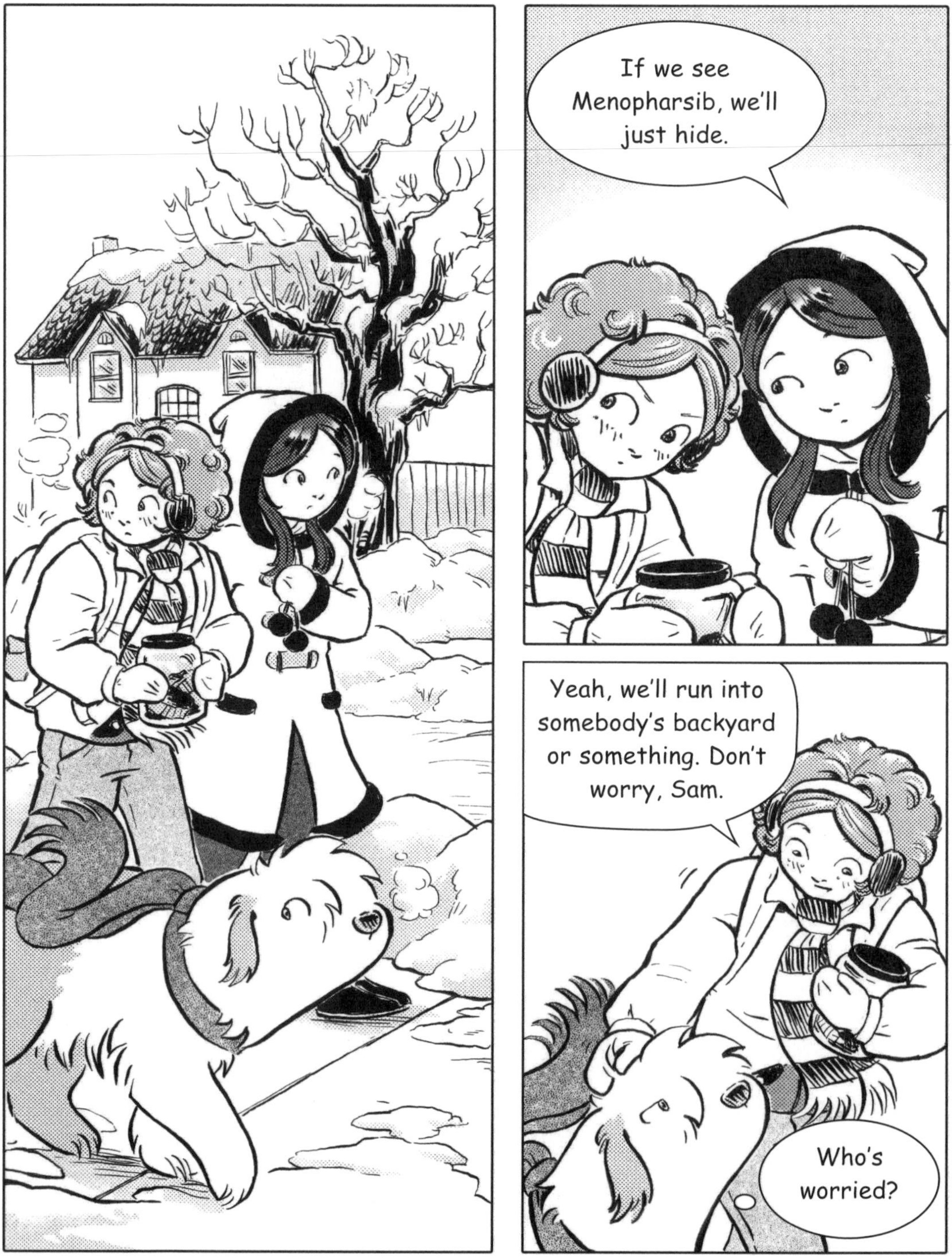
If we see Menopharsib, we'll just hide.
Yeah, we'll run into somebody's backyard or something. Don't worry, Sam.
Who's worried?

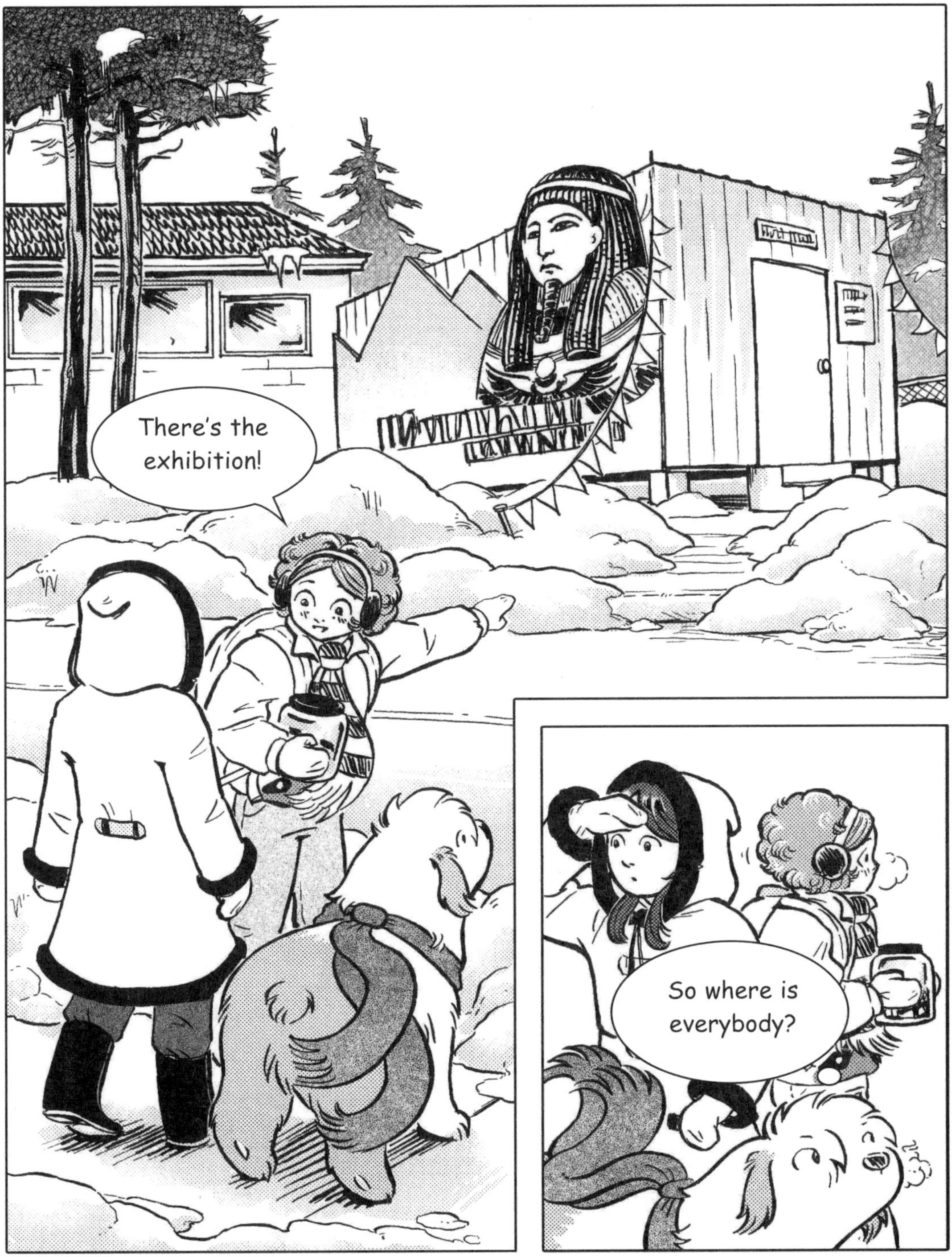
There's the exhibition!
So where is everybody?

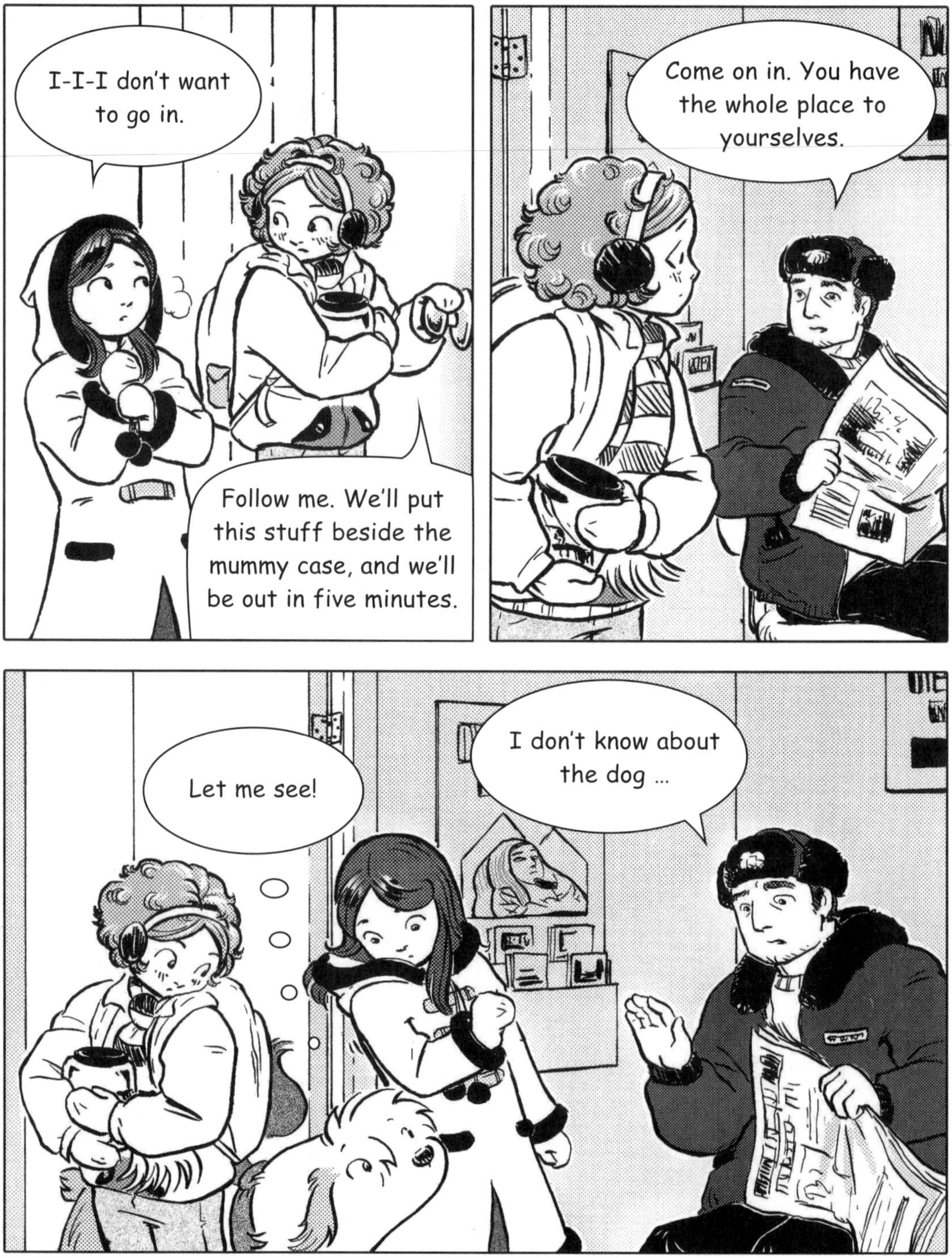
I-I-I don't want to go in.
Follow me. We'll put this stuff beside the mummy case, and we'll be out in five minutes.
Come on in. You have the whole place to yourselves.
Let me see!
I don't know about the dog ...

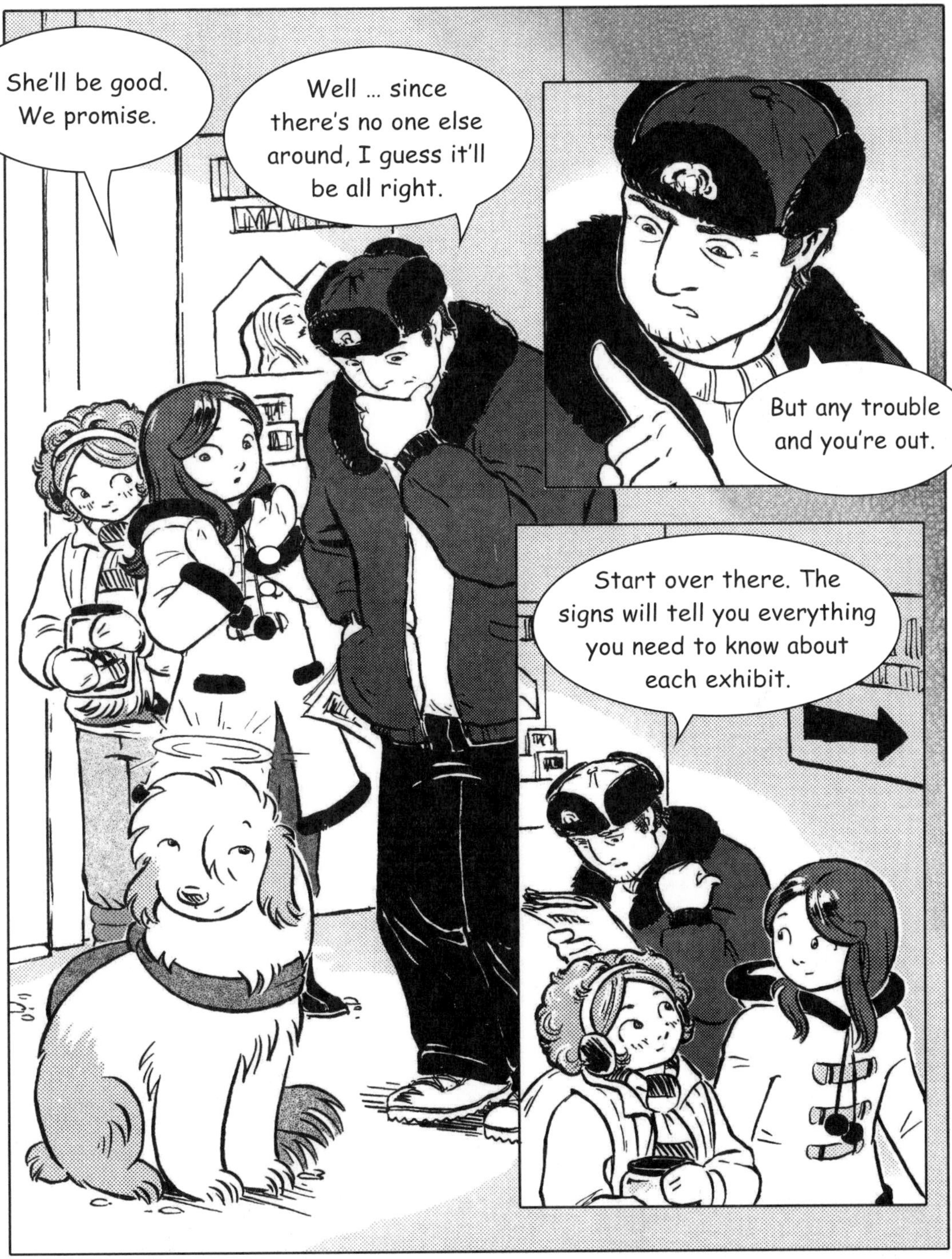
She'll be good. We promise.
Well ... since there's no one else around, I guess it'll be all right.
But any trouble and you're out.
Start over there. The signs will tell you everything you need to know about each exhibit.

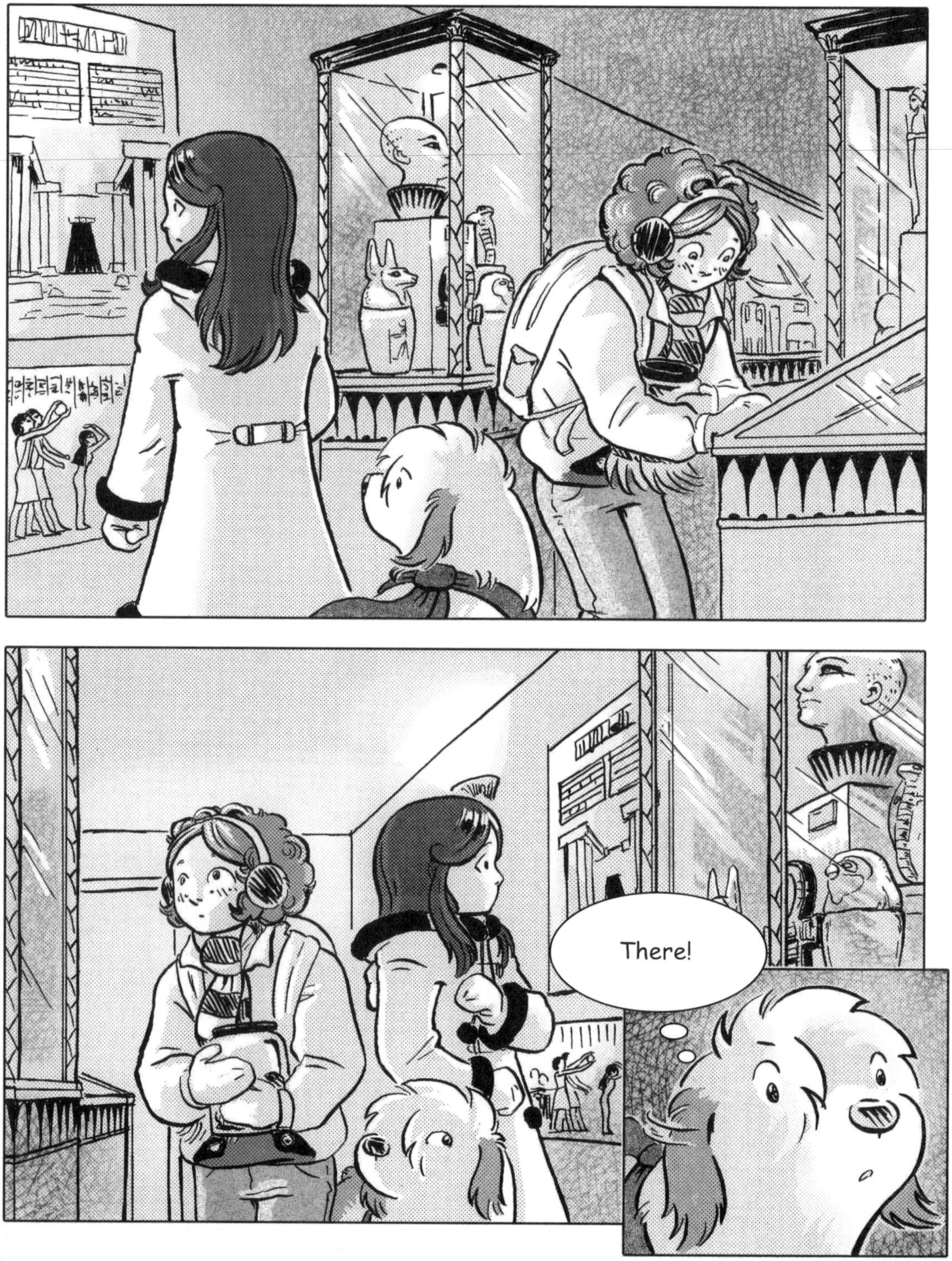
There!

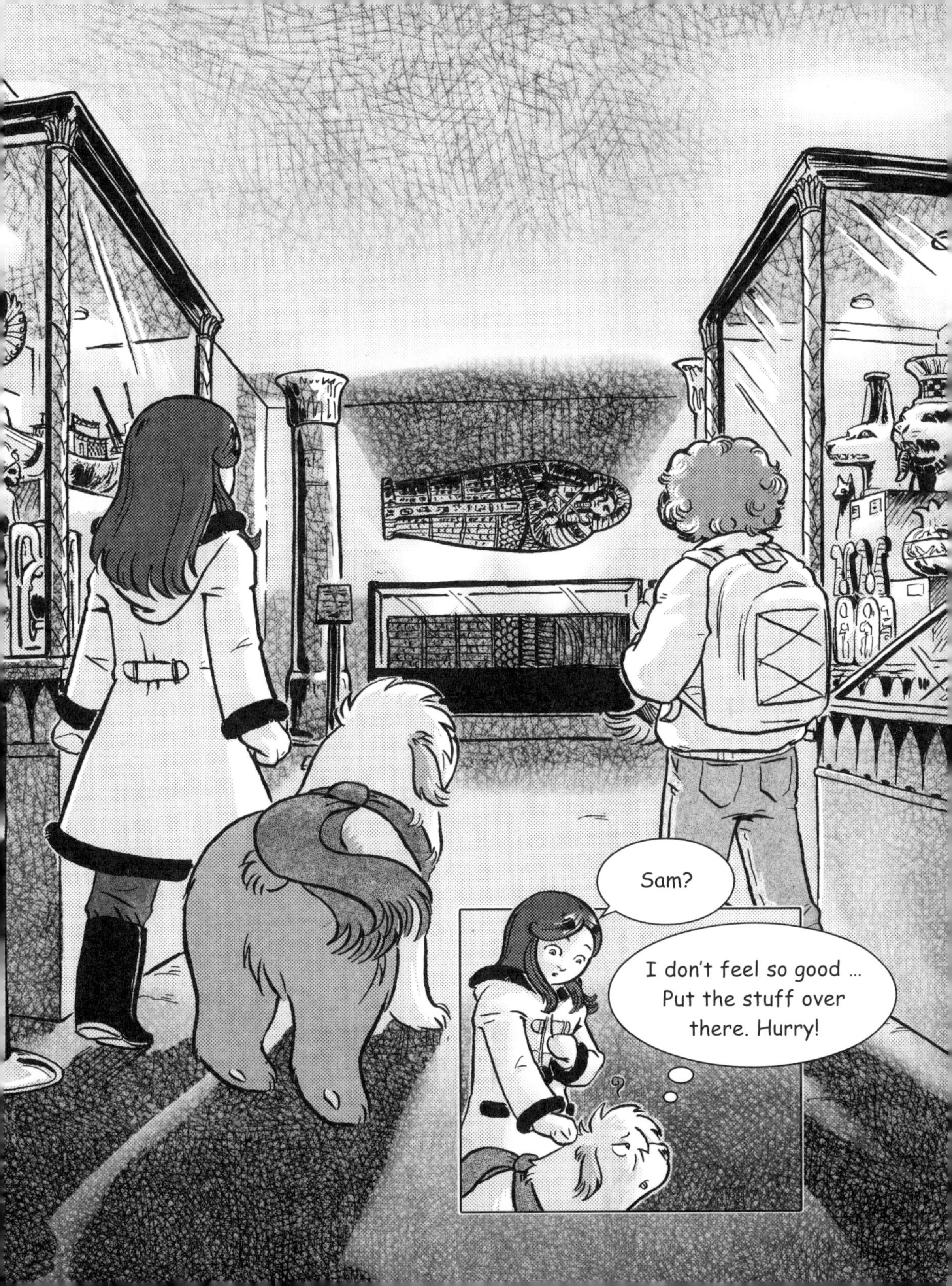
Sam?
I don't feel so good …
Put the stuff over
there. Hurry!

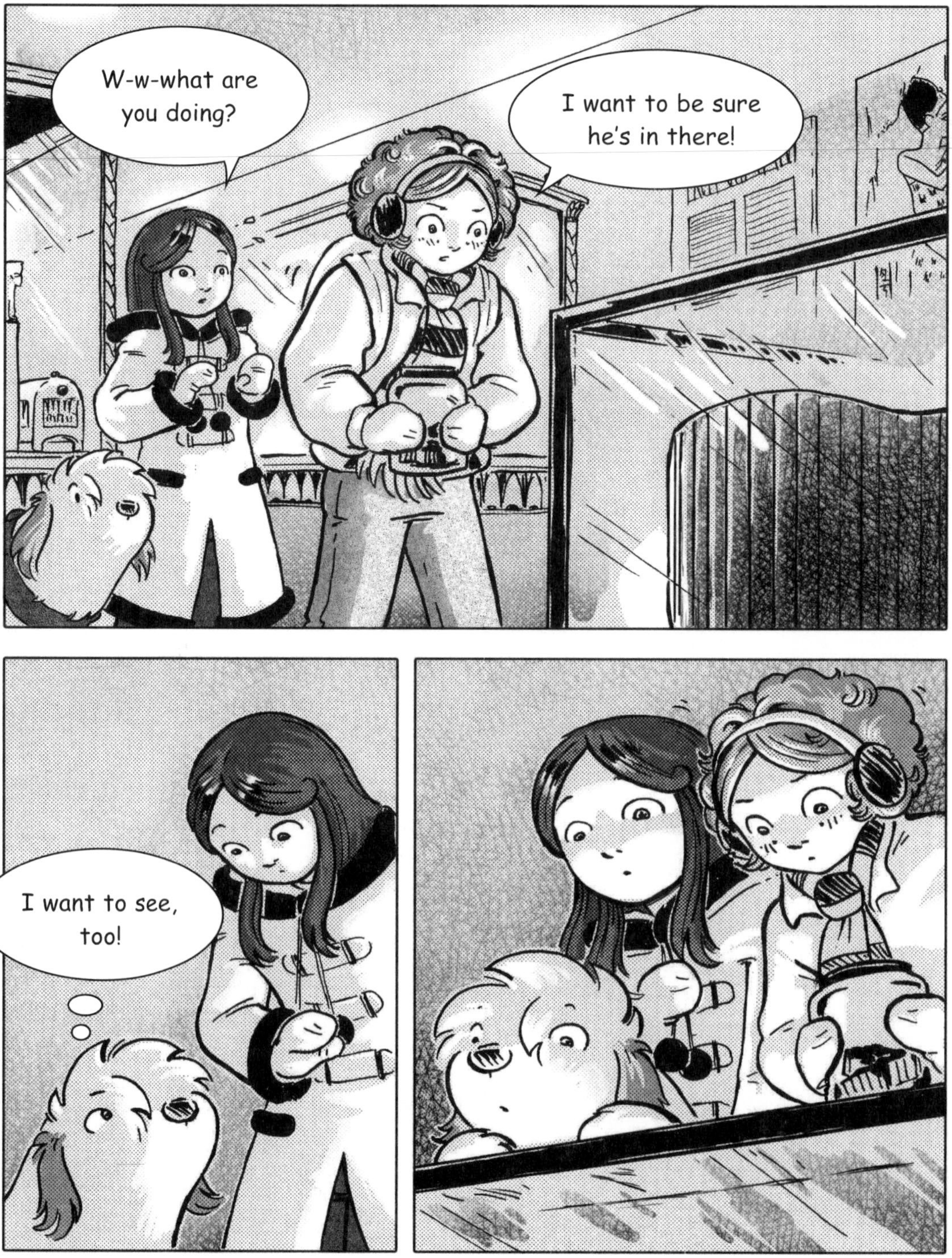
W-w-what are you doing?
I want to be sure he's in there!
I want to see, too!

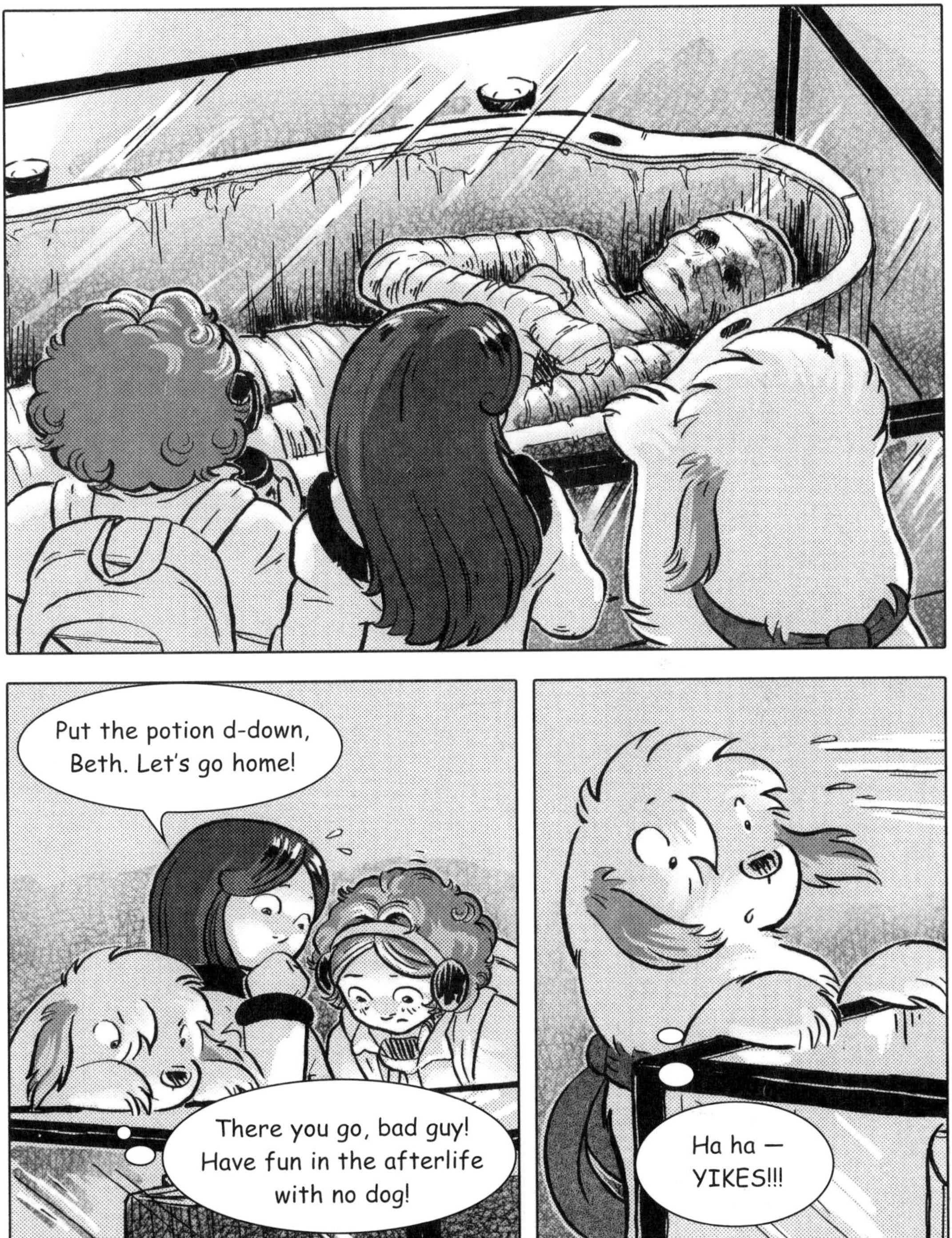
Put the potion d-down, Beth. Let's go home!
There you go, bad guy! Have fun in the afterlife with no dog!
Ha ha — YIKES!!!

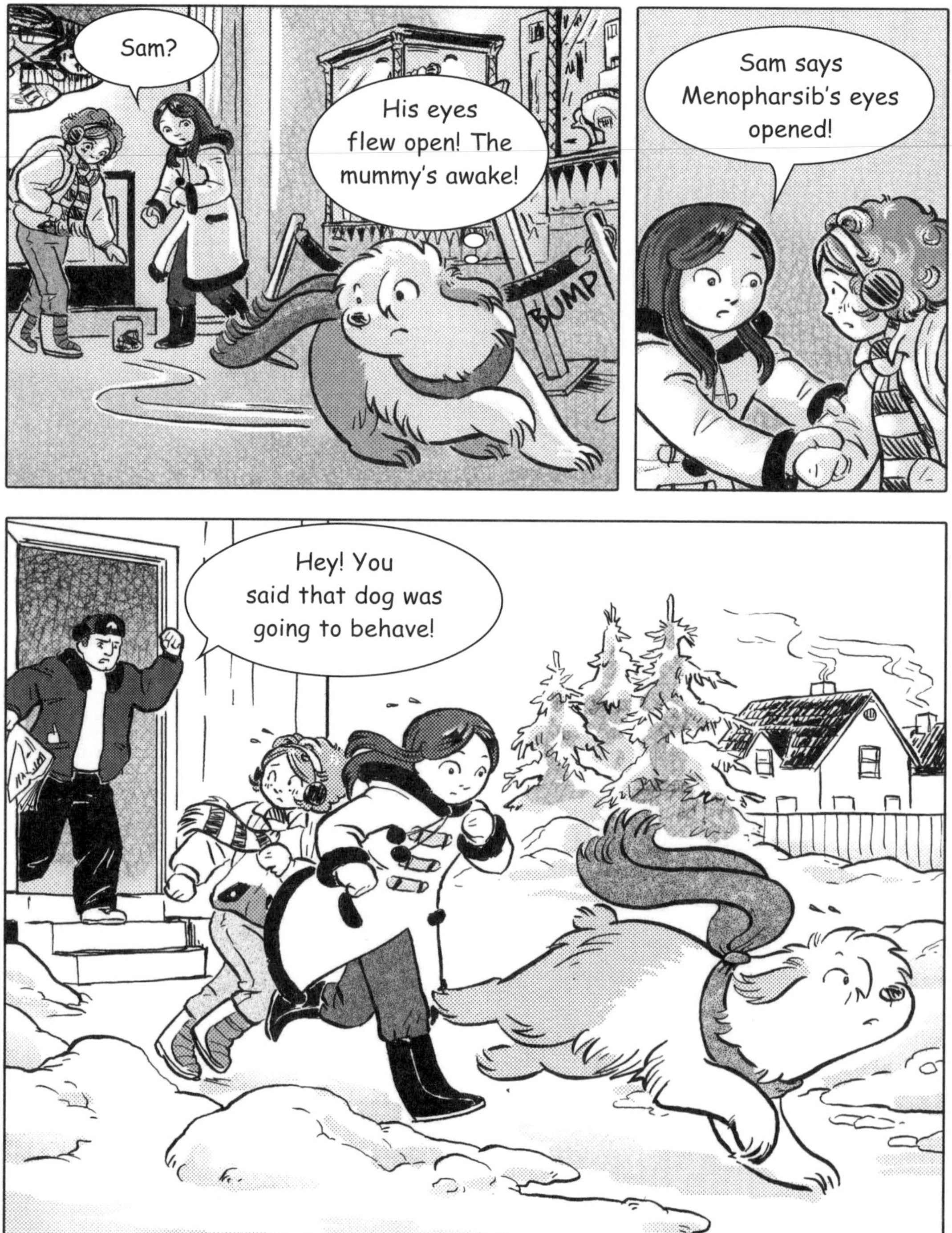
Sam?
His eyes flew open! The mummy's awake!
BUMP
Sam says Menopharsib's eyes opened!
Hey! You said that dog was going to behave!

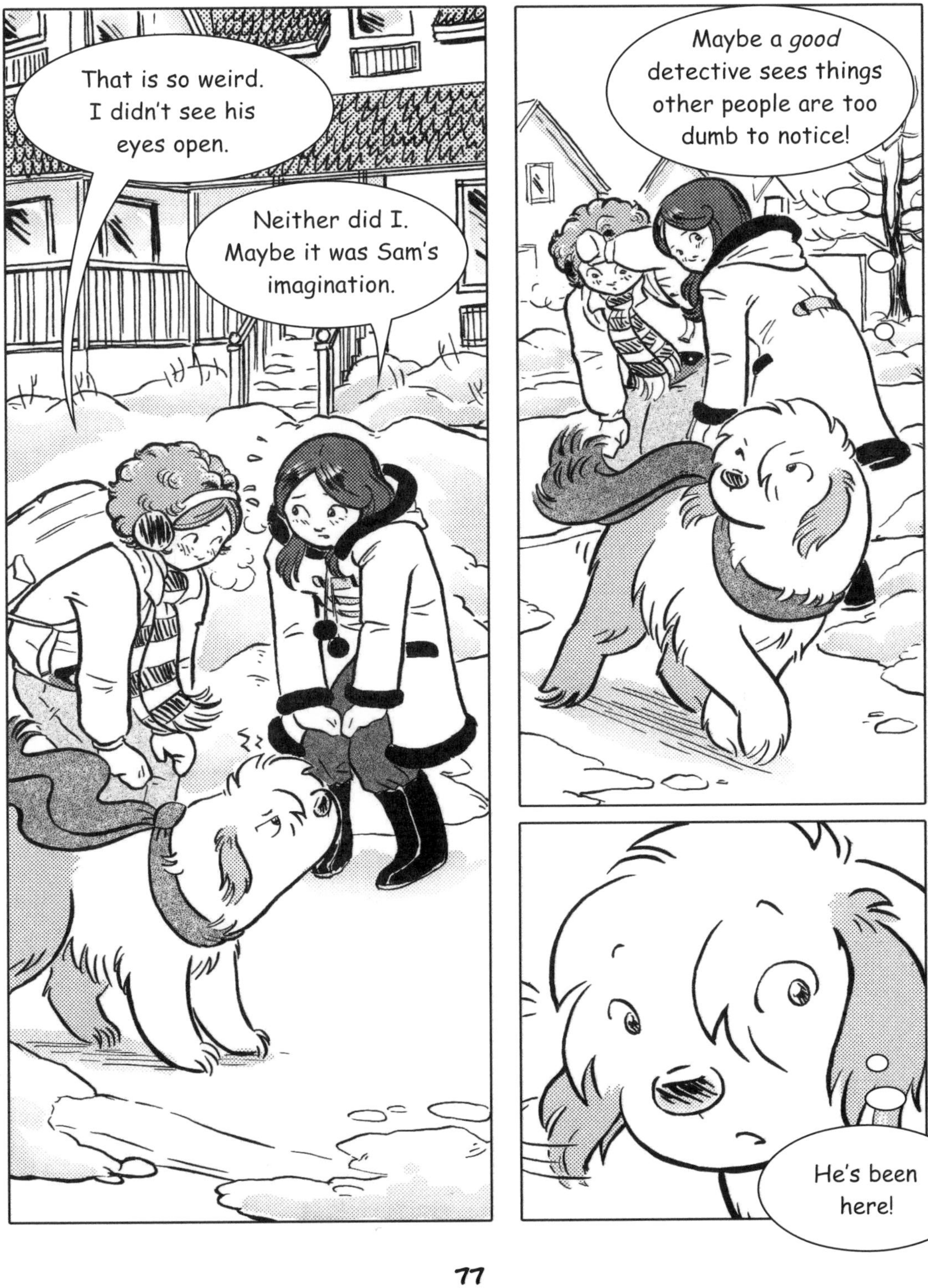
That is so weird. I didn't see his eyes open.
Neither did I. Maybe it was Sam's imagination.
Maybe a *good* detective sees things other people are too dumb to notice!
He's been here!

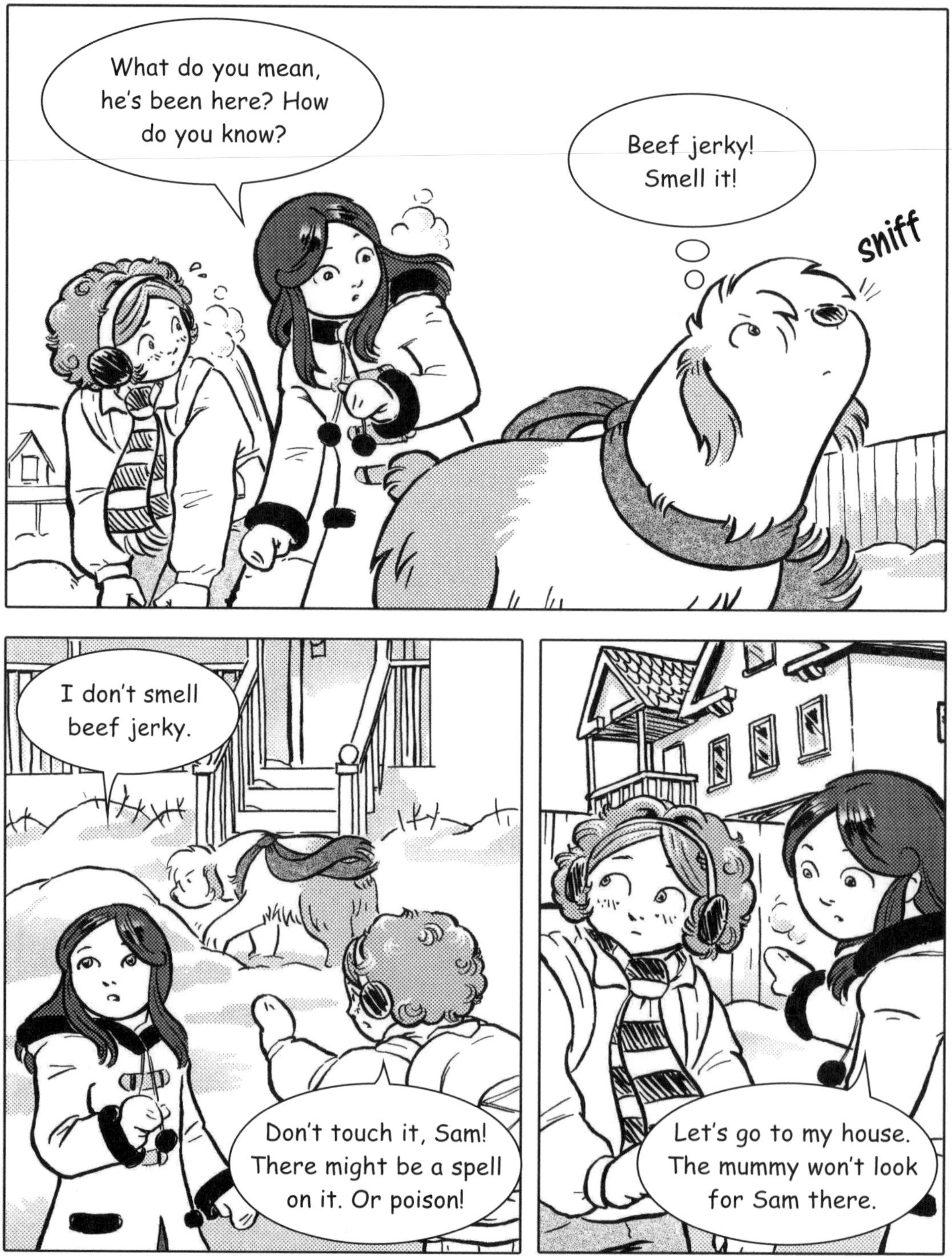
What do you mean, he's been here? How do you know?
Beef jerky! Smell it!
SNIFF
I don't smell beef jerky.
Don't touch it, Sam! There might be a spell on it. Or poison!
Let's go to my house. The mummy won't look for Sam there.

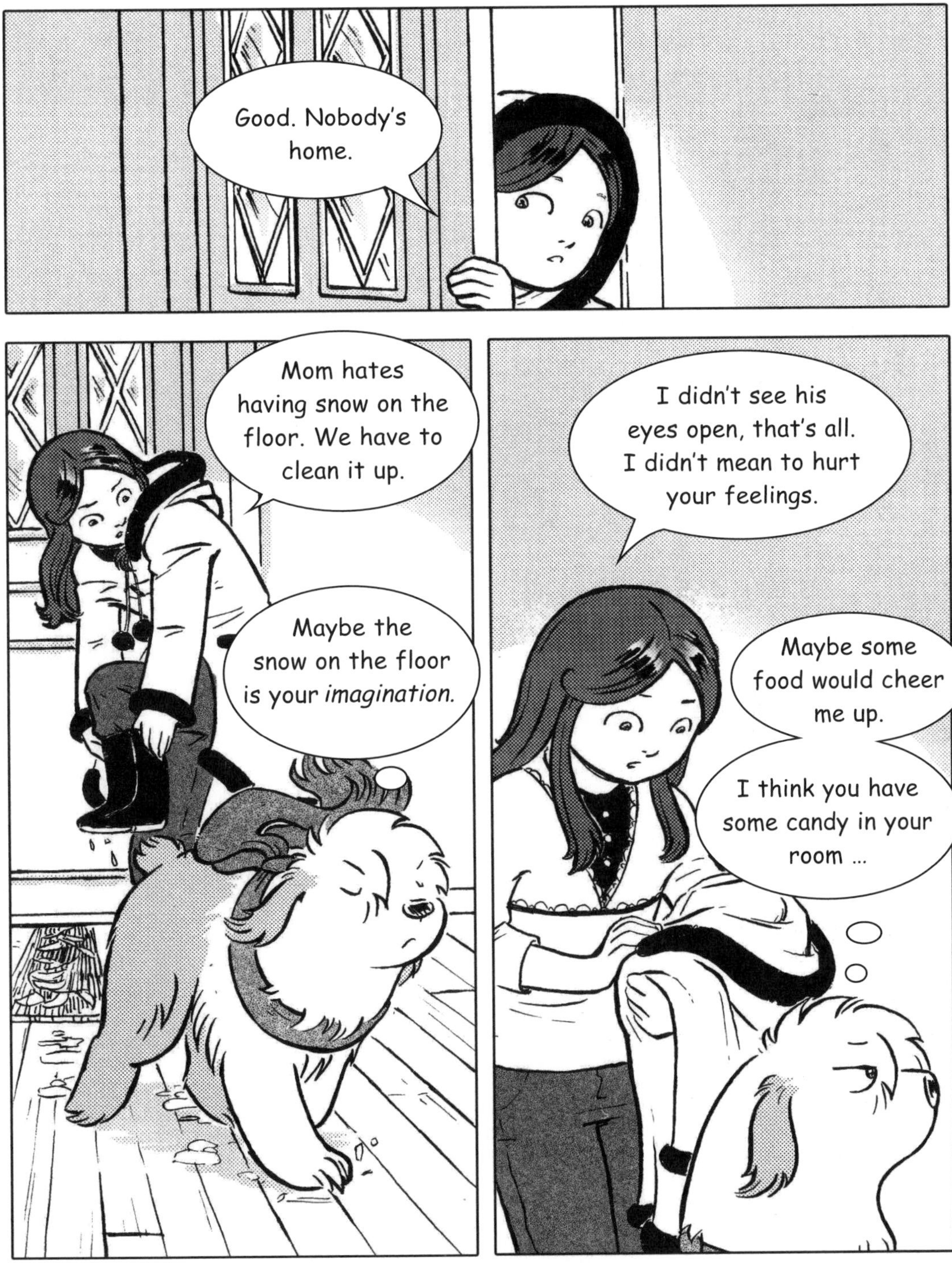
Good. Nobody's home.
Mom hates having snow on the floor. We have to clean it up.
Maybe the snow on the floor is your *imagination.*
I didn't see his eyes open, that's all. I didn't mean to hurt your feelings.
Maybe some food would cheer me up.
I think you have some candy in your room ...

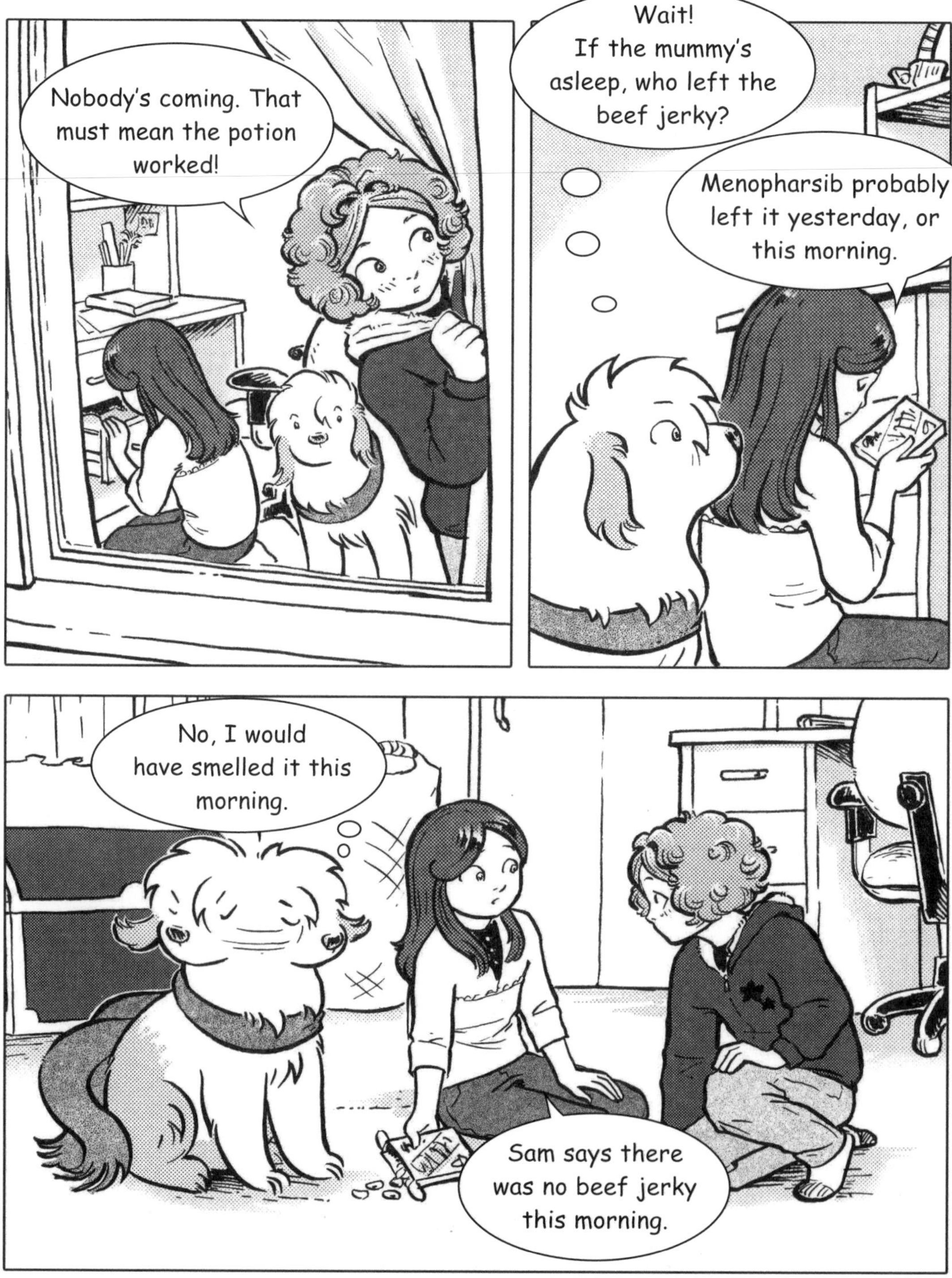
Nobody's coming. That must mean the potion worked!
Wait! If the mummy's asleep, who left the beef jerky?
Menopharsib probably left it yesterday, or this morning.
No, I would have smelled it this morning.
Sam says there was no beef jerky this morning.

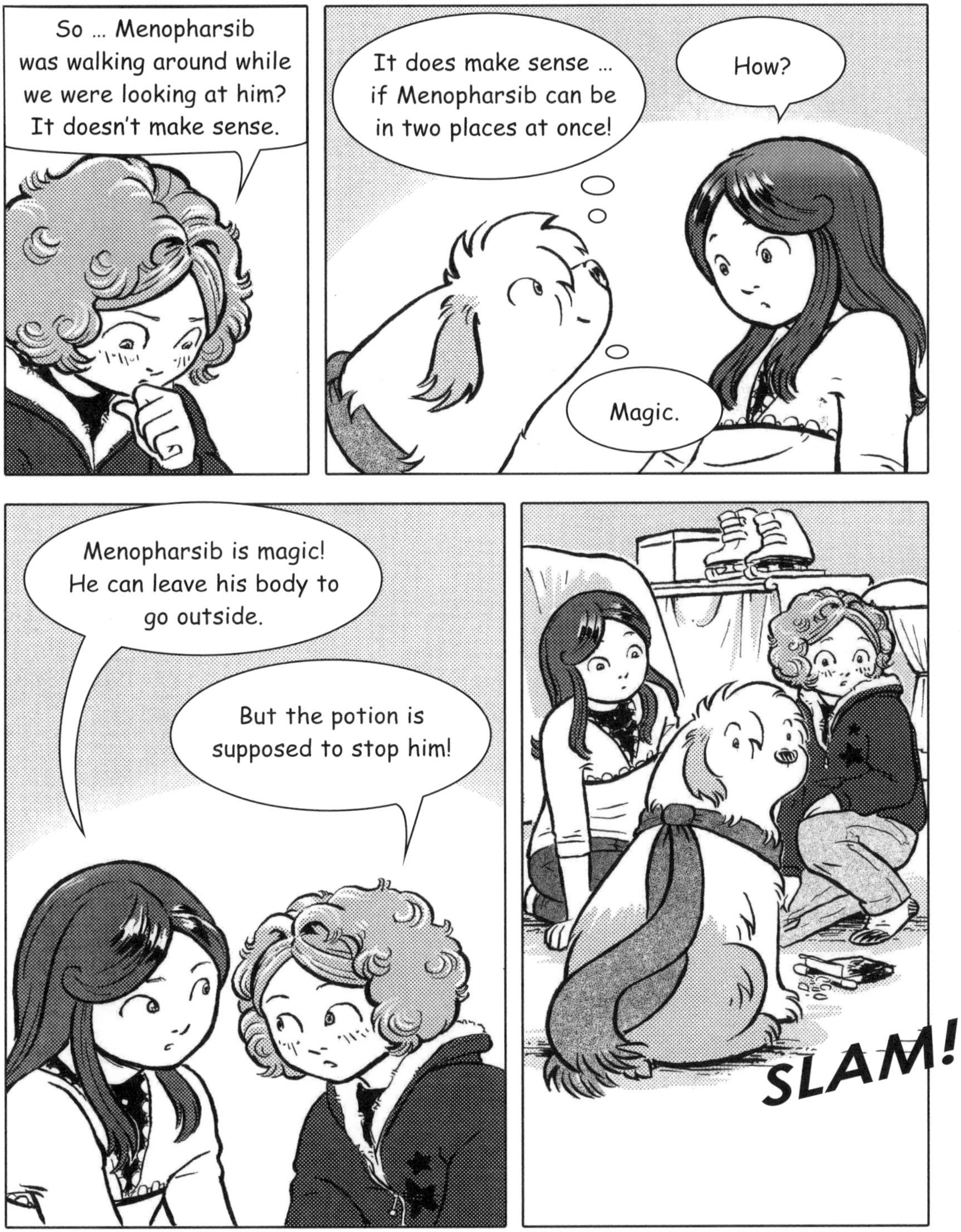
So ... Menopharsib was walking around while we were looking at him? It doesn't make sense.
It does make sense ... if Menopharsib can be in two places at once!
How?
Magic.
Menopharsib is magic! He can leave his body to go outside.
But the potion is supposed to stop him!
SLAM!

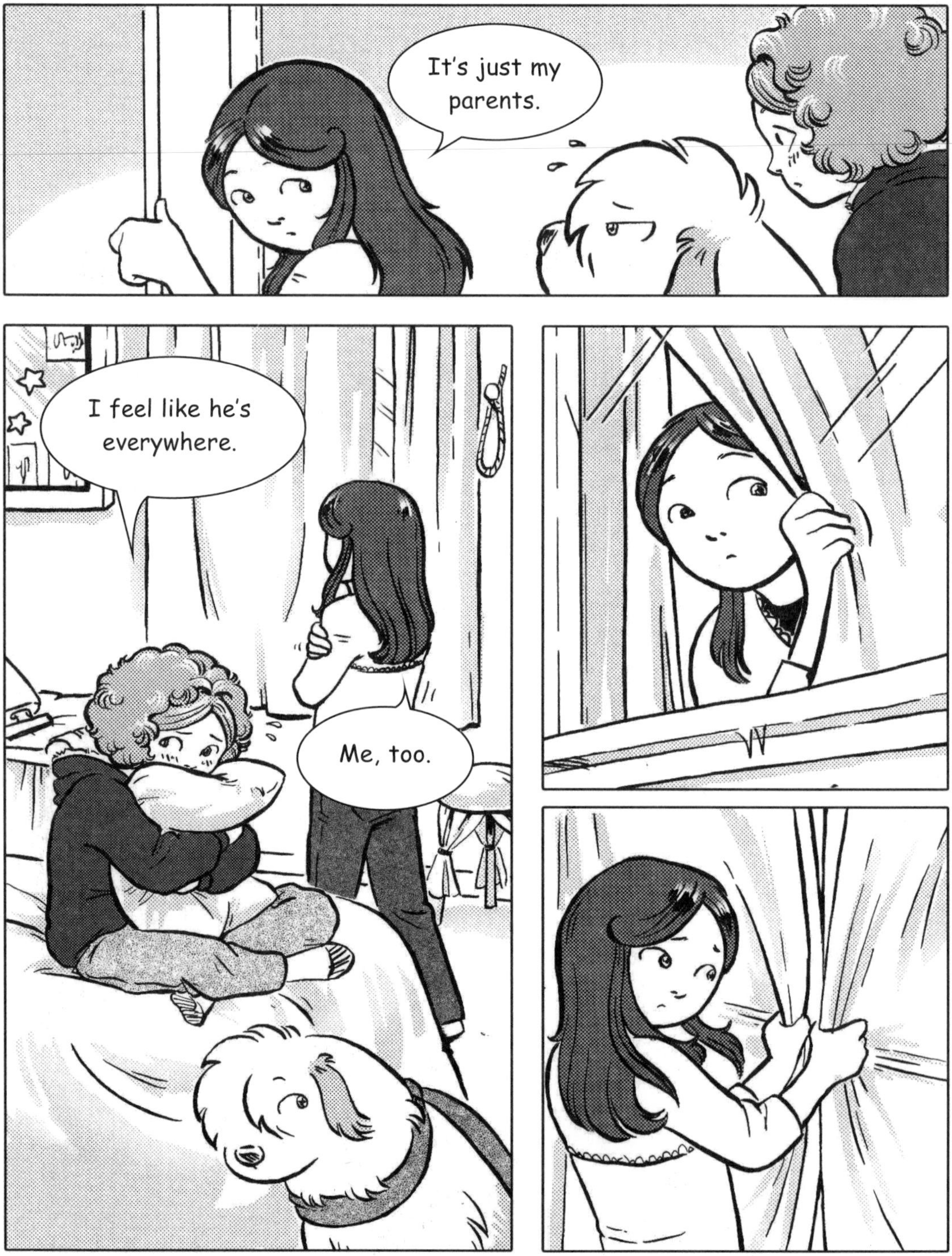
It's just my parents.
I feel like he's everywhere.
Me, too.

Hours later ...

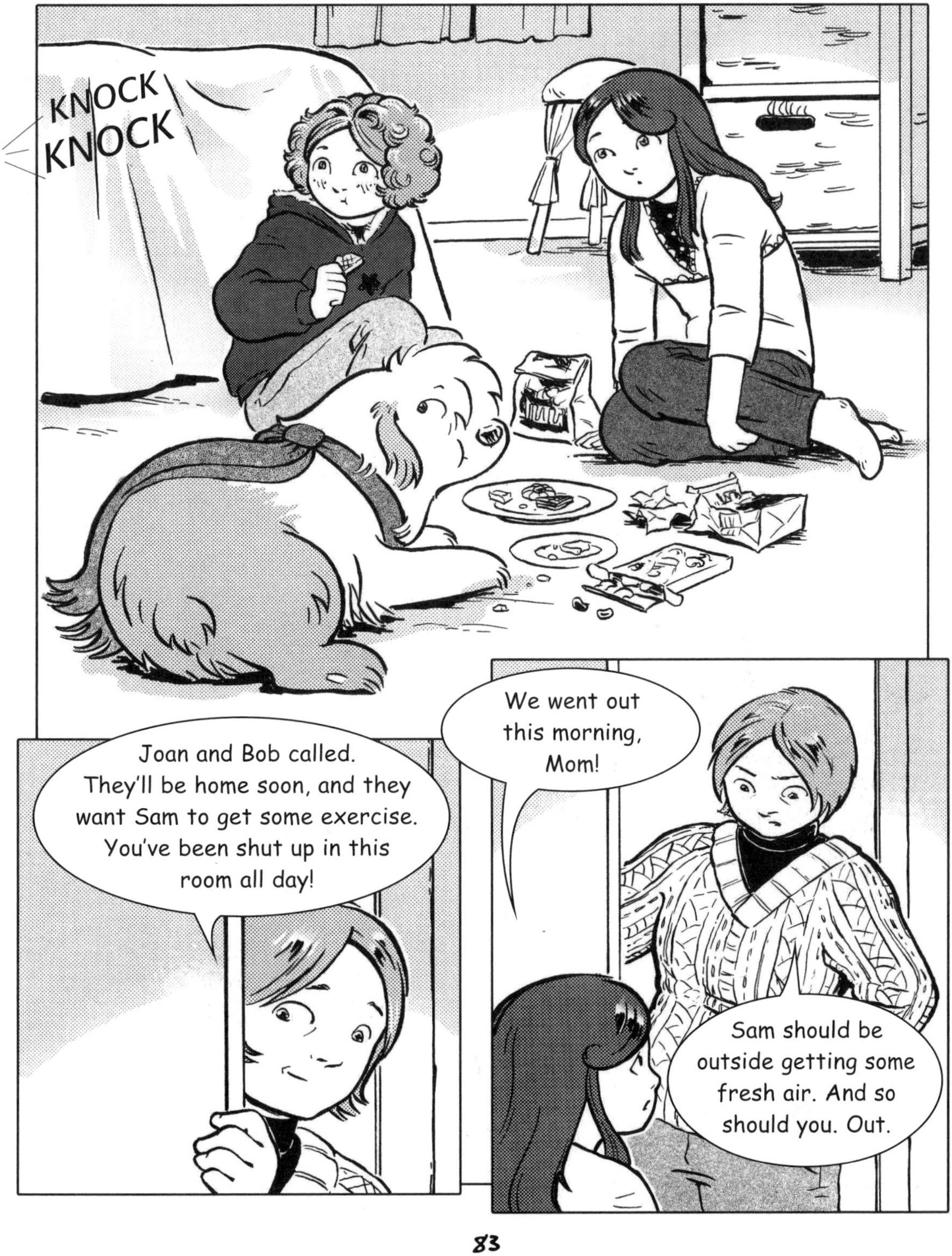
KNOCK
KNOCK
Joan and Bob called. They'll be home soon, and they want Sam to get some exercise. You've been shut up in this room all day!
We went out this morning, Mom!
Sam should be outside getting some fresh air. And so should you. Out.

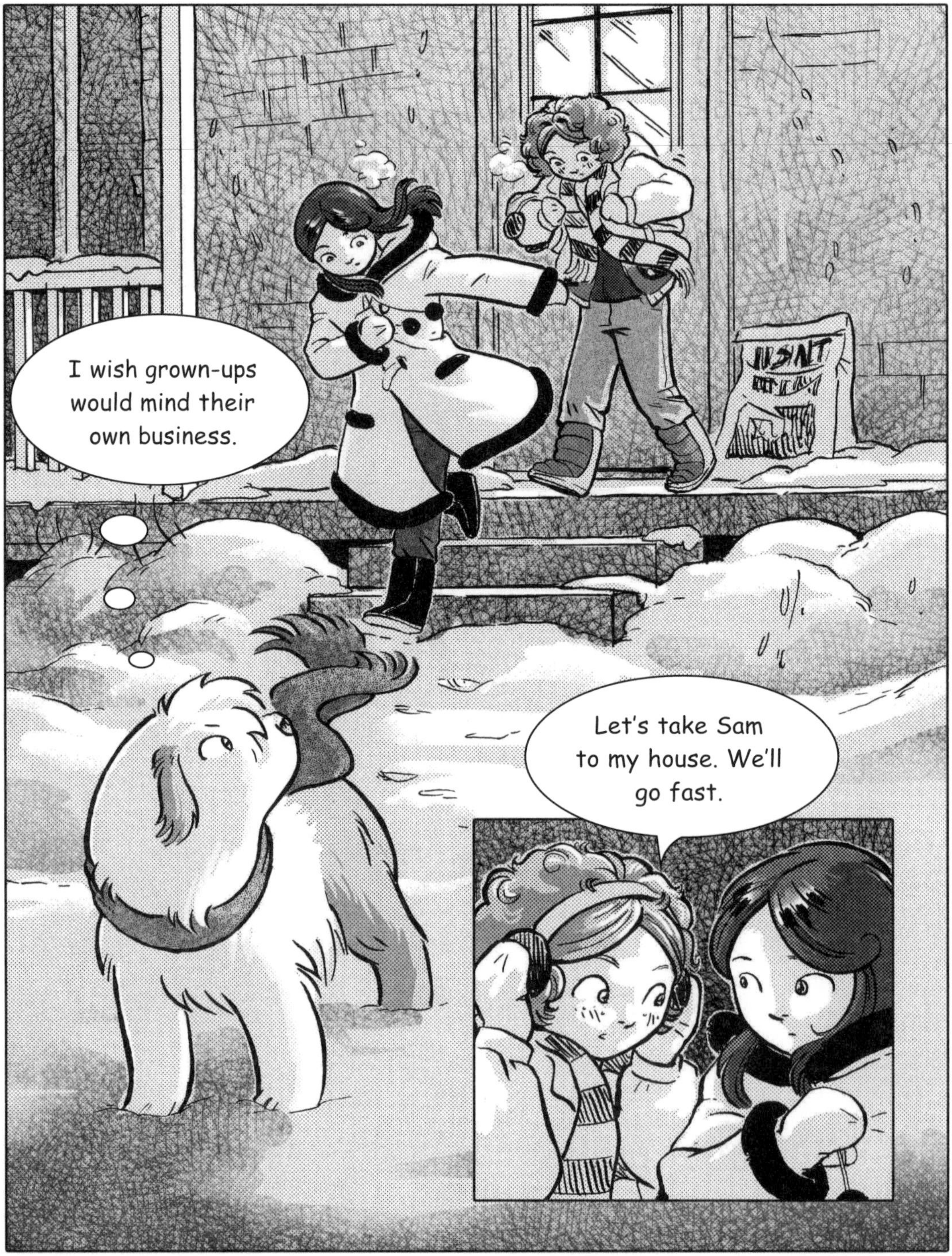
I wish grown-ups would mind their own business.
Let's take Sam to my house. We'll go fast.

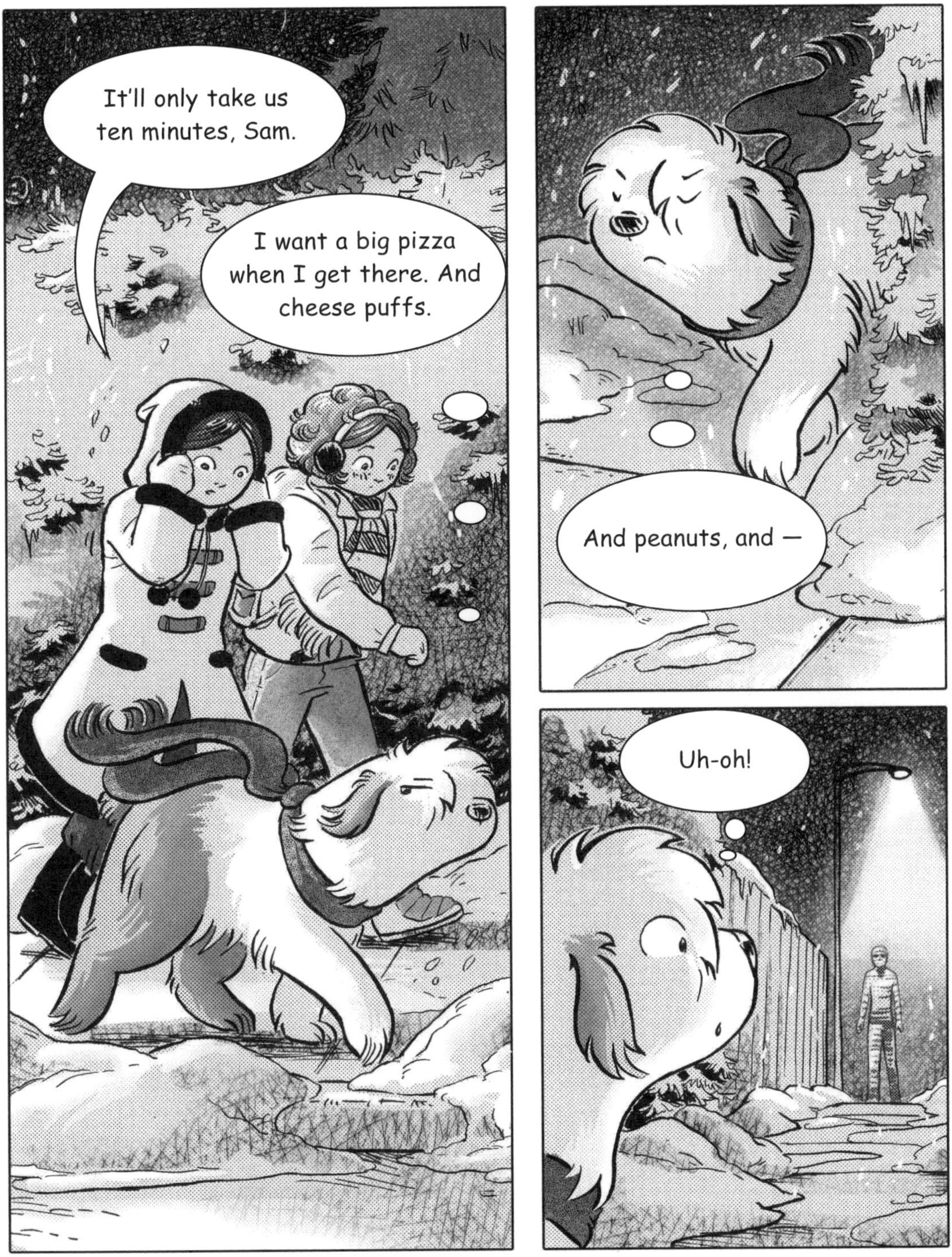
It'll only take us ten minutes, Sam.
I want a big pizza when I get there. And cheese puffs.
And peanuts, and —
Uh-oh!

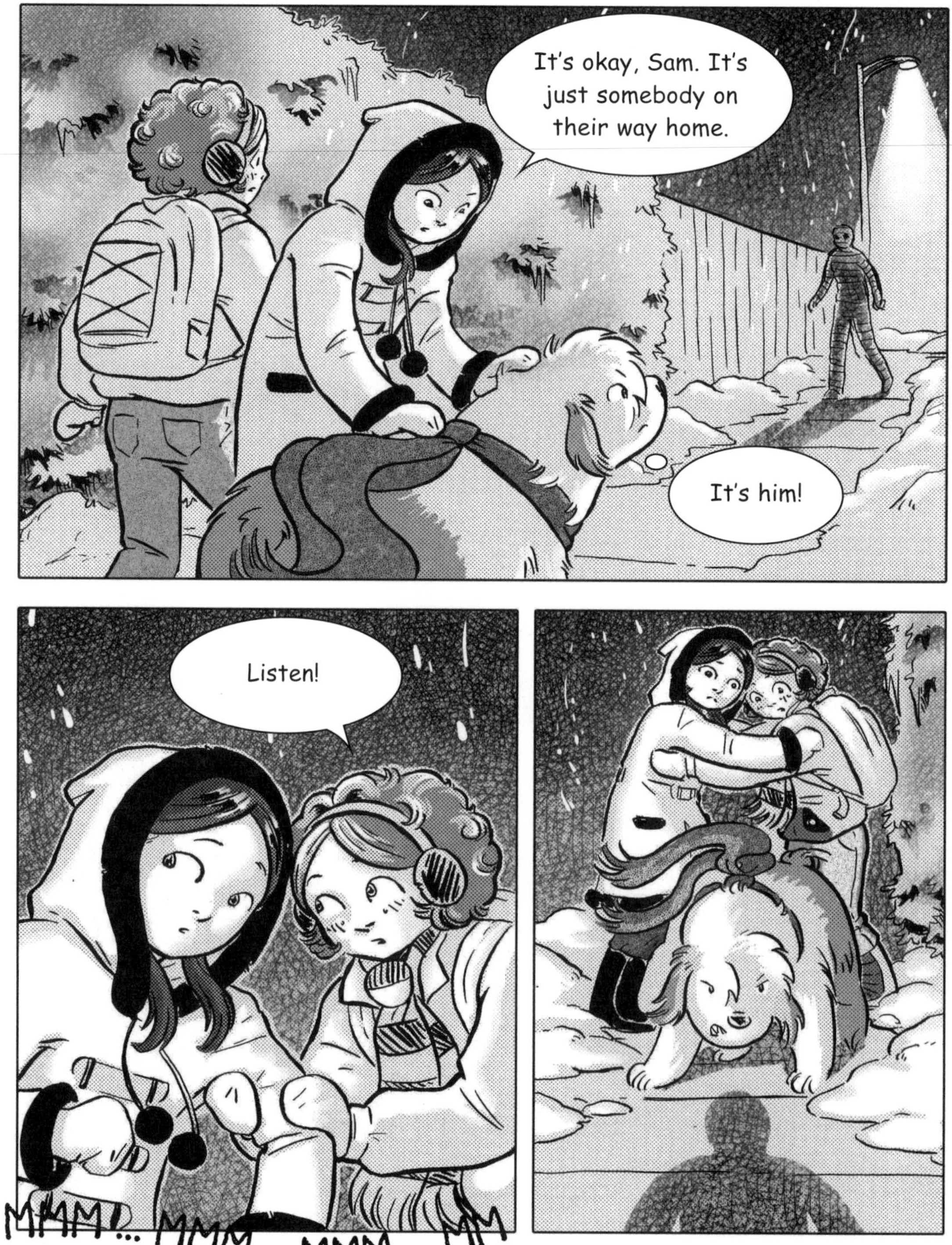
It's okay, Sam. It's just somebody on their way home.
It's him!
Listen!
MMM ... MMM ... MMM ... MM

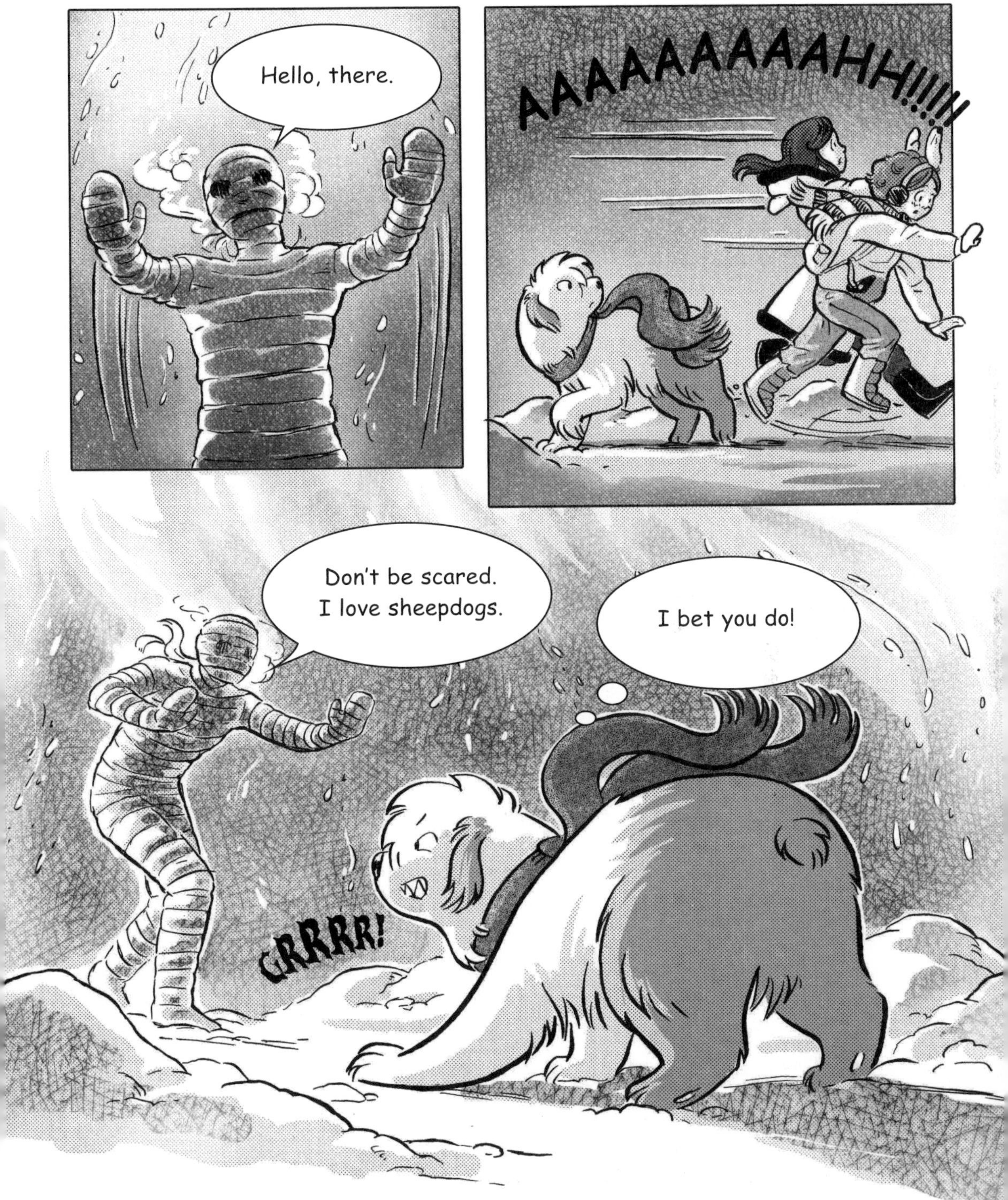
Hello, there.
AAAAAAAAAHH!!!!!!
Don't be scared. I love sheepdogs.
I bet you do!
GRRRR!

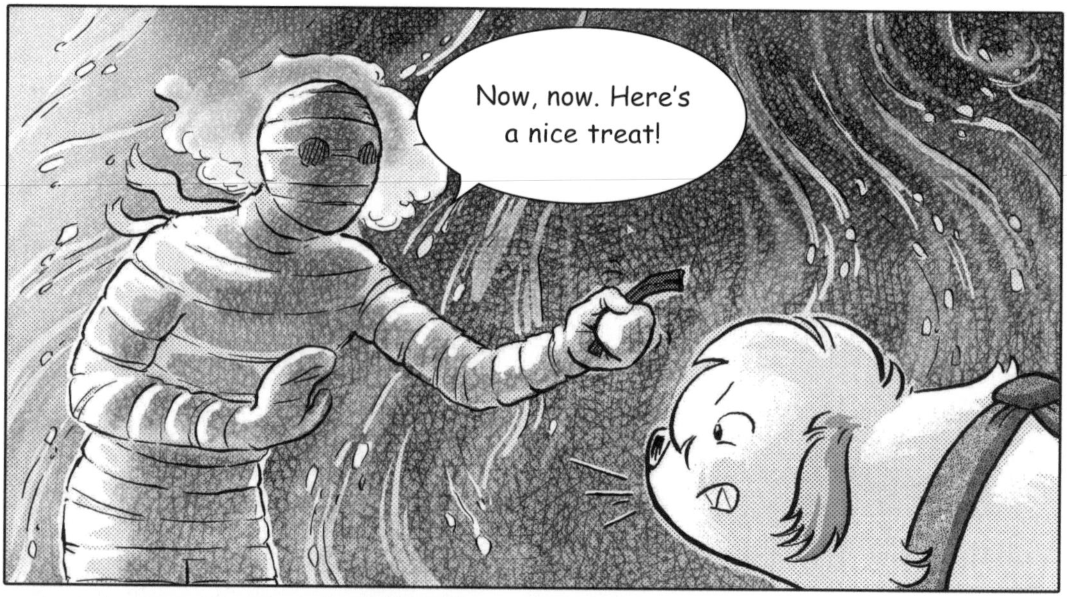
Now, now. Here's a nice treat!

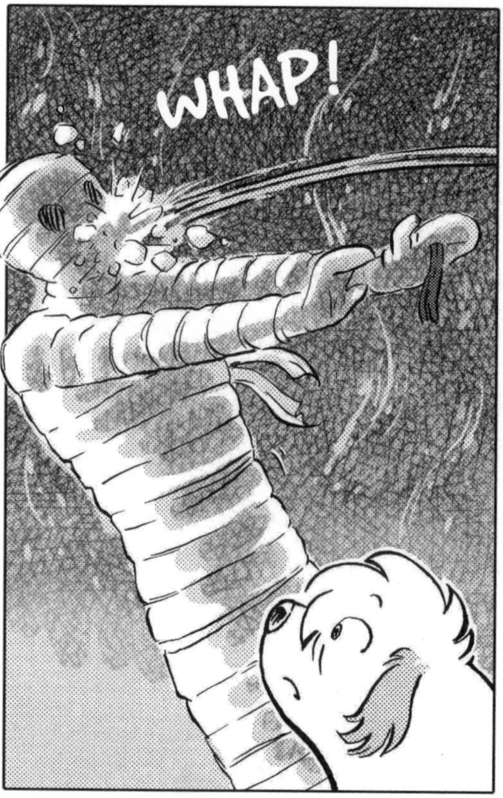
WHAP!

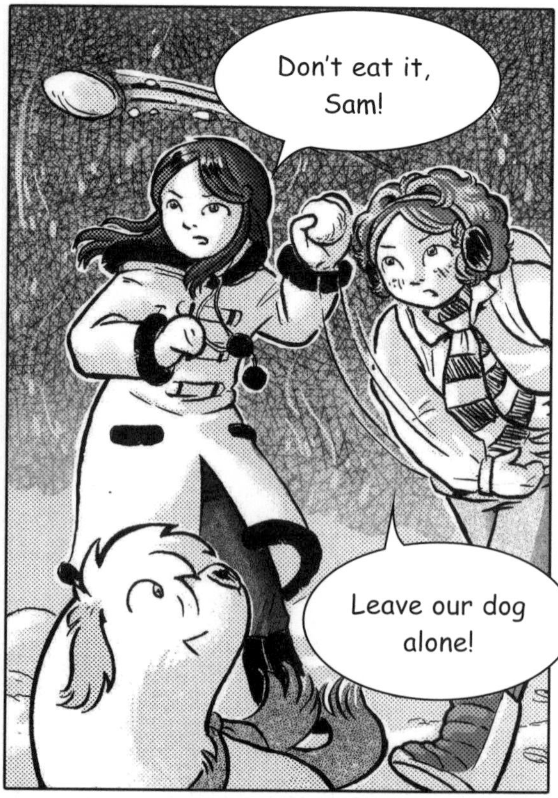
Don't eat it, Sam!
Leave our dog alone!

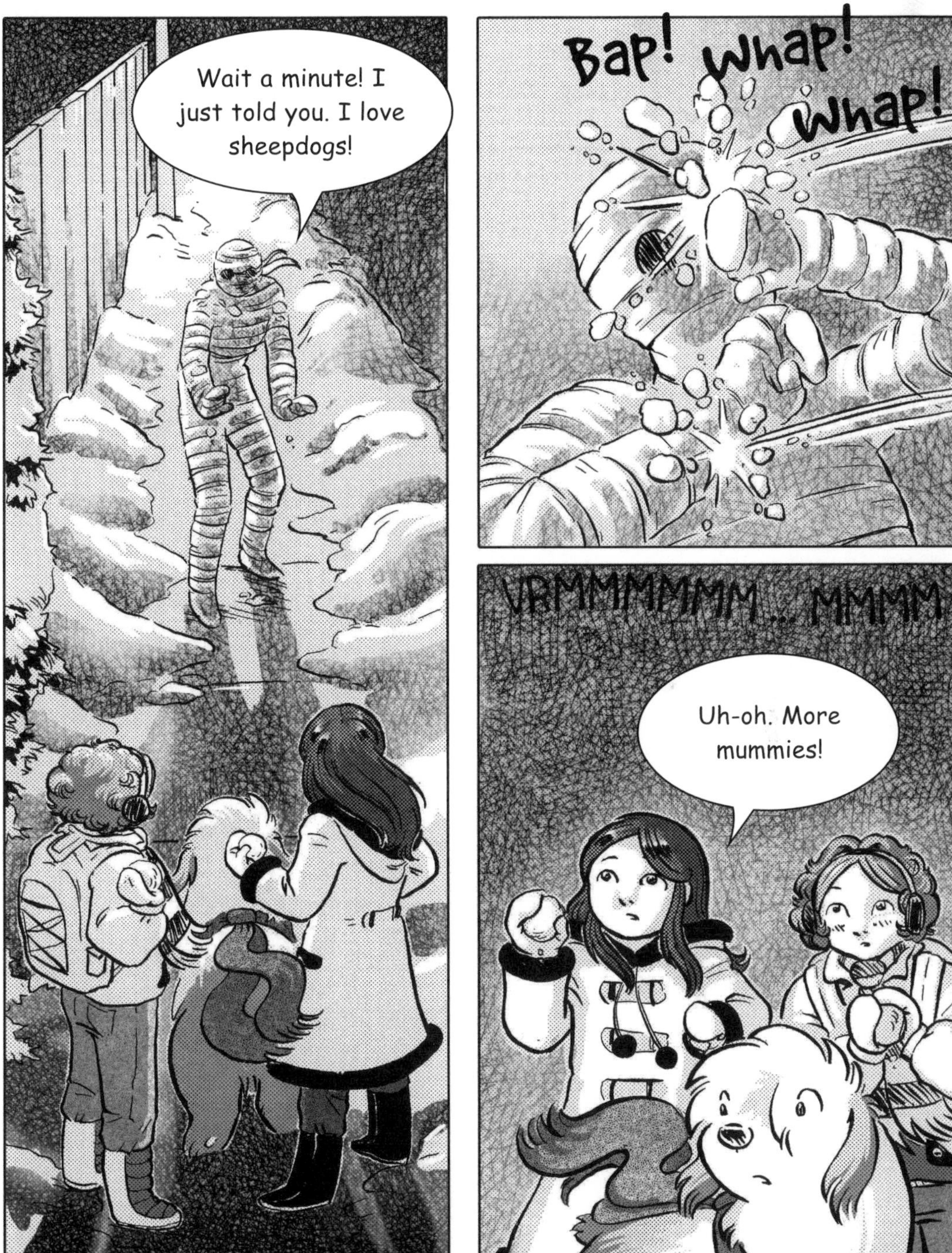
Wait a minute! I just told you. I love sheepdogs!
Bap! Whap! Whap!
VRMMMMMMM ... MMMM
Uh-oh. More mummies!

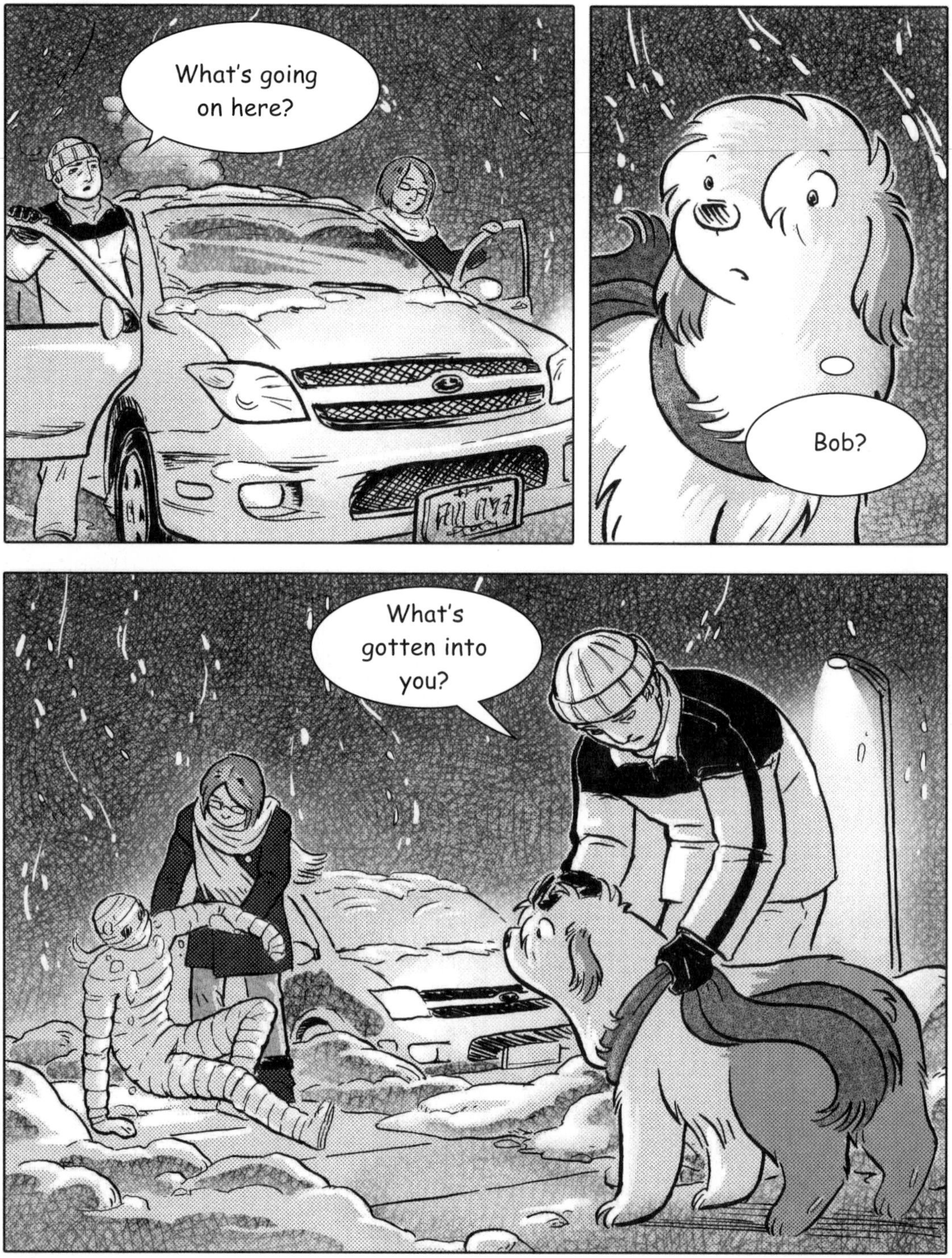
What's going on here?
Bob?
What's gotten into you?

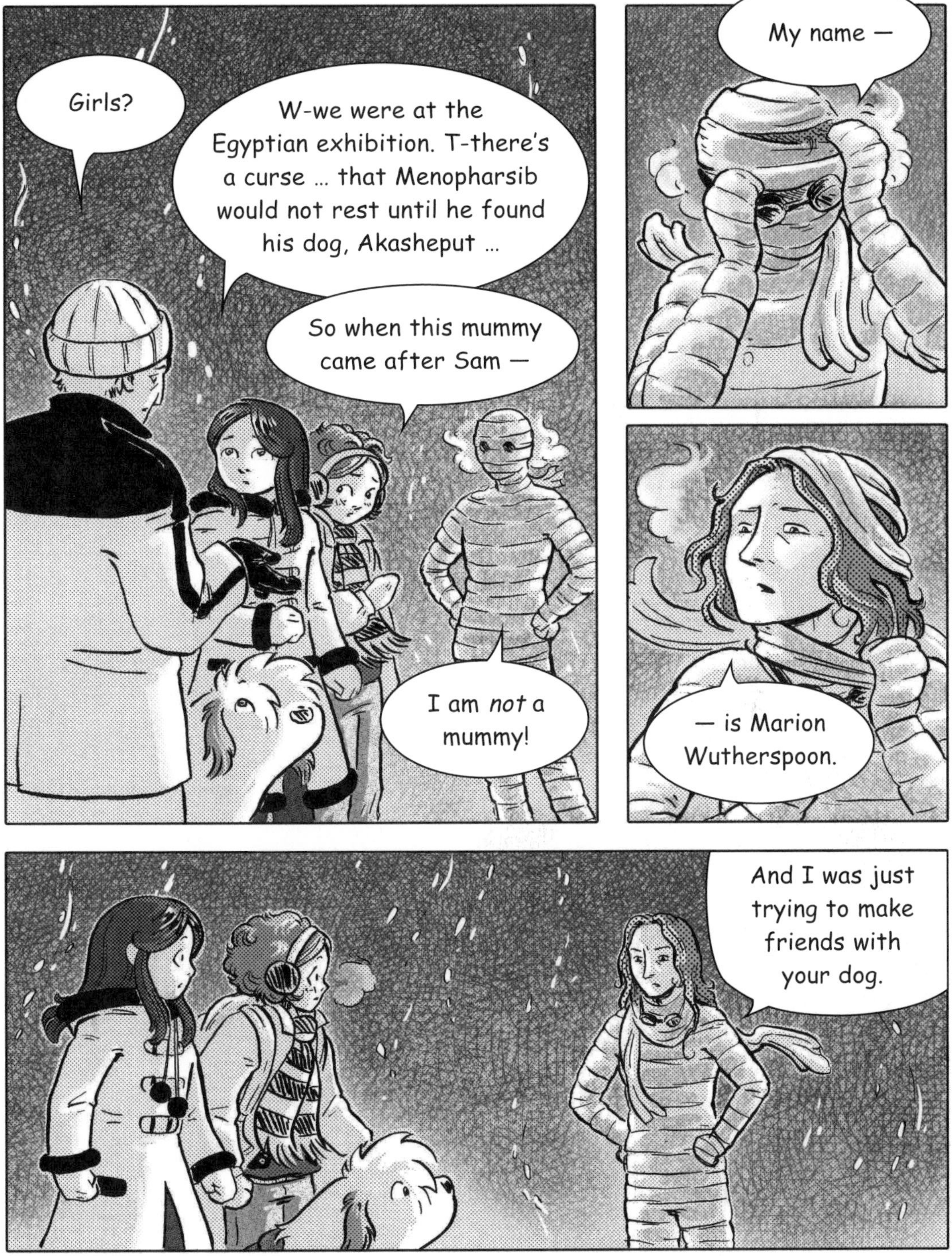
Girls?
W-we were at the Egyptian exhibition. T-there's a curse ... that Menopharsib would not rest until he found his dog, Akasheput ...
So when this mummy came after Sam —
I am *not* a mummy!
My name —
— is Marion Wutherspoon.
And I was just trying to make friends with your dog.

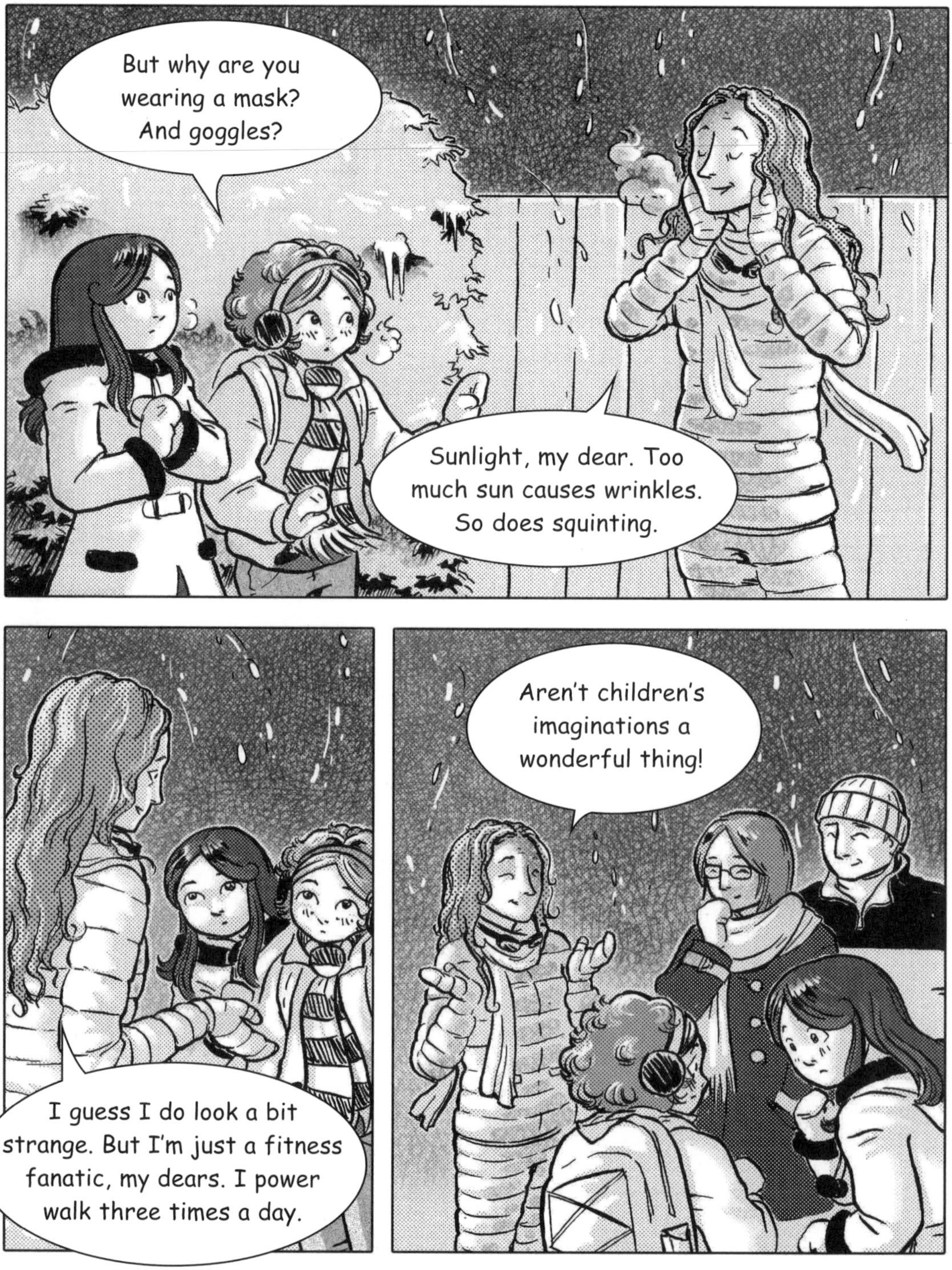
But why are you wearing a mask? And goggles?
Sunlight, my dear. Too much sun causes wrinkles. So does squinting.
I guess I do look a bit strange. But I'm just a fitness fanatic, my dears. I power walk three times a day.
Aren't children's imaginations a wonderful thing!

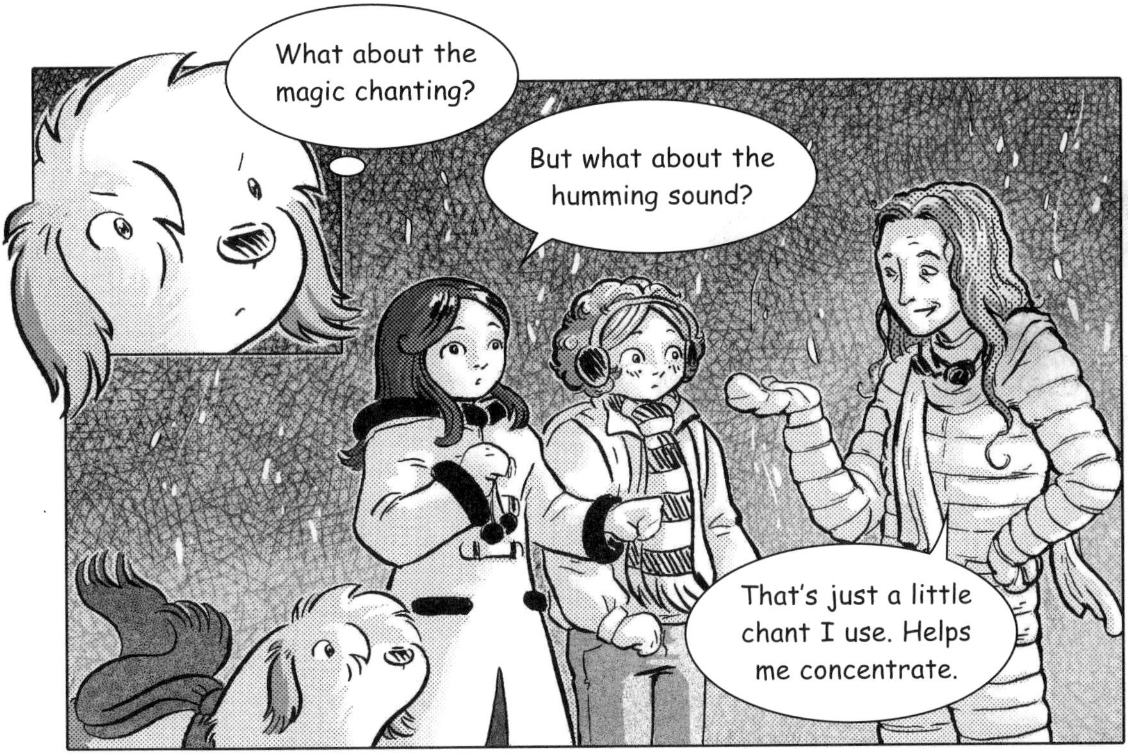
What about the magic chanting?
But what about the humming sound?
That's just a little chant I use. Helps me concentrate.

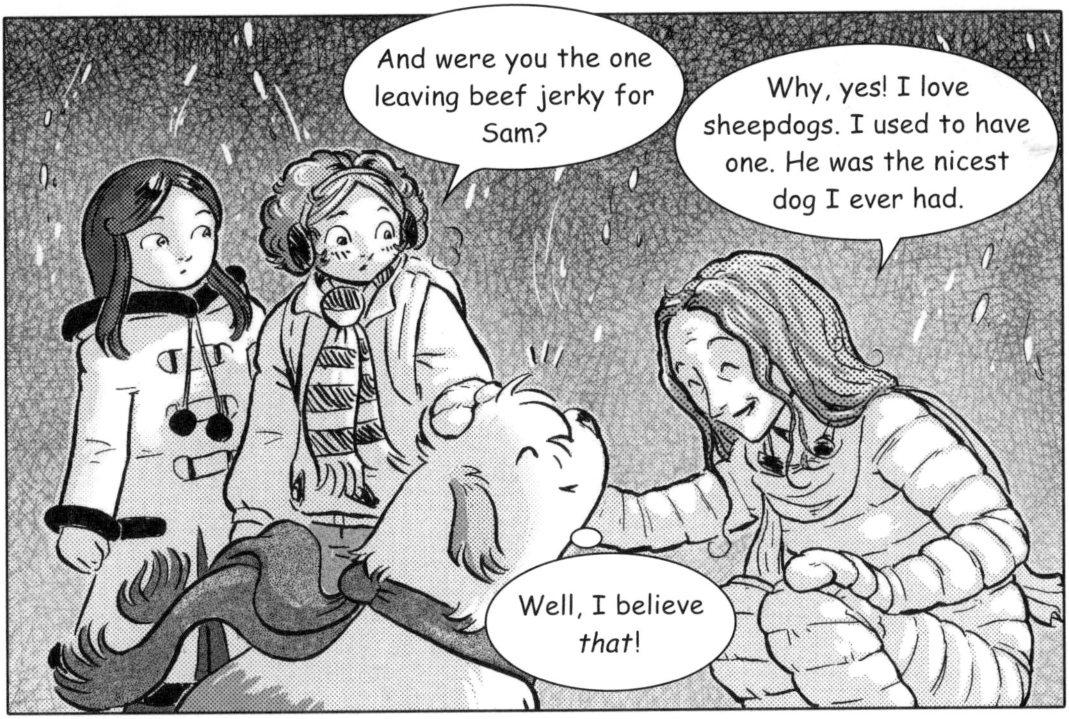
And were you the one leaving beef jerky for Sam?
Why, yes! I love sheepdogs. I used to have one. He was the nicest dog I ever had.
Well, I believe *that*!

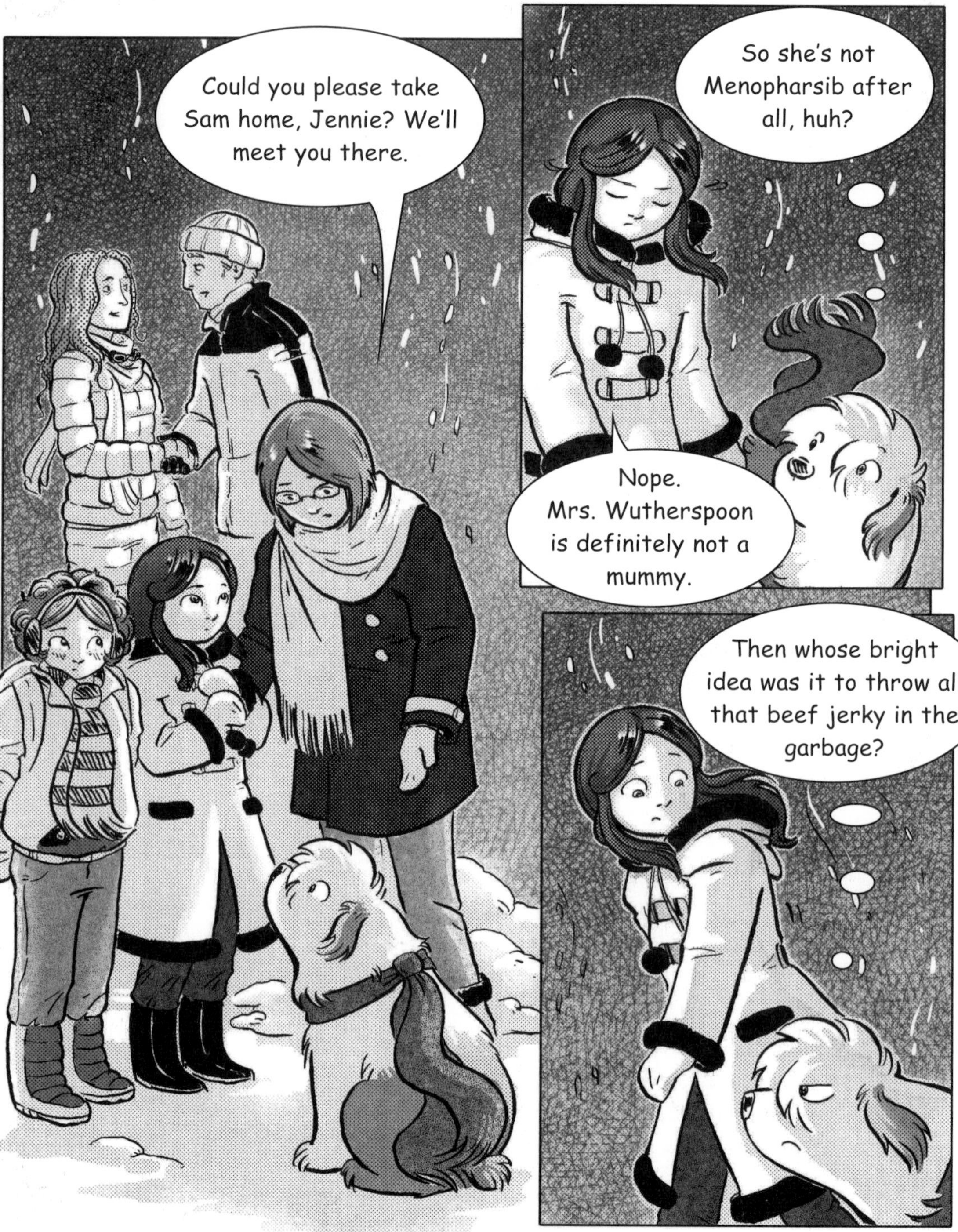
Could you please take Sam home, Jennie? We'll meet you there.
So she's not Menopharsib after all, huh?
Nope. Mrs. Wutherspoon is definitely not a mummy.
Then whose bright idea was it to throw all that beef jerky in the garbage?

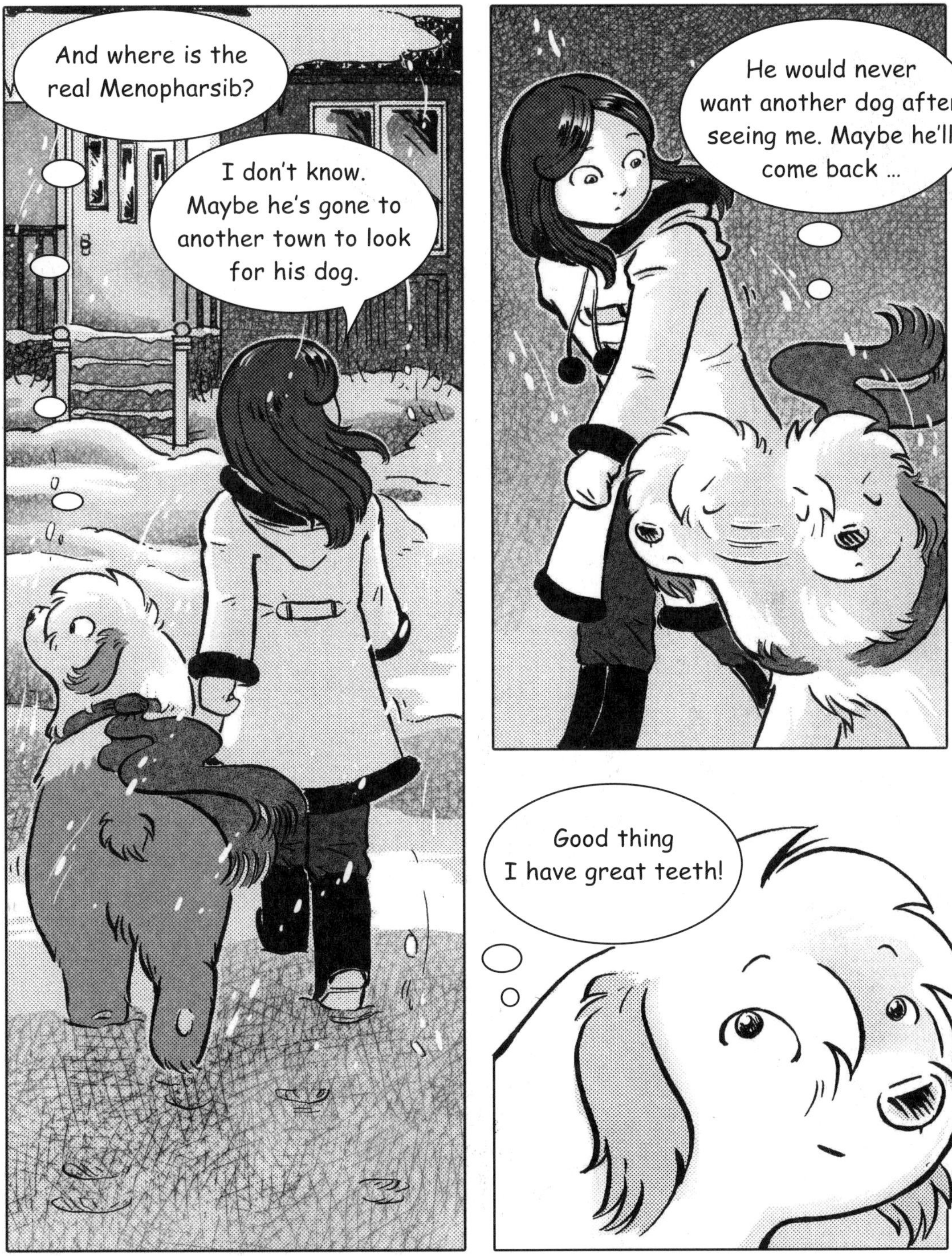

And where is the real Menopharsib?
I don't know. Maybe he's gone to another town to look for his dog.
He would never want another dog after seeing me. Maybe he'll come back ...
Good thing I have great teeth!

Join Claire and her friends for action-packed fun!

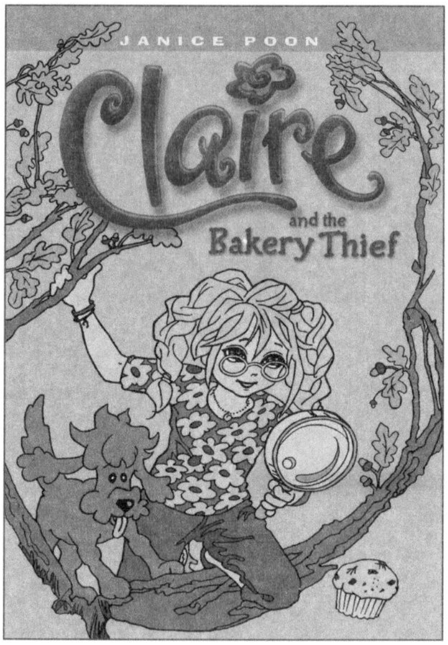
JANICE POON
Claire
and the
Bakery Thief

Claire and the Bakery Thief

Claire, her dog, Bongo, and her best friend, Jet, must catch the Bakery Thief — a recipe for fun and adventure.

Written and illustrated by Janice Poon

Hardcover 978-1-55453-286-5
Paperback 978-1-55453-245-2

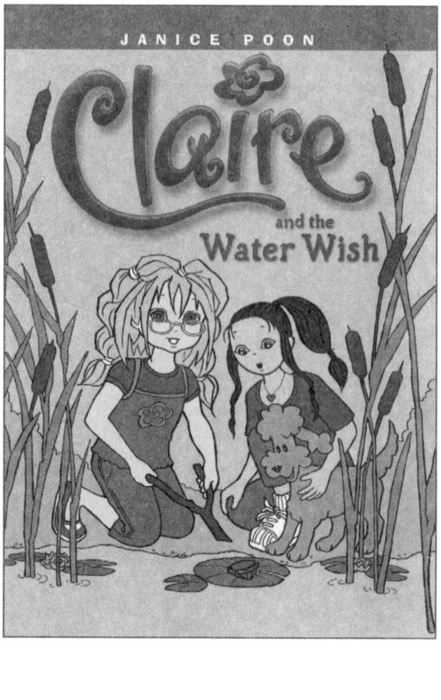
JANICE POON
Claire
and the
Water Wish

Claire and the Water Wish

After Claire and Jet's friendship hits a bumpy spot, the girls need to put their differences aside to help bring the Lovesick Lake polluters to justice.

Written and illustrated by Janice Poon

Hardcover 978-1-55453-286-5
Paperback 978-1-55453-245-2

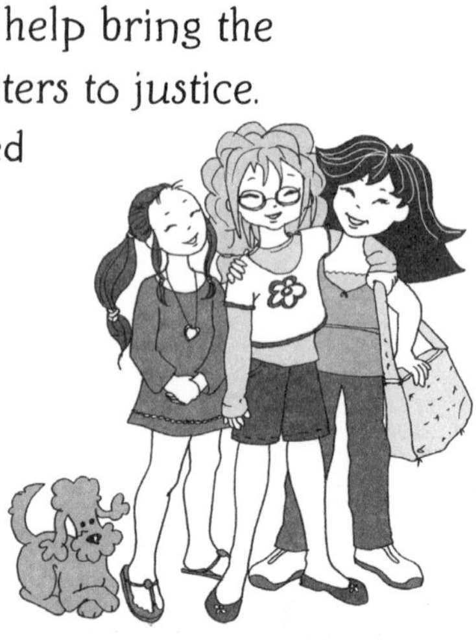